STORM RISING

BOOK THREE OF THE SHOAL CREEK SAGA

LANNY BLEDSOE

BLEDSOE PUBLISHING

1

May Hobb stood in the club parking lot and watched Storm Gill get in his car and drive away. Tears streamed down her face as she thought of their conversation, especially what he had said about her choice. He was standing by her car when she came out of the club. She was surprised; she had not expected him to be there. She had walked toward him, stopping a few feet away, her eyes on his face. "I'm surprised to see you here."

He nodded. "I expect you are."

"You followed me?"

Storm shook his head. "I didn't, but I had someone follow you."

"You didn't trust me?"

Storm shook his head. "Why would I trust you. You're a Hobb."

She smiled. "That's true. Sometimes I forget." She stared at him. "You saw the show?"

"I did."

"So, why are you standing here talking to me? You want to tell me what a terrible person you think I am."

He shook his head. "No, it's not up to me to judge you, May. It seems you've made your choice."

"What other choice did I have?"

He half smiled as he looked at her. "May, did you think I was playing with you? That all I wanted was to get you in my bed?" He shook his head. "I was the other choice you had. All you had to do was accept me." He started away and looked back at her. "I'm sorry that choice wasn't good enough for you." He walked to his car, got in and left.

She stood there until he was out of sight, got in her car and headed toward River Bluff. She had to go talk to Star.

Star was sitting on the sofa when she heard May's car drive up. Ruby had already gone to bed. She jumped up, ran to the door and opened it. When she saw May's face, she knew something bad had happened, her eyes were red and wet. Star's first thought was that Walt had done something to her. She imagined the worst. "What's happened? Tell me about it," she said.

May walked to the sofa and sat down. She looked at Star. "Storm came to the club last night and saw me on stage. He saw me naked on stage. When I came out of the club, he was waiting for me in the parking lot." Tears flowed down her face.

Star handed her a handkerchief and looked at her. "What did you expect? Did you think you could play around with him during the week, be in that club every weekend and he wouldn't ever find out? How long did you think that would last?"

"He had me followed."

Star shrugged. "You said he wanted to do something special for Friday and Saturday night, but you had something else to do and wouldn't tell him what it was. Storm is not a fool, May. If he was really interested about you, he would want to know what you were doing. You knew that eventually he would find out where you were."

May nodded. "Well, he certainly found out."

"What did he say to you?"

"He said he wasn't judging me, but I had made a choice. I asked him what other choice I had. He said he was my other choice."

Star nodded. "Sounds like he was serious about you if he said that. You could stay at the club, or you could have him, that seems to be his message."

"That's what he said."

"So, what do you do now?"

May looked perplexed. "I don't know. For one thing I don't know if the choice is there after he saw me tonight. He may not want me. Secondly, I don't know that I want that choice if he's still offering it."

Star stared at her. "What does that mean?"

May shook her head. "I don't know if I want to stay in River Bluff. Even if it was with Storm, I don't know. Right now, I don't want to live here." She stopped and didn't say any more. Growing up in River Bluff hadn't been good for her. Her family had been most of the problem; she was embarrassed to be a Hobb. She had thought going to a new place would be better.

She didn't tell Star, but the stage was a special place for her. She was drawn to the excitement. Her feelings were intoxicating and powerful, unlike any she had ever felt before. She could move the crowd by taking off her clothes. Each time she took off a piece, the crowd roared for more. She could tease them and excite them even more until she stood almost naked before them. The men wanted her. They were under her control and she loved it.

She had never had any power before. She had grown up knowing people looked down on her because of her family. She was never accepted for who she was. But that wasn't true when she was on stage. She was the main attraction, and she liked being the star.

She was attracted to Walt and that bothered her. She realized he was a dangerous person; Star had warned her about him. Despite knowing better, she was drawn to him. She had been attracted to him since she met him that first day at Josie's. She still remembered the feel of his hands on her. She knew her having these feelings about Walt wasn't good.

All these thoughts and feelings were in her head. She knew what she was doing was wrong in so many ways. Her situation with Storm was also confusing and her feelings for him were mixed up among the other feelings and that made everything worse.

Star leaned back and stared at her sister in disbelief. "You do understand what you're saying. You'd rather be on stage, half-naked in front of a bunch of drunks than have a normal life here with Storm."

May laughed. "That sounds really stupid, doesn't it?"

Star nodded. "Sounds really stupid to me."

"What if Storm is not interested in me after he saw me on stage?"

"I can't answer that," said Star. "You made this mess; you have to clean it up -- if you want it cleaned up. Otherwise, forget about him." Star got up and looked down at May. "I can't help you and nobody else can. You have to make up your mind, then talk to Storm if you want to and see where he is on this." She walked away toward her room. "What you want may not be up to you anyway. You misled him. I damn sure would hate to have to face him now." She stopped, thought for a moment and walked back to the sofa. "What about Walt? How did he act tonight?"

May looked up and Star knew something had happened there too. "He was all over me when I came off the stage. He put his hands all over me and tried to kiss me, saying I was going to his house with him. He's been after me more and more lately. I pushed him away, but he wouldn't stop touching me. He said I had promised him I'd go with him. I finally managed to get away and went out the door. He followed me outside, screaming and trying to pull me back inside. That's when I saw Storm waiting in the parking lot."

Star shook her head. "What did you expect Walt to do? You've led him on because you wanted him to put you on the stage. You've let him see you naked and feel all over you. Now you want him to leave you alone and be a good boy? That's not going to happen. Walt is used to having his way with women at the club and he wants you. If you stay at the club, he's gonna have you even if he has to force you." She nodded. "You have two choices right now, either give in to him or leave because Walt ain't gonna change." Star turned and went to her room.

May sat on the sofa with her head in her hands. She knew what choices she had, either to stay on the stage and face all the danger that went with that choice or stay with Storm in River Bluff. She knew, even though Storm was upset with her now, all she had to do was offer herself to him long-term and he would respond to her. She sat and thought about each choice. Later she got up and went to bed with Star. She didn't know what to do.

~

Storm left May and headed toward River Bluff. He had listened to Win Clark describe what he'd seen the night before when May was on the stage. Win had spoken plainly and explicitly about what May had done. But he wasn't prepared for what he saw when he watched her himself. She not only came out on the stage and took off her clothes, she reveled in it. She stood almost naked before the crowd and let men pay money to run their hands over her. She laughed and invited them to share her body without any shame. He couldn't help but wonder, after he had seen her on stage, what had she been doing when she was off the stage?

He thought about the man he had seen follow her out the door at the club, grabbing at her and yelling. It seemed something had to be going on between that man and May to generate such strong feelings on the man's part. Based on what he saw, the man didn't want May to leave the club and was trying to pull her back inside. It seemed he thought he had the right to keep her there.

But when he had faced her and talked to her, he didn't see any regret for her actions. There was no regret in her face or in what she said to him. Like he had told her, she had chosen her path – a path directly away from him.

He arrived home, went inside and went to bed. He was disappointed in May, for himself and for her. He thought about her until sometime in the night, then he finally went to sleep.

~

Rep and Mose went out the Shoal Creek Farm gate, waved to Big'un and headed south. Rep was excited but worried. He had no idea what he was going to find when he got to his old homeplace. Based on the bit he remembered when he ran away that night six years ago, he was expecting the worst. He couldn't imagine that his daddy had changed from the man he'd been when he left. And if he hadn't changed, there certainly was no hope for him or his family.

When they neared the Shoal County line, he thought of the general store where he'd stopped and the old man he'd talked to. The old man had directed him to Shoal Creek, all the time warning him not to go there. He wondered if he was still there. He thought about stopping but he had other things on his mind.

"Do you know how to git to yo' house?" asked Mose as they went down the road.

Rep thought for a minute. "I'm not sure exactly but if we follow this road we'll get there. When I got on this road that mornin', I never got off it on another road. I stayed on this road going north till I got to Shoal Creek." He looked at Mose. "Now somewhere down yonder the road we lived on runs into this road. I'm sure bout that but I don't know exactly where it is."

As they rode Rep thought about the four years he had walked on this road. It took him that long to get to Shoal Creek and they would get back to his house in the truck in one day. Lila had told him it was about two hundred miles to the area where he had lived. That seemed like he traveled mighty slow, but he was walking, and he didn't travel in wintertime. He had always holed up when he saw cold weather coming, he'd been smart enough to do that. He thought of the winter he'd spent with the loggers and then the winter he'd been with Tess. There wasn't any doubt the time with Tess in his bed had been more enjoyable. But he'd learned from both experiences.

He had done little traveling from spring through fall weather because that was when planting and then harvesting took place. These were the times when jobs were available, and he had worked every year. Most of the time he worked for room and board and ended up with little money in his pocket. The only exception was the winter he worked with the loggers and Jake had paid him. That winter with the loggers had been important, he had grown up and especially had learned to defend himself.

The times between working and wintering was when he traveled. During these times he would stay in one spot, usually on a creek where he could get fish and gig frogs, for several days. When he felt the urge to move, he moved. He never had a destination, never had a schedule so he had no reason to hurry. One place was as good as another, so why move?

The sun was straight up when Mose stopped in the woods by a creek and they ate the lunch Hattie Mae had fixed for them. Rep thought of the ham biscuits she had fixed for him the last time he was on the road. Today they ate fried chicken, slaw and biscuits with a gallon of sweet tea. They both agreed Hattie Mae was a fine cook.

They got back on the road. "What you thank you gonna find with yo' family?" said Mose.

Rep shook his head. "I don't know, Mose. I been gone almost six years and there ain't no tellin' what has happened to 'em since. I'll just have to wait and see."

They were riding about midafternoon when Rep saw a building ahead and he recognized it. "That's the school where I went, Mose," he said as he pointed at the building. Now he knew where he was. He'd walked from his house to this building on the few days when he went to school.

Past the school building was a dirt road to the right. "That's the road right there," said Rep. "Turn on it." Rep knew his house was about a mile down the road. He stared ahead, his heart pounding. He had no idea what he was about to find, but he didn't feel good about it.

He first saw the fields across the road where he'd spent so many miserable days plowing, hoeing and harvesting. They were nearing a bend in the road and he knew they were getting close. "The house is right around the bend, Mose." He leaned forward as they rounded the bend and he saw the house. “Damn,” he said as Mose stopped.

Where he had left a dilapidated, two room shack some six years ago, he was now looking at a larger frame house painted white with flowers in beds along the front. He looked at Mose, his face showing his surprise. “The old house is gone, Mose. Somebody else lives here now. They done tore the old house down.”

He opened the door and slowly got out. He looked around, staring at the house and the yard. He saw electric wires running to the house where there had never been any before. There was a barn painted red in the rear of the house. He looked around again. It had to be the right place. The fields across the road were as he remembered; they were the same. He was completely puzzled, wondering how this had come about.

As he shut the truck door, a young boy came out the front door of the house and stood on the steps looking at him. He looked to be seventeen or eighteen years old. He walked down the steps toward them and stopped, his face questioning. “What y’all be lookin’ for,” he asked. He stood staring at Rep.

“I’m lookin’ for the family that used to live here,” said Rep. “Lookin’ for the Doe family.”

The boy was staring at Rep with a puzzled look when a young girl came out the door, stopped on the porch and looked at them. “Who you be lookin’ for?” the boy asked.

“Harry Doe’s family, they used to live here.”

The boy shook his head, confused by the question. “I’m Owen Doe,” he said, “I live here. Harry Doe was my daddy, but he be dead.”

Rep was shocked. “You’re Owen Doe?”

The boy nodded. “I am. Who you be?”

Rep didn’t know what to say. “You had a brother named Rep Doe. Do you remember him?”

The boy nodded. “I remember ‘im. Mama said he run away years ago.”

Rep smiled. “He did run away,” he said. He walked toward the boy and stuck out his hand. “I’m Rep, Owen. I’m yo’ brother.”

Owen shook his hand, but his face showed his uncertainty. "You're Rep?"

"I am."

"You done got big."

Rep laughed and hugged him. "You done got big too."

Owen looked at Mose.

"This is Mose," said Rep. "He's my friend."

The girl had walked off the steps toward them and was looking at them, unsure what was going on.

"And who is this?" he asked.

"This is Louise," said Owen.

Rep walked to her. "I'm your brother Rep, Louise. I remember you when you were a little girl." He hugged her, although she wasn't sure who he was.

"Where's yo' mama?" Rep asked, as he held Louise's hand.

"She up Mr. Joe's. She works for 'im now, cooks and keeps house for 'im."

"You said Daddy died."

Owen nodded. "He died bout three years ago. Doctor said the whiskey got 'im."

Rep looked at the house, he was puzzled. "Who fixed up the house?"

"Mr. Joe done it. After Daddy died, Mama started working for 'im and he's been mighty good to us."

Rep looked at him, puzzled by his statement. He had never remembered Mr. Joe ever being nice about anything. "What does Mr. Joe's wife say about him doing all this for y'all?"

Owen shook his head. "She don't say nothin' cause she had a stroke and she be in the bed. She don't know nothin', Mama says. That be why Mama be up there, to help look after her."

Rep listened but didn't say anything else. He had no idea about this, but it sounded strange to him.

"Where's your brother, Brooks and your sister, Kathryn?"

"They be with Mama."

He looked across the road at the fields. "Who works the fields now?"

"I do and Mr. Joe has some men now. Brooks works too."

"So y'all get along all right now."

Owen nodded. "We do good, Mr. Joe looks after us."

"You say Mama is up Mr. Joe's house?"

"She goes early ever mornin'. Some nights she stays all night to look after Mr. Joe's wife."

Rep looked at Mose but didn't say anything else. He thought about his mother who was fifteen when he was born. So, she would be around thirty-seven now, still a young woman. He didn't know how old Mr. Joe was, as a boy he'd thought of him as being old back then. He was probably getting close to sixty now, still not an old man. If his wife was sick, chances are he was looking for a woman. He didn't know for sure, but it looked like that might be the case with his mother.

"I'm gonna ride up and see Mama," he said. "We'll be back after we talk to her." Rep and Mose went to the truck and rode on up the hill to Mr. Joe's house. When they pulled in the driveway Rep got out. Mose stayed in the truck.

He was walking toward the back door when it opened, and his mother walked out. He stopped and waited. She stepped out on the steps and stared at him. "Can I help you?" she said.

Rep looked at her. She was dressed well with makeup on and was a nice-looking woman. He had remembered her when he left home as a woman without hope, doing her best to survive to look after her children. "You don't recognize me, do you?" he said, watching her face.

She was puzzled as she stared at him. "No, I don't believe I do," she said. "Have I met you before?"

Rep smiled. "I'm Rep, Mama," he said.

Her eyes widened and her hand flew over her mouth. "Oh my God," she said. "I thought you was dead," she said as she rushed forward and wrapped her arms around him, tears flowing down her face. She hugged him, then finally pulled back and looked in his face.

"We all thought you was dead after all these years. Where have you been?"

Rep took her by the hand, led her to the truck and introduced her to Mose. Then they went inside and sat at the kitchen table and he started telling her about where he had been and what he had done. "You're a grandmother, Mama. I have a son."

She stared at him. The shock of him suddenly appearing, alive and well, after all these years had confused her mind. She was having difficulty taking in all he was saying. "You're married?" she asked.

"Her name is Lila. Our son's name is Rip, Mama." He didn't say anything about Bess. He would cover that later; it was too complicated for right now.

They talked for another hour, Rep talking and his mother asking questions. Brooks and Kathryn, his brother and sister came in and were introduced to him. Neither of them remembered him, since they had been too young when he left.

The door opened and Mr. Joe walked in. Rep and Mose were introduced. Rep was surprised at how friendly the reception was from Mr. Joe, completely different from the way he remembered him. He told Rep how he appreciated his mother helping look after his wife since she had been sick. Rep nodded but didn't comment. He seemed to be a good man and when Rep saw how he looked at his mother, it was obvious he was fond of her.

They talked for a while with Mr. Joe. Then Rep and Mose, along with his mother and the children, went to her house. It had been decided that Rep and Mose would sleep in Mr. Joe's bunkhouse and their beds had been fixed. Mose was glad they weren't going to sleep in the woods as Rep had said they would do. His mother fixed supper with some of the food they had brought, and they all ate together. Mose went to the bunkhouse, the children went to bed and Rep sat with his mother and talked.

She wanted to hear about Lila and little Rip. She was most surprised that he was married and had a son. After talking about Lila, he told her about losing Bess and that made her sad. She couldn't believe he had survived on the road all those years and then ended up with a wife and a son.

He asked about his daddy. She told him how he had continued to drink until it killed him.

She looked at Rep. "You've seen that I'm working for Joe and his wife is sick."

Rep nodded and watched her face.

"When yo' daddy died I had nothin' left. You was gone and I had four kids to feed and without the farm I had no place to live. I didn't know what to do. Joe's wife had the stroke and was in the bed all the time and he needed somebody to look after her. He come to me and asked me to help. I hadn't never talked to him much in the past, but he needed help and I did too. He said if I would help him, I could stay in the house and he would help me out." She looked at Rep. "That was all it was to start with."

Rep nodded.

"After I had worked for a while, I saw he was a good man, and I grew to like 'im. His wife had been a domineering woman and made his life miserable. Their two children had moved away, and he was alone." She stared out the window for a moment and then looked back at Rep. "He was good to the children, that was important to me. One day he come to me and said he knew he was older than me, but he liked me and knew I was a good woman. He said he was gonna look after his wife as long as she lived but if I was willin', he would like to be with me."

Rep could see tears swelling in her eyes as she talked.

"I listened to him talk for a while, then I took his hand and I led him to his bed, and I loved him. I've been sharing his bed at times ever since." She looked back at Rep. "I'm not ashamed of what I've done. I be happier right now than I've ever been."

Rep smiled and leaned over and kissed her. "You done what you thought was best. Mr. Joe seems like a good man and he's been good to you and the children." He shook his head. "I think you done right."

They talked on until late in the night. She asked him about Mose and he told her about him being Lila's uncle and all Mose had done for him since he had been at Shoal Creek. Finally, he had told her all he could think of and went to the bunkhouse.

The next morning, he and Mose ate breakfast with his mother and the children. When they finished his mother asked him to walk outside with her.

"I need to ask you to do somethin' for me, Rep," she said.

"I will if I can," said Rep.

"Owen is seventeen now and he don't like this farm life. He's getting' a little wild now and I can't handle 'im. He needs a man around 'im." She stared in Rep's eyes. "Will you take 'im with you and give 'im a job?"

"Does he want to go?"

She nodded. "I talked to 'im last night. He said he wanted to go with you."

"I'll take 'im if you want me to. Let me talk to 'im."

Rep walked outside. Owen was sitting on the steps. Rep sat down beside him. "Yo' Mama tells me you want to go with me and work where I am."

"Yes, suh," said Owen.

Rep shook his head. "Don't say sir to me, Owen, I'm yo' brother. If you want to go, I need somebody to fish on the river. The boy doin' it now is bout to go to college. I'll teach you how to fish, I used to do it myself. It's a good life, living on the river and fishing." He looked at him. "You reckon you'd like to do that?"

Owen nodded. "It sho' would be better than walking behind that mule."

Rep stood up and looked down at him. "I want you to know this. If you won't work or if you get in trouble, I'll whip yo' butt. Do you understand what I'm sayin'?"

Owen looked up at Rep towering over him and nodded.

"Then go get yo' stuff and get ready to go."

Owen jumped up and ran in the house.

Later the whole family gathered outside and said their goodbyes.

Rep hugged his mother and his brothers and sisters. He took his mother to the side. "You know where I am now. If you need me or need help, just let me know. I can help you if you need me, but it looks like Mr. Joe will look after you."

She nodded. "Look after Owen."

Rep smiled. "Don't worry bout 'im. I'll look after him."

He and Mose loaded up with Owen in the truck and headed north toward Shoal Creek.

2

May woke up early on Sunday Morning. Star was still asleep, so she slipped out of bed and quietly left the house. She drove to the dormitory and parked. She went in the room and Alva was getting ready to go to church. She looked at May, she could see her eyes were red and puffy. "Are you alright?"

May nodded. "I haven't felt well and had a restless night."

"You do what you want to," said Alva. "I'm going to church."

May knew she didn't want to sit in this room alone with her thoughts, so she dressed and went to church with Alva. Throughout the service her thoughts were on Storm and what she should do. There was no way she could go through the coming days without facing him and she couldn't hide forever. But she couldn't go to him without looking like a fool, she had to maintain some of her pride. After what he had said to her, she doubted he would ever come to see her. She decided the best plan would be to go about her business each day and eventually they would run into each other. When that happened, she would deal with it.

Her second quandary was deciding what she really wanted to do with her future. She had said she didn't want to live in River Bluff and she still felt that way. If Storm was serious and wanted to marry her, then she would have to because that would be where he was going to live. If she married Storm, she'd never have to worry about anything ever again. He would look after her and she'd have anything she wanted. Also, if she married him, she would be a Gill and not a Hobb.

Storm was everything a girl might want in a man. He was handsome, smart and wealthy. He was educated and would be successful in his job. She enjoyed being with him, she liked him, and she might be somewhat in love with him. But she knew she wasn't madly in love with him. If she was, she wouldn't be thinking about all these details; she would just run off with him and never look back. She thought that was what people in love did.

She had enjoyed kissing him and felt she would enjoy going to bed with him. While she'd no experience in bed, she felt sure he had so there'd be no problem there. So, she wasn't exactly sure why this debate was going on in her head.

Storm had said she had made her choice. To him the choice she had made had been to dance half naked on stage in front of a crowd of drunk men. If that was her choice, then she couldn't have him. She understood that. She couldn't be with him during the week and dance naked on stage on the weekends. Star had said that wasn't a compromise Storm would accept and May knew it.

What if this debate she was having with herself was a waste of time? Maybe, when he saw her on stage with her breasts bared, he had decided she was not for him and was through with her forever. If that was true, why did he wait for her in the parking lot? Did he face her to tell her he was through with her? He never said that. In fact, he didn't say anything about his choice in the matter. He only talked about her choice. He said she had made the choice to dance naked on stage rather than choose him.

By the time the pastor finished his sermon, May had decided. She wasn't scheduled to go to the club until Friday afternoon. She had until then to run into him and see what happened. If he wouldn't speak to her and ignored her completely, she would have her answer; he was through with her. But if he did talk, then she would wait and see what his message was. If he threw down an ultimatum, then she would have to decide her direction. But she knew if it came to that, there was no middle ground. She knew that already.

When she and Alva walked out of the church and turned toward the dormitory, she saw Storm's car parked in front of Jim's bench at the gym. He was sitting on the gym steps, his eyes on her. Alva saw him too. "There's Storm on the gym steps," she said.

"I see him," said May.

"You didn't see him this weekend, did you?"

"No," said May, "I didn't see him," as they walked out the road.

"He's looking at you," Alva said as she glanced at May. "Are you supposed to meet him?"

"No, I'm not supposed to meet him."

Alva looked at her, surprised by her tone.

They walked on toward the gym; May was watching Storm out of the corner of her eye."

He was still staring directly at her.

When they got directly in front of gym steps, May stopped, turned toward Storm, put her hands on her hips and stared at him. Alva, standing beside May, looked at her and then at Storm, not understanding what was happening.

Storm sat on the steps, his eyes on May's eyes. He didn't move nor did May. This stymie continued for more than a minute, then May turned and started out the road. Alma hesitated, then followed her.

"What was that all about?" asked Alma when they got to the dormitory.

"I don't want to talk about it," said May as she went in her room and shut the door.

Alva stood looking at the door and then went to her room.

On Monday May went to school. When she got out, she was determined to prove to Storm that she wasn't intimidated by him. She left the dormitory and walked to the stores. Jim Hawke was sitting on his bench as she approached.

May didn't know it but Jim and Win Clark were best friends and confidants. Jim, as the constable and Win, as director of security for the mill, had shared information about what was going on in town with each other for years. They shared everything they knew. So when Win trailed May to the club in Phenix City and saw her act, he told Jim everything about it. Win did this with no thought about his pledge to Storm to not tell anyone. The good of the town outweighed any individual's rights, even if the person was a Gill.

Jim watched May approach. He had been surprised when Win had told him about May's actions at the club. He had never been surprised at anything Star did, she'd always been what she was. But although May was a Hobb, he thought that somehow she was different. It seemed he had been wrong, the Hobb blood was stronger than he had thought.

"Morning, Mr. Jim," she said as she walked up.

"Morning, little girl. Where you be headed?"

She shook her head. "No place special. Just walking."

He nodded. "I didn't see you this weekend. You musta been gone somewhere."

She looked at him. "I was. I went to see a friend."

"Thought you musta been gone cause I saw Storm and he was by hisself." He cut his eyes at her.

She turned and looked at him. "What does that mean? I don't stay with him all the time."

"I thought y'all had a little case goin'."

She shrugged. "Well, you thought wrong." She looked at him. "Did he say that to you?"

Jim shook his head. "He ain't said nothin' to me bout you, but I saw ya'll together more than once last week. Seemed like somethin' was goin' on."

"Sometimes you're worse than a gossipy woman, trying to get something started."

Jim laughed. "You be mighty touchy bout 'im, it seems. Somethin' botherin' you?"

"Why do you say that?"

"You talked about Storm worrying about you being a Hobb and

he ain't never said one-word bout that." He looked at her. "You be the only one been worried bout that."

May shook her head. "What are you talking about?"

"Yo' folks always acted like white-trash and yo' brothers did too. And Star damn well acted like a Hobb; she was bout sorry as hell." He nodded. "But that boy don't care about them Hobbs, he just cares that you ain't gonna be like 'em."

May stepped toward him and stared in his eyes.

"What the hell are you saying?"

"I never said a word about you shooting that man cross the river. I figured there was a reason for it, and it wasn't my business." said Jim. "But if you're gonna go to Phenix City and be part of that sorry ass business down there, don't come to me when you're in trouble."

May's face was red, she was embarrassed that he knew what she had done. "What did he tell you about me?"

"He ain't told me nothin'. I ain't seen 'im." Jim looked at her. "I know what's goin' on about most everythin' in this town, little girl. Didn't Star tell you that?"

"You didn't talk to Storm?"

"I didn't."

May knew he was telling her the truth. Somebody else in town knew about Phenix City. She had no idea who. She shook her head; she hadn't expected this from Jim. She turned and started walking toward the Methodist church. She hadn't gone ten feet when Storm's car came around the church and headed toward her. She stopped, her eyes on the car, she could see his eyes on her. The car slowed and came to a stop beside her. Storm leaned over, opened the passenger door and looked at her. "Get in," he said. He watched her eyes, waiting for her reaction.

She hesitated, her eyes on him, unsure what to do. Then, without thinking, she got in and shut the door. She didn't look at him but kept her eyes straight ahead.

He didn't speak, turned the car around and headed to the river. He tuned on the dirt road to the landing, went past the group gathered there and drove upriver to where they had parked before.

May kept her eyes straight ahead and waited. They sat for several minutes, neither spoke.

Finally, Storm broke the silence. "Will you explain to me what you're doing?"

May looked at him. "You saw me Saturday night. You know what I'm doing."

"I know what, that was obvious, but I don't know why."

May shrugged. "I don't have to explain or apologize to you for what I do. Why do you think it's your business?"

"I realize that you don't owe me an explanation or an apology," said Storm. He sat for a moment. "I thought that maybe there was something between us more than just friendship."

"We have been out a couple of times," said May, "That's all. I never made any kind of commitment with you to do or not do anything."

"So, the time we've been together hasn't meant anything to you?"

"What does it matter to you what I do?" she asked.

Storm shook his head. "Damn, May. I saw you on a stage almost naked. You were taking money from men and letting them run their hands over you."

"So?" she said, looking at him.

"I have serious feelings about you. How do you think I felt when I saw that?"

"What are you saying?"

"I've been to strip clubs before, May. I've seen naked women on stage, and I know what they do. I also know what they do when they're off stage too."

She turned toward him. "What are you accusing me of?"

"I'm not accusing you of anything, but men that pay money expect more than just touching you."

"All I've done is what you saw me do on the stage, nothing more." She glared at him, daring him to say more.

He figured he needed to get away from this subject. "Who was the woman on stage with you?"

"That was Josie, she's from Shoal Creek."

"Who was the man that chased you out the door at the club and you were running from?"

"That was Walt Wend. He owns the club."

"Why was he after you? He seemed mighty upset, grabbing at you and yelling."

May turned and stared directly in Storm's face. "He wanted me to go to his house with him. I wouldn't go."

"Why would he expect you to go? Have you been with him before?"

May took a deep breath. "No! I have never been with him."

Storm thought for a moment. "I've heard that name, Walt Wend. The people at Shoal Creek said he is the man that buys the whiskey they make. They don't like him."

"That's right, Walt owns the club and buys whiskey." She stopped. "Josie is his girlfriend."

"But he wants you too," said Storm

"Yes, he wants me," said May. "But I don't want him."

Storm reached and took her hand. "May, surely you know what kind of people you are dealing with here. They are mean people, and they will hurt you."

She looked at him. "I know that, but I can take care of myself."

"Are you going back to the club?"

"I'm supposed to go Friday night."

"Are you going?"

May nodded as she looked at his face. "Yes, right now I plan to go."

Storm stared at the river water rushing by for a minute, then he started the car. "Then there's nothing else for me to say." He looked at her. "I did try." He pulled back on the dirt road and headed for the dormitory. Neither one spoke as they passed the gym. He pulled in at the dormitory, she got out and he drove away.

. . .

Jim Hawke was on his bench as Storm got back to the gym. He pulled over, parked, got out and walked over and sat by Jim.

"You don't look real happy, boy," Jim said. "I just saw you go by with May."

Storm grimaced. "I don't understand her, Jim."

Jim rubbed his hand across his face. "I'm gonna tell you, Storm. I know about her being in Phenix City in that club."

"Figured you might know about that," said Storm. "Why does she do it?"

"Don't know that," said Jim. "Women ain't logical critters like men, so there ain't no way to figure them out. They mostly act on emotions and you can't catch emotions and put them in a bucket, cause you can't see 'em." He looked at Storm. "I understand you went down and saw her on stage."

"Yes, I did."

"She's among some bad people down there and she's likely to get in bad trouble before it's over. Them people she's dealing with don't care about nobody."

Storm nodded. "I know that."

"If you care bout her, you can't just walk away and leave her. You need to keep her close to you. If you leave her, she won't have nobody else."

Storm listened to Jim; he knew he was right. He got up, went to his car and headed down the road toward Pot Licker Lane. He pulled up in front of the Hobb house and parked. When he knocked on the door, Star opened it. "I'm Storm Gill," he said. "I'd like to talk to you."

Star smiled. "I know who you are, Storm," she said as she walked out on the porch. "Let's sit out here." They walked to the end of the porch and sat down.

"I'm sure you know that I went to Phenix City and saw May on stage."

Star nodded. "She told me."

He looked straight at Star. "Why is she doing this?"

"I've asked her that same question and she never gave me an answer." She shrugged. "I don't know that I can tell you why."

"You did all that sort of thing. Is that what she's trying to do, copy you?"

Star smiled ruefully. "That's probably part of it. She was always asking me about what I had done." She laughed. "She told me one time she had made a list of the things I had done, and she was going to match it. I told her I was ashamed of most of the things I did."

Storm stared at her. "She may be trying."

"Why are you here and asking me all this?" asked Star.

Storm shook his head. "I have feelings for her. Don't ask me why but she has captured me." He looked at her. "Don't take this the wrong way but it really bothers her that she's a Hobb. She told me I'd never really have anything to do with her because it would upset my parents for me to be seen with a Hobb. I think she really believes that."

"I'm sure she does," said Star. "This family has been one sorry ass bunch of white trash. May had to live with it every day. She moved out to try to get away from being a Hobb." Star shook her head. "I was certainly a part of that by the things I did."

"When I saw her come out of the club a man was chasing her, grabbing and yelling at her. She said he was the owner, Walt Wend. The people over at Shoal Creek said he buys whiskey," said Storm.

"Walt is a mean bastard," said Star. "He's also handsome and charming. He likes women and is used to having his way with them at the club. He has his eyes on May. I've warned her about him.

"Jim says she'll get in trouble if she stays there."

Star agreed. "That's probably true."

"She told me she's going back Friday night."

"I expect she will," said Star. "What are you going to do?"

Storm shrugged. "I don't know. I don't know if I should try to talk to her again or not."

"She's strong minded," said Star. "She's also hardheaded and tough."

"I know that. Thank you for talking to me," said Storm as he got up and went to his car. He had no idea what he should do.

Star sat on the porch after Storm left. When she had met with Walt at Shoal Creek, he agreed to leave her family, and especially May, alone. Based on his recent actions, he wasn't doing it. She understood that May had walked into his territory of her own free will and that clouded the issue somewhat. However, he had agreed to leave May alone regardless, so he was breaking their agreement. She knew that regardless of what he did with May, she would have to kill Walt eventually. It was just a matter of when.

3

Rep talked to Owen as they went north. He found him to be intelligent but his upbringing, as his had been, was lacking in social skills most people took for granted. His father was an uneducated drunk.

He was possibly driven that way by a hopeless sharecropper life that had no chance of success. His mother, married at fourteen and a mother a few months later, was a child trying to raise children. He and the other children were born into this family, and their future at birth was bleak at best. Rep knew he was fortunate to have escaped. By accident he had run into families that helped him and he had managed to survive to this point.

The trip was exciting for Owen. He had never been more than two miles from his home and had no idea there was a large world out there. He had gone to the eighth grade, and that only part time before his daddy had put him in the fields full time, so he had little education. As they rode up the road, he constantly asked questions and Rep tried his best to answer them.

By the time they got to Shoal Creek Rep had a good feel for Owen and felt he would fit well on the river. With Rolley scheduled to begin college in January, Owen would have time to learn and be ready to take his place. He also planned to spend as much time with him as he could.

They stopped at the barn and Lila was inside at the desk. When they walked in, she jumped up, ran to Rep, hugged and kissed him and then looked at Owen.

"This is my brother, Owen" said Rep. "He's gonna be staying with us now."

Lila didn't question Rep. She turned and hugged Owen, telling him how welcome he was and how glad she was he had come to live with them. Owen was overwhelmed. The trip through Georgia, seeing so many things he'd never seen before, had been great. Talking to Rep and having a chance at a new life in a new place was more than he had ever hoped for. And now, this beautiful woman hugging him and welcoming him into their lives was the best of all. He was looking forward to what came next.

Rep knew Lila was waiting for him to tell her about his folks and about his trip, so he asked Mose to take Owen to Hattie Mae and get him fed. He would meet them later and take Owen to the shed and get him set up. Mose left with Owen.

Rep sat down with Lila. He told her about the trip going down. Then finding the house and his surprise when he saw it, all new and painted with flowers all around. Lila was interested in his story as he talked about the children and seeing his mother and how she had looked and what she was doing. But she was especially interested in the relationship between his mother and Mr. Joe.

"So, she said she was cooking and cleaning plus helping Mr. Joe look after his wife," said Lila. "Then she told you that in addition to these duties she was sharing his bed?"

Rep nodded. "She had been there for a while and he came to her and told her he had feelings for her. It seemed that she felt the same way." He looked at Lila. "When I watched them together it was plain they cared for each other."

"So, it would seem that when his wife dies, they would marry."

"That would seem to be what will happen," said Rep. "Then Mama would be set up good."

"You never expected to find this, did you?"

Rep smiled. "No, I didn't. I was expectin' the worse when I got there. But I reckon that Daddy dying and Mr. Joe's wife having the stroke set it all up to work this way."

Lila shook her head. "We don't ever know what is coming next in our lives."

Rep looked at her. "Look at us, at all that happened. Look at how we ended up together."

Lila leaned over and kissed him. "You're right. We've gone through a lot."

Rep got up. "I better go find Owen and get him set up at the shed. He can stay down there, and I'll show him around and teach him about the fishing. Rolley can help him too."

"He seems like a good boy," said Lila.

Rep nodded. "He's like I was when I left home. He's got a lot to learn." He kissed Lila and went out the door.

Rolley Hill had fished the trotlines and all the set hooks and headed back to the landing. When he came out of Back Slough, he was surprised to see Rep and a boy he had never seen standing by the shed. He beached the boat, got out and walked up the bank.

Rep and the boy met him. "Rolley," said Rep, "this is my brother, Owen. He's gonna be staying here in the shed." Rep then explained to Rolley that Owen would be taking his place with the fishing when he went to college. He explained that he would be showing Owen around and teaching him about fishing, but he wanted him to also help with the training.

Rolley shook hands with Owen and told Rep he would do all he could to help. "Have you heard anything from Karen?" Rolley asked.

Rep smiled. "Lila said she is coming for Thanksgiving for a few days. I thought you might be interested in that news."

"That's good," said Rolley. He went to the boat, got out several catfish and took them to the table.

Rep looked at Owen. "This is what you do when you catch fish. Every day you clean them and take them to Hattie Mae in the kitchen." He showed Jim how to cut off the head, gut the fish and get it cleaned for the kitchen. By the time they finished Own had caught on and Rep thought he would do well. He asked Rolley to take Owen with him for the next few days and show him what to do. Rep told Owen he would also show him around too. He told him they would be bird hunting the next few weeks and he wanted him to learn that too.

The rest of the week went fast, there was no trouble and then it was Friday.

May got home from school Friday afternoon, went to her room and told Alva she would be gone Friday night. She would stay with her friend, Josie Friday night and with Star Saturday night as she had done last week. Alva looked at her but didn't say anything. She knew something was going on with May and she was worried about it. The fact she wouldn't share any details with her bothered her greatly. She decided that if May didn't come forward after the weekend about what she was doing, she was going to have to confront her. She couldn't have May live with her if she wasn't honest with her.

May got in the car and headed toward Phenix City. She had not seen nor talked to Storm since Monday. She had avoided Jim Hawke too, not wanting to have to listen to him chastise her again. She knew her actions were cowardly, but she had done a lot of thinking about her situation and didn't want either Storm or Jim messing with her mind.

She tried to watch behind her as she drove since she had been followed before, but she didn't see anybody behind her. She got to the club, pulled into the parking lot and got out. She stood and looked around but didn't see any cars she recognized. She went in the club and headed for Walt's office. She had thought all week about what she would do.

Walt was sitting behind his desk when she walked in and she could see the surprise on his face when he saw her. She walked over to the desk. "I want to talk to you," she said.

He leaned back in the chair and looked up at her. "All right, talk."

"I want to have an understanding with you. I'm not like Josie and the other girls that work here. If they want to go to bed with you, that's their business but I'm not going to do it," she said. "If I ever do go to bed with you, it will be my decision, not yours."

She watched his face. He stared at her with no emotion. "I enjoy being on the stage and that's what I want to do, nothing more. I want to do that without you bothering me and threatening me." She stared across the desk at him. "I want to be left alone."

He smiled. "So, I'm supposed to keep my hands off you."

May nodded. "You don't need me; Josie will keep you satisfied for now. That should keep you happy."

He stood up and walked over to her. "What if I don't want to do this? What if I don't want to leave you alone? You remember I've already had my hands all over you." He grabbed her arm and held her. "I could take you right now."

May shrugged. "You could, but if you force me or hurt me, either I will kill you or Star will." She looked in his eyes. "You know we will, we've already decided that."

He laughed, pulled her to him and kissed her. "I know you would." Then he pushed her back and patted her on the rear. "I'm going to have you and I'm not going to wait forever."

She shook her head. "Go take a cold shower." She walked out of the room.

May was pumped up when she went downstairs and dressed. She felt that she had got Walt off her back at least for a while and could enjoy being on stage which was what she liked. She found Josie and told her what she had done. "I'm depending on you to keep him happy and wore out so he won't be bothering me," said May.

Josie laughed. "I don't thank he ever gets wore out."

Josie went on first as usual so the crowd was already stirred up when May came out. She was more excited than usual, and the crowd reacted to her. By the time she got to the final part of the act the crowd was almost out of control.

She saw a nice looking, well dressed young man standing at the edge of the stage holding up money and motioning for her to come over. She walked over and leaned over near him, which she didn't normally do, but he didn't look dangerous.

"I have a hundred dollars if you'll come sit and talk to me," he said.

The crowd was so loud she could hardly hear him. "Why would I do that," she asked.

"I'm not going to bother you," he said. "I just want to meet you."

May had never been off the stage and in the crowd and met with anybody after the act before. She backed away and moved near Josie. Josie had been watching her talking to the man. "Who is he?" May asked.

Josie moved closer. "He's Harry Rinkley, the third or fourth, or somethin' like that," said Josie. "His family owns half of Georgia. What did he want?" she yelled as they moved about.

"He offered me a hundred dollars to come sit and talk to him."

Josie laughed and took off her top. "Damn, tell Harry I'll spend the weekend with him for less than that."

May laughed and looked at Harry, he was still holding up the money, his eyes on her. She eased that way, moving slowly toward him. His eyes didn't leave her. She stood in front of him and leaned over right above him and took off her top. He stared at her nakedness, standing six inches away. She smiled at him. "Maybe I will another day," she said as she backed away.

He smiled, nodded and watched her as she walked away.

When she went off stage through the curtain Walt was hugging Josie and telling her how great they did. He turned when he saw May, hugged her and tried to kiss her, all the while his hands were moving over her. She let him go for a moment and then pushed him away. She didn't want to start a scene in the dressing room with other people around. She had already told him how she felt about him having his hands on her. She started dressing.

He whispered in her ear. "I felt the cold bumps. You were enjoying it."

She smiled and whispered. "You're wrong about that," she said as she walked to the door. He watched her go.

May went outside and walked to her car. She had parked under a light because she knew it would be dark when she came out. When she got into the lighted area, she saw Storm standing by her car looking at her. She stopped, her eyes on him and her mind searching for a reason for him to be here. "What are you doing here?" she asked, her eyes searching his face as she walked toward him.

"I was worried about you and came to see if you were all right."

She stared at him, her face showing her doubt about what he was saying. "You drove all the way down here because you were worried about me?"

He nodded.

She still didn't understand his reason for being here. "Did you watch the show? I was on stage tonight."

He shook his head. "I knew you would be on stage. I didn't watch the show." He looked at her. "I had already seen it."

She stood there, completely confused. "So, what are you going to do now?"

"It is late and it's dark. I am going to follow you home."

She walked over to him where she could clearly see his face. "You knew I was going to be on stage tonight. You knew what I was going to do because you have seen me do it. You knew I was going to take off my clothes in front of a crowd of men and stand there naked." She stared in his face. "Yet you came because you were worried about me?"

He smiled and nodded. "Yes, that is right."

"You are going to follow me home?"

"Yes, I am."

She didn't know how to reply to him because she knew he had been against her coming tonight. She had thought he was mad with her, yet here he was. She didn't know anything else to say, so she got in, started her car and headed toward River Bluff. Storm ran to his car and followed her.

As she drove, she thought about what Storm had done and was doing. She had never had anyone show this type of concern for her in her life. Alva had, but that was different, she was a woman. The men she had known in the past, those in her family and others, didn't really care about her. She certainly knew what Walt was concerned about. By the time they reached River Bluff, May knew what she was going to do.

When they got to the outskirts of town, she pulled into the dormitory drive. Storm pulled in behind her to make sure she was alright. May got out of the car, ran to his car, opened the door and got in the passenger's seat. She was carrying a small bag.

Storm was surprised and looked at her. "What are you doing?" he asked.

"I was supposed to stay with Josie at her apartment tonight. But when you showed up and were so sweet, I decided to come with you." She looked at him. "Do you have an extra bedroom?"

Storm was surprised at the question. "I do. Why do you ask?"

"I have no other place to stay. I told Alva I would be gone, and Star doesn't expect me." She looked at him. "I thought I might stay with you."

"You are kidding, aren't you?" he asked.

"I'm serious," she said. "You don't want me to go with you?"

"No," he said, "I didn't say that. This is so sudden that I'm confused." He stared at her. "You are going to my house and stay with me."

"Yes, I am, if you want me to."

Storm stared at her and shook his head. "Exactly how do you expect this to work?"

May shrugged. "I've never done this before so I'm not sure, but I need a bath. After I bathe, I'll dress, I have clothes with me. Then if you have an extra bed, I'll go to sleep."

He stared at her. "You intend to sleep in my house tonight?"

"Yes. If you let me." She watched Storm's face.

"I don't know what I think," he said. "It seems I have no idea about you and what you think."

She reached up and kissed him. "Let's go to your house, we can figure it out."

Storm backed out of the drive and headed out the road. All the way to his house his mind was churning. He pulled into his driveway and got out.

May got out and took his hand.

"You sure this is what you want to do?" he said as he walked up and opened the door.

She laughed. "Yes, I've already told you that. Quit talking so much." She followed him inside. "I like your house." she said.

He led her through the house to the bathroom. "You have a shower," she said as she looked around. She was surprised, none of the mill houses had showers, only tubs.

"Yes, Daddy had that put in for me. I like a shower." He looked at her. "There's towels here and soap. If you need anything else let me know."

She laughed. "You've already pretty well seen all of me on the stage." She cut her eyes at him. "You want to take a shower with me?"

He stared at her and shook his head. "You've already confused me enough tonight. I couldn't take any more." He walked out and closed the door.

She smiled, undressed and got in the shower. She came out in a nightgown and house coat. He was sitting on the sofa.

He got up and met her. "I have your bed ready," he said as he led her to the bedroom.

"You were sweet to be worried about me tonight," she said. "I thought you were mad with me and would never speak to me again. But then you showed up."

He smiled. "It didn't make much sense, did it?"

"Maybe not, but it was nice of you."

"People will talk about you if you spend the night with me."

She turned up her nose. "I'm not worried about my reputation; you know I'm a Hobb."

He shook his head. "I wish you would stop saying that." He leaned over and kissed her. "I'll see you in the morning." He closed the door and went to his room. He sat on the bed and thought of her being in the next room. *I may never go to sleep*, he thought.

He was still awake when he heard the door open and she tiptoed across the room, pulled the cover back and crawled into the bed.

He turned over. "What are you doing?" he asked, staring at her.

"Don't talk," she said as she kissed him. She nestled up against him. "Just hold me and be real quiet."

He felt her warmth against him. He put his arm around her and pulled her body tighter against him. Her body against him aroused him. He looked in her face and her eyes were on him. She kissed him, turned over and sat up in the bed. He watched her, wondering what she was doing.

She reached down, grabbed her nightgown, pulled it over her head and threw it on the floor. She stared at him. "I've never done this before, but I wanted it to be with you." She lay down beside him, wrapped her arms around him and kissed him."

"Are you sure about this?" he asked.

"Yes," she said as she kissed him again, put her leg over him and pulled him to her.

He didn't say anything else.

The early sun was lighting the room when he woke up. He looked at her as she slept, slipped out of bed, took a shower and dressed. He came back in the room and she was awake, lying there looking at him when he walked in.

"Good morning," he said.

She smiled up at him. "Good morning."

He sat on the bed and leaned over and kissed her. "Are you alright?"

She kissed him back. "Yes, I'm fine."

He stared in her eyes, searching her face. "You surprised me last night."

She chuckled. "Surprised me too. I didn't know last night that I would do that. It just sort of happened."

"I'd be glad to have you surprise me anytime."

She looked up at him and patted his face. "You are sweet, but I don't think that would be a good idea."

"Why not?"

"I might get to liking you too much and that wouldn't be good."

"I think it would be very good." He leaned over and kissed her. "I would like to talk to you about it."

She turned over, jumped out of bed and started toward the door. "No, you don't," she said as she went to the bathroom. After she dressed, she came back to him on the couch and they went out the front door. She looked up at him, her face questioning. "I'll see you tomorrow?"

Storm stood there, his eyes on her. He knew she was going back to the club tonight and she was putting the subject in front of him with her question. He pulled her to him and kissed her. "I'll see you tomorrow."

She smiled. They got in his car and headed to Star's house. They didn't see anybody on the way.

"You spent the night and slept with Storm at his house?" asked Star.

"Yes, I did."

"What brought this on?"

"He knew I was on stage at the club last night and he was against me going, but he came down there to make sure I was alright. He followed me home." She looked at Star. "I thought that was sweet."

"He was sweet, so you decided to reward him by sleeping with him."

May nodded. "I did. I wanted him to be the first. I like him."

Star sat and looked at her. "But you don't know if you want to marry him and stay with him. Now what?"

"I'm going to the club tonight." Then she told Star about her conversation with Walt and the understanding they had agreed on. "At least I have him off me for the moment."

"Maybe so," said Star, "but he's not gonna wait forever." She looked at May. "What are you gonna do then?"

"I can't answer that until I get there," said May.

Star shook her head. "You better think about it before he comes after you. I know him. Once he's had enough of your delays, he's gonna come after you and he's not gonna fool around."

May knew Star was telling the truth.

May went to the club Saturday night. Walt was not there, and Josie didn't know where he was. May certainly didn't miss him and had a good night on stage, drove to River Bluff and spent the night with Star. She was tired and slept late. All church services were over when she walked to the dormitory. When she went in the room Alva was sitting on the sofa and when May looked at her, she knew Alva had something on her mind. She waited for her to speak.

Alva put her book down beside her and looked up at May. "Will you please sir down, May? I would like to talk to you."

Mat sat down; she could tell Alva was bothered.

Alva looked at her with that schoolteacher look she used with her students when she had suspicions about their actions. "May," she said with her eyes on her face, "I may be wrong, but your recent actions have led me to believe you are hiding something from me. These mysterious weekends with no explanations worry me." She paused. "I realize I am not your mother and therefore you don't have to answer to me for your actions. But you came to live with me and therefore I feel I have a right to know what you are doing."

May looked at Alva. There was nobody she owed more to than Alva who had rescued her from her family when she had no hope. She knew Alva would be disappointed in her and she was sorry, but she had gone to the club and to Storm's house knowing what she was doing.

Alva sat in thought for a minute, then looked at May. "You've been gone two straight weekends and you weren't with Storm. What is going on?"

May got up off the sofa and looked down at Alva. "I have things going on in my life that I have to work through. I have to make decisions and you might not like what I decide. I think the best thing for me to do is go live with Star for right now. She's there with mother now and there's room. You'll never know how much I appreciate what you've done for me."

Alva got up. "You don't have to leave, May. You can stay. I'd just like for you to be honest with me."

"This is best, Alva," said May. She hugged her. "Believe me, I don't want to disappoint you anymore." She walked to her room, packed her clothes, loaded them in the car and went to Pot Licker Lane.

Later that afternoon May left Star and walked up to the gym. It was deserted as it usually was on Sunday. She had promised Storm she would see him on Sunday. She had no intention of going to his house, but if he was looking for her, she was making herself available. Several people came walking by and she spoke to them.

She was about to decide he wasn't looking for her when his car came around the church. He came on, parked by Jim's bench, got out and walked to the steps and sat down beside her.

"Are you alright?" he said, looking at her.

She smiled. "I'm alright. Are you?"

He nodded. "I'm still trying to figure out Friday night."

"What about it?"

He looked at her. "You know what I'm saying. You decided to spend the night and sleep with me. It was your decision."

She nodded. "Yes, it was my decision.

He shook his head. "Just all of a sudden you decided."

"No, that's not true. You were sweet to me and I decided it was time."

He looked at her. "You know I'm in love with you."

May let his hand go and stared out across the street, tears welling up in her eyes. "You can't mean that Storm. I don't want you to tell me that."

He took a deep breath. "That's not what I wanted you to say."

She put her arm around him and laid her head on his shoulder as the tears flowed. "You don't want me, Storm." She kissed him on the cheek. "You know what I am."

"No, I don't know what you are because you don't know what you are," said Storm. "Are you trying to prove you're like Star or you're a real Hobb? Is that what you're doing in that club?"

May shook her head. "I don't know. I just know you don't want me."

"That's up to me to decide. I love you and I want to marry you." Storm grasped her shoulders and turned her to face him. "Do you want me to get on my knees and ask you?"

Tears ran down May's face as she looked at him. "No, I don't want you to do that." She shook her head. "I can't marry you, Storm. I don't love you like that, and I'd make you miserable. I like you too much to do that to you."

He stood up, pursed his lips and looked down at her. "I've never told another woman that I loved her before." He stepped back. "I damn well won't ever make that mistake again." He turned, walked to his car and drove away.

May sat on the gym steps, watched him drive away and cried.

Star looked at May, her face showing her amazement. "He asked you to marry him and you turned him down?"

"Yes, I did. I told him I didn't love him, and I would make him miserable."

Star got up and walked across the room. "Why the hell would you do that without at least getting to know the man?"

"I like Storm," said May, "and I didn't want him to get hurt, so I thought it was best to stop it now."

Star laughed. "Well, he said the other night you had made a choice and he gave you a second chance. You turned down that second chance. I hope you're ready to live with it because I question if you'll ever have another chance."

May nodded. "I knew that when I told him no."

"I gather you are going to stay at the club," said Star. "I hope you're ready to deal with Walt."

May looked at her. "I can handle Walt."

Star turned over and said no more.

May went to school Monday and Tuesday and both days came home after she got out and never left. She didn't want to see nor talk to anyone. She had seen Alva at school but hadn't talked to her. Of all that had happened recently, being apart from Alva hurt her the most.

Her conversation with Storm had upset her greatly, more than she had thought it would when she was talking to him. His blurting out that he loved her had surprised her and she had told him what she had planned to tell him if the subject ever came up. But then he had asked her to marry him and that threw everything haywire. That was a question that required an answer immediately and so she had given one. Now it seemed she had to live with it.

When school was out on Wednesday, she left the house and went to the stores. She was ready to face the world and deal with what came. As she passed the Methodist Church, she thought that Alva would be coming to prayer meeting tonight. That thought and remembering what Alva had done for her took over her mind. She saw that Jim was sitting on his bench watching her. She crossed over to the opposite side of the street from him and waved at him as she passed. She was headed for the dormitory.

She knocked on Alva's door. It opened and Alva was looking at her. "Alva," she said, "you have been the best thing that ever happened to me. I have repaid the help you gave me by not been honest with you. I want to tell you the truth about what I've been doing."

Alva looked at her, turned and went to the couch. "Come and sit with me."

May went in and sat down beside her. "You asked me what I've been doing the last weekends and I didn't tell you because I knew it would disappoint you." For the next thirty minutes she told Alva everything about the club, about Josie and about Walt. She didn't leave out a single detail, from Walt touching her to the excitement of being on the stage naked. She told her about Storm coming to the club and watching her on stage.

Alva sat quietly and listened.

"Star asked me why I'm doing this, and Storm asked me, but I couldn't answer because I'm not sure why." She looked at Alva. "Even as I'm telling you this, I plan to go to the club on Friday and Saturday nights and go on stage."

"You realize how dangerous this is?" said Alva.

May nodded. "I do." She took a deep breath. "I'm sure you think I'm as bad as I can get, but that's not all. Friday night Storm knew I was at the club and he was waiting for me in the parking lot after the show. He said he was worried about me getting home safely so he followed me home."

"He must really care for you," said Alva.

May shook her head. "Yes, he does." She breathed and looked at Alva. "I went home with him and slept with him." She didn't go into more detail. "He asked me to marry him on Sunday, even though he knew I had been to the club Saturday night."

"What did you tell him?

"I told him no. I told him I didn't love him, and I would make him miserable."

"So, it's over?"

May nodded. "That would seem to be the case."

"You know that I don't understand why you are doing this at the club, and I don't condone it," said Alva.

"I know that."

"Having said that, you know I love you."

May nodded. "I know that."

"I am here for you if you need me and I would like for you to stay with me." She looked at May. "I can't do that as long as you go to that club every Friday and Saturday night."

May smiled. "I understand. I love you and I'm sorry I've disappointed you." She got up, hugged Alva and went out the door.

4

Rolley and Owen loaded up the boat early Monday morning and headed down Back Slough to fish the set hooks and trotlines. They got to the first hooks and started paddling along the bank. They passed several hooks but had no fish. Rolley couldn't understand it. He looked at Owen. "We always get several fish along this bank and we don't have a one," he said. "Something's not right here."

They paddled on down to the first trotline, pulled it up and started across. He felt nothing pulling on the line, all the bait was gone, and he didn't have one fish. He shook his head; he knew something was wrong. He looked at Owen. "Let's paddle around the bend and check that line," he said.

"If it don't have fish, then something's going on." He got the paddle and started down the slough. When he rounded the bend they saw a man in a boat in the middle of the slough. He was fishing their trotline.

Rolley reached back, cranked the motor and headed for the boat. The man looked up when the heard the motor. He sat and watched them approach, the trotline across the bow of the boat. He was a big man with a scraggly black beard and long, greasy hair down his back.

Rolley pulled up beside the boat. He looked at several catfish plus two flatheads in the bottom of the boat. "You're fishing our trotline," he said, his eyes on the man's face.

The man looked at him, turned and spat tobacco juice into water. He stared at Rolley. "Ain't yoren' no more," he said. "This be my territory now and all the hooks on it up Back Slough." He spat again.

"You can't do that," said Rolley. "I put these lines and hooks out myself."

The man shook his head. "Don't make a damn with me what you done. I done told you these be mine now." He reached down and picked up a double-barreled shotgun and pointed it at Rolley. "Listen, you little shit. You git the hell outta here and if I see you back down here again, I'll damn well shoot you."

Rolley knew he couldn't argue with the shotgun, so he turned around, cranked the motor and started up the slough. He knew he had to find Rep. When he landed, he told Owen to stay with the boat and he went up the hill, past the kitchen and on to the barn. He ran up on the porch and burst in the door.

Rep, Lila and Mose were sitting at the desk and they all turned and looked at him when he barged in. Rolley caught his breath and quickly told them what had happened. He described the man and the threat he had made.

Rep looked at Mose, his face questioning.

"Sugar Boy," said Mose.

"Who is he?" Rep asked.

"Sorry white trash," said Mose. "He live in Lost Man Swamp down below where Lick be livin'. Ain't never done nothin' but cause trouble. He ain't been up here for a while, cause Red run him off." He quicky explained that Sugar Boy Hogg, that was his name, had a reputation for drinking, fighting and fishing other people's hooks. They had caught him some years back and Red had told him that if he was caught on Back Slough again, he would hang him. Sugar Boy wasn't scared of much, but he was scared of Red because he knew Red would kill him. This was the first time he'd been on Back Slough in several years.

Rep and Mose jumped up, got their rifles and headed for the door with Rolley behind them.

"Please be careful", Lila yelled out as they went out the door.

They started running up the road toward the landing. "We might catch 'im still there," said Rep as they ran. "He run the boys off and he won't expect them back so soon."

Rep jumped in the boat with Rolley and Owen and Mose followed in the other boat. They headed down Back Slough and when they rounded the last bend, Sugar Boy was still sitting in the middle of the slough. He was surprised to see the boats.

Rep told Rolley to stop about fifty yards away. Rep looked at Rolley. "All he had was a shotgun?"

"That's all I saw," said Rolley."

Rep stood up and fired close over Sugar Boy's head. "I got you outgunned," he yelled. "Stand up."

Sugar Boy stood up, staring at Rep. "Who the hell are you?" he yelled back.

"I'm the man with the rifle," Rep said as the boat drifted nearer. "Reach down real slow, pick up the shotgun and throw it in the water," said Rep.

Sugar Boy shook his head. "I ain't gonna throw my gun in the water."

The next shot hit the wooden gunnel next to Sugar Boy's leg.

"The next bullet will be in yo' knee. Git rid of the shotgun."

Sugar Boys face was filled with hatred as he stared at Rep. "I'll git you, you son'na bitch," he said as he tossed the shotgun in the water.

Rep's boat was now abreast of Sugar Boy's boat. "You threatened these boys with a shotgun," he said. "That was a stupid thing to do."

Sugar Boy didn't answer, just stared at Rep.

Mose looked at Rep. "You better kill 'im now, Rep. If you don't he gonna come back later and you'll have to kill 'im then."

Rep shook his head. He knew what Mose said was true, but he couldn't kill him like this with Rolley and Owen looking on.

Mose picked up his rifle, stood up and looked at Sugar Boy. "You don't want to kill 'im, Rep, I'll do it." He looked at Rep. "Ain't no need to let 'im go."

Rep looked at Sugar Boy and pointed the rifle at him. "You give me half an excuse and I'll blow you out of the boat. Red told you before that if you're ever caught in Back Slough again, he'd hang you, I'm telling you the same thing," said Rep. "I'll sho' hang yo' ass."

Sugar Boy moved to the back of the boat, his eyes on Mose. He cranked the motor and headed down the slough.

They rode back to the landing. Both Rolley and Owen kept their eyes on Rep the entire way. Neither one had ever seen anything like they had just witnessed. Both were glad they hadn't peed in their pants when Mose told Rep he'd better kill the man. They both now had insight into Rep's thinking, and they would never forget it.

Rep and Mose left the landing and headed back to the barn. "You know 'im?" Rep said.

Mose nodded. "I know 'im. "Ain't seem 'im in a long time though. He be afraid Red was gonna hang 'im. Now Red be dead, I reckon he thank he can come back." He looked at Rep. "You oughta kilt 'im, cause you done hurt 'im bad now and he gonna come after you."

Rep nodded. He knew Mose was right. "Don't you say nothing bout this to Lila."

They walked on to the barn.

Mose did know of Sugar Boy, but not much about the man and his background. Sugar Boy Hogg lived in the backside of Lost Man Swamp, located about a mile below Walnut Creek where Lick Shell lived. He was born in the swamp twenty-five years before to Lizzie Hogg, a young run-away girl from the Alabama side of the river. Lizzie had run away from a terrible life hoping for a better life but all she found was a worse life. She had taken up with several men in the months prior to Sugar Boy's birth and had no idea which one was his father. She had ended up in the swamp by chance. The man she was living with when Sugar Boy was born had found her down river at a fish camp where she was waitressing and selling herself to anyone with a few cents. Chester Wild was his name. He was looking for a live-in woman, he wasn't real picky and Lizzie was available.

Chester took her to the swamp where he had a ramshackle house on land he didn't own. He catfished, made moonshine and trapped muskrats for a scrape by living. He was not a bad man, except when he got drunk and Lizzie learned to stay away from him when he was drinking. The three of them lived in the swamp until Sugar Boy was about eighteen. One night, Chester got drunk and came after Lizzie with a butcher knife. Sugar Boy grabbed a twelve-gauge shotgun, shot him in the back and killed him.

They dragged his body into the swamp and left it, then went back to the house and went about their business. Chester was not missed. Sugar boy knew how to fish, run traps and operate the still so that was what he did.

For the next several years he was a fixture along the river. He sold whiskey, fought in the beer joints and bars on both sides of the river and stole anything in sight. Most people knew him, disliked him and stayed away from him. He was accustomed to doing as he pleased downriver. But then he made a mistake; he went upriver to Back Slough.

The man who was fishing for Shoal Creek at that time went for two or three days without catching any fish and he reported to Mose that something was wrong. Mose set up men on the bank to watch the lines and they caught Sugar Boy. They held him at gunpoint until Red Hogan got there. He had the men untie Sugar Boy and then Red beat him until the men thought he would kill him. He didn't kill him, but then got a rope, put it around Sugar Boy's neck, threw the end over a limb and hoisted him into the air. He let him hang long enough to put the fear of dying in Sugar Boy and then let him down. Red told him that if he ever caught him on Back Slough again, he would hang him.

Red had the men take the motor off the boat and throw it in the river. Then he threw Sugar Boy, half beat to death and with rope burns around his neck, into the boat and set it adrift. Somehow, he survived but he never came to Back Slough again while Red Hogan was alive.

~

The next three days were quiet on the river. Rolley and Owen fished each day and although they were nervous and watched for Sugar Boy, nothing happened. They were dressing fish when Rep came walking down the path toward them. "Owen," he said, "I'm going down to Lick Shell's place to get a bird dog and I want you to go with me. You need to know where his place is."

When they finished cleaning the fish Rolley headed back to River Bluff and Rep and Owen headed toward Walnut Creek. He had told Owen about Lick and Mattie and Bess on the way to Shoal Creek, so Owen knew about his involvement with the Shell family.

When they landed up Walnut Creek, they didn't see any activity at the house. They got out, tied up the boat and walked toward the house. They got to the steps leading to the porch and Rep yelled out. Immediately the front door opened, and Lick walked out followed by Mattie.

"Rep," said Lick, "what you doin' down this way?" He turned his eyes on Owen.

"Came to get the dog," said Rep. "This is my brother, Owen. He'll be fishing for us and I wanted him to know where you lived."

"Didn't even know you had a brother," said Mattie.

"He just came to live with us," said Rep.

"You come to see us anytime, Owen," said Mattie.

Lick turned and yelled out, "Sassy, git out here."

The door opened and Sassy walked out. When she saw Rep, she ran down the steps and hugged him. She looked over Rep's shoulder and saw Owen. She stepped back. "Who he be?" she said.

"That's Owen, my brother," said Rep. "He lives with us now."

Sassy stepped back, keeping her eyes on Owen.

"Sassy," Lick said, "they want that boy dog, the one with the black head. You go git 'im."

"Go with Sassy, Owen," said Rep. "You need to know where the dog pens are." He watched as they walked away. Then he turned to Lick. "You know Sugar Boy Hogg, don't you?"

Lick nodded. "Yeah, I know 'im. Sho'nuff sorry bastard, if there ever was one." He looked at Rep. "How come you be askin' bout 'im?"

Rep told him about the encounter on Back Slough.

"He be trouble," said Lick. "I know 'im. He was sho' scared of Red. Red bout beat 'im to death and he didn't come back this way no more." He looked at Rep. "I reckon he ain't scared of you yet. He gonna be back."

"We'll just have to wait and see," said Rep.

"I've been to Sugar Boy's place in the swamp. He makes whiskey." Lick shook his head. "Bad place, that swamp. He was born and raised up in it. I wouldn't never go in there lookin' for 'im. He be done kilt you fore you got ten feet." He looked at Rep. "You oughta kilt 'im when you had 'im in Back Slough and been done with 'im."

"That's what Mose said," said Rep. "He was probably right."

"Ain't no doubt Mose be right," said Lick

Sassy started walking away toward the barn and Owen fell in behind her. Sassy cut her eyes at him. "How old you be?" she asked as they walked.

"I be eighteen next month," said Owen. He was walking behind Sassy and thought she was about the prettiest girl he'd ever seen. She was filled out more than any girl he'd ever been around, and he couldn't keep his eyes off her.

"I be almost seventeen," she said. "Bess got married when she be sixteen."

Owen looked at her. He had no idea what Bess getting married at sixteen had to do with what they were talking about.

"You got a girlfriend?"

Owen shook his head.

Sassy turned up her nose. "You ever kissed a girl?"

Owen looked at her thinking this was about the strangest girl he had ever talked to. He nodded. "Lots of times," he said. He felt like she was teasing him, and he wanted to put her in her place. "It ain't none of yo' business no how."

She looked at him and laughed. "You be lying," she said. "You ain't never kissed no girl." She hurried on past the barn to the dog pen.

Owen followed. He wasn't sure how to deal with her.

Sassy went in the pen, got the leash and clicked it on the dog's collar. Owen could tell she knew what she was doing, and he was impressed. The only girls he had ever been around were his sisters and they didn't know how to do anything.

She came out of the pen, stopped beside him and stared. "I seen you lookin' at me while ago, like I was a piece of fried chicken you wanted to eat. You better watch yo' eyes." She walked away with the dog.

Owen stood for a moment, then hurried after her. He'd never been around a girl that talked like she did, and he surely didn't know how to deal with her.

They got back to the house where Rep and Lick was waiting. Sassy handed the leash to Rep and looked back at Owen. "That boy ain't got no manners round no girl," she said. Without another word she went up the steps and went in the house.

Rep looked at Owen. "What did you say to her?"

Owen shook his head. "I didn't say nothin'. She said I was looking at her like a piece of fried chicken."

Rep laughed. "You can't pay no attention to Sassy. She might say anythin'."

As they walked back to the boat and rode back up Back Slough, Owen couldn't get the thought of Sassy out of his mind.

5

Lila was concerned about Sugar Boy Hogg and the confrontation Rep and Mose had with him. She talked as they were getting ready for bed. "I'm worried about Owen and Rolley being on the river now. From what Mose said that man is really mean and Mose said he would come back and be after you."

Rep shrugged. "He might. If he does try something, we'll deal with it."

Lila shook her head. "Sometimes you bother me," she said. "You know that man is dangerous and yet you act like it's nothing."

Rep laughed. "You stop worrying. I'll take care of it."

"Well," she said, "don't say I didn't warn you." She walked over to Rip's crib, picked him up, walked to the bed and laid him down. She crawled in and cuddled him.

Rep walked over and looked at them. "What are you doing?"

"Rip looked lonely. He wanted to sleep with us."

Rip got in the bed and looked at her. "He has a bed and you already have somebody to sleep with, in case you forgot."

Lila laughed. "You've been taken care of very well, I think. You just turn over and go to sleep." She leaned over and turned off the lamp.

Storm had left the gym steps upset with himself. He felt like an idiot. He had blurted out that he loved May and then she had told him that wasn't what she wanted to hear. That would have stopped anybody with any sense from saying more, but he didn't stop, he asked her to marry him. Without any hesitation she said no, and not a simple no, she said she didn't love him.

He should have had enough sense to walk away from her after he saw her at the club but after Friday night at his house, he felt that he had a chance to change her direction. He had been wrong, and she had told him he was wrong. She had told him repeatedly that she was a Hobb and he didn't want her, and he should stay away from her. But he hadn't stayed away, and he felt like a fool. Anyone but a fool would have known what she was. Any woman that would go on a stage and stand naked before a crowd of drunken men wasn't suddenly going to put on an apron and be a housewife. May had proven without a doubt that she was indeed a full-blooded Hobb.

Storm went to the mill early Monday morning and stayed late. He did the same each day for the rest of the week, losing himself in work. The mill was going to be his responsibility for life, and he needed to learn all he could. Friday afternoon he knew May was heading to Phenix City and the club. Knowing that, he left the mill early and headed to Atlanta. He had friends there from school and he needed to get his mind straight. May had chosen what she wanted, and it wasn't him.

Friday afternoon May headed to Phenix City and the club. She was excited as usual. The anticipation of getting on the stage with the crowd and the music always pumped her up, but today she was even more excited. She was especially looking forward to tonight. After talking with Storm, she needed something else on her mind. Storm telling her he loved her and asking her to marry him had clouded her thinking and she wanted to get everything straight again. She felt like some time on stage would do that.

When she walked in the club and the dressing room Josie was already getting dressed. She walked over and hugged her. She had not seen her since last Saturday night and a lot had happened in her life since then. She was looking for some sense of normalcy and Josie was part of that.

Walt was also waiting for her. It had been a week since he had seen her, since the Friday night she had talked to him. He had not been at the show on Saturday night. He immediately came over to her as he always did and put his arms around her. He pulled her around and tried to kiss her, but she turned her head and pushed back against him.

"What the hell's wrong with you?" he said as he jerked her back around.

May looked up at him. She knew it was always going to be this way as long as she wouldn't do as he wanted. She didn't want this harassment to go on forever, so she made a decision. It was a spur of the moment decision that she hadn't thought out completely. She leaned against him and whispered. "Just wait till after the show."

He frowned, looked at her and let her go.

"I've got to dress," she said.

He had turned her loose but stood right beside her and watched her. As she started undressing, she was aware of him being so close and his eyes following her every move. When she took off her panties, he grabbed her again and pulled her against him, his hands running up and down her body. She stood still for a few seconds, then pushed him away. She dressed and joined Josie outside.

"Are you alright?" asked Josie.

May nodded. She heard the crowd yelling when Josie went out on stage and it pumped her up.

When she walked through the curtain and joined Josie on stage she was walking on air. It was as though someone else had taken over her body. She'd never been more excited; the crowd sensed her excitement and they responded. After a few minutes of dancing and stripping, she was down to her top and G-string. She walked to the edge of the stage, knelt in front of a young, uniformed soldier and took off her top. Then she leaned over, pulled him to her and kissed him. She'd never done this before with anybody nor had any of the other girls. The crowd went berserk. Several men grabbed at her, and she had a hard time getting away. From then on, the crowd was hers and she put on a show. Soon the stage was covered with money and men were offering more. Then, completely out of control, May stood in the center of the stage and took off everything. She stood in the middle of the stage for everyone to see. Josie ran over, took her by the arm and led her through the curtain.

"Damn, May," said Josie. "Have you gone crazy? Them people bout to tear this place apart."

May laughed and ran to the dressing room. That was the best night she'd ever had on the stage and she was caught up in it. Her actions were out of control and she didn't care. Walt followed her into the dressing room. She grabbed a house coat, wrapped it around her and looked at him. "Wait for me in your office."

He looked at her, questioning.

"Go on," she said. "I'll be there in a minute."

He looked at her one more time and walked out.

May gathered up her clothes and purse, looked at Josie, shrugged and walked out of the room. She went up the stairs to Walt's office. When she walked in, he got up from behind his desk and walked toward her.

May knew Walt had a small bedroom and bath next to his office he used when he slept over. "I need to take a bath," she said. "I'm all sweaty."

He took her arm and led her into the bathroom. She took off the house coat and stood before him. "I'll be out in a minute." His eyes went up and down her, he nodded and walked out.

She ran water in the tub, bathed and dried off. She walked into the bedroom with the towel wrapped around her. Walt was in the bed. He pulled the covers back and looked up at her.

"It is my choice to do this," she said. "You leave me alone from now on and let me be on stage. I'll choose when we do this again." She stared at him. "You understand?"

He nodded. "I understand."

She dropped the towel and crawled in the bed. She moved against him and kissed him.

Later, Walt turned over and went to sleep. May lay beside him and listened to his breathing. Her mind was back, and she was in control again. She felt nothing for him. The desire she had felt to have him was gone. She slipped out of the bed, dressed and left the office. She went downstairs, out the door into the parking lot, got in the car and left. As she drove home, she thought that now Walt would leave her alone and she could do what she wanted. If he didn't do as he promised, she would kill him.

Sugar Boy loaded his boat, left the swamp before daylight and headed up the river. He passed the mouth of Walnut Creek, continued on and beached the boat several hundred yards below the mouth of Back Slough on the Georgia bank. The eastern sky was light enough so he could see to walk through the trees and brush. It took him thirty minutes to be in position on Back Slough just below the trotline where Rep had run him off.

He had brooded over that incident for days now and the more he thought about it, the madder he got. He'd never got over the way Red Hogan had treated him years before, but he'd done nothing about it because he was afraid of Red. Hanging in that tree with that rope around his neck had put a fear in him that he couldn't overcome. But this time was different. He intended to kill whoever came to fish the lines today and then head for the swamp. There was no way any man could find him there and if they came after him, he would kill them too. He settled down in the trees and waited with his rifle.

. . .

Rolley and Owen left the Shoal Creek landing and headed down Back Slough. It had been several days since the incident with Sugar Boy and nothing had happened, so they went about their fishing as usual. They were having a good day with several catfish and one flathead. They came to the last trotline and Rolley ran the boat against the tree where the line was tied. He stood up. As he did the bullet clipped him in the top of his shoulder and knocked him into the bottom of the boat. Two more shots were fired. Both rounds hit the tree above Owen's head. Another shot was fired, and it splintered part of the wooden gunnel above Owen's head. "Stay down," said Rolley. "Don't get up." The pain in his shoulder washed over him and he fought to stay awake.

The willow tree where the trotline was tied hung out over the water. The boat, with Rolley and Owen lying in the bottom, was pushed by the current into its overhanging limbs where it was caught in the limbs.

Mose was at the kitchen talking to Hattie Mae when he heard the first shots fired. He immediately knew it was a high-powered rifle. Then when there were more reports, he knew something was wrong. He thought about Rolley and Owen being on Back Slough and he started running toward the barn. Rep and Lila were at the desk when he rushed in. "Rifle shots down Back Slough," he said as he grabbed his rifle

Rep jumped up, went to the rifle rack, grabbed his rifle and they both went out the door. Lila ran to the door and watched them run up the hill toward the kitchen. Rep yelled back at her, "Call the sheriff."

They ran past the kitchen and down the path to the landing. They jumped in the boat, pushed away from the landing and headed down Back Slough with the motor wide open.

. . .

Sugar Boy was frustrated. He knew he had hit one of the boys but wasn't sure of the other. They were both out of sight in the bottom of the boat. The boat was now hidden behind thick willow tree limbs on the far bank and he couldn't get another clear shot. Then he heard a motor coming down the slough at full speed. He knew help was coming, probably armed and he didn't want to get in a firefight, so he gathered up his gear and headed through the woods toward his boat.

As Rep rounded the last bend Mose was in the front of the boat with his rifle ready. They had no idea what they would find. Rep didn't see Rolley's boat at first but then saw it behind a willow tree against the Big Island bank. He turned and headed toward it. He was relieved to see Owen's head raise up and look at them. They pulled up beside the boat and Rep saw Rolley lying in the bottom of the boat with blood all around him.

Mose jumped in the boat and turned Rolley over. "He's hit in the meaty part of his shoulder," Mose said. "It went through. He's lost blood but it ain't too bad."

Rolley roused up and looked at Rep. "He was on the Georgia bank," he said. "We didn't ever see him."

"Don't worry bout it," said Rep as he helped Mose pull Rolley into his boat. He and Mose put their rifles in the boat with Owen; he didn't want to go to River Bluff armed. He looked at Owen. "You take the boat back to the landing and tell Lila we're taking Rolley to the doctor in River Bluff." He cranked the motor and waited to make sure Owen had the motor running before he started up the slough. He looked back and Owen was following him. Mose was in the bottom of the boat holding Rolley who was alert. Rep was glad to see him looking around.

When they got near the Shoal Creek landing, he turned into the river and headed toward the River Bluff landing. He could see a crowd at the landing and knew there would be people there to take

Rolley to the mill nurse's office. He had made this trip before with Bess. When he neared the landing, he started yelling and the men ran to the water and were waiting when he beached the boat. He quickly told them Rolley had been shot and needed a doctor. The men said the best thing was to take him to the nurse's office. They put Rolley in the back of one truck and Rep and Mose jumped in the back of another truck and followed them to the mill.

Several men carried Rolley into the office and put him on the table and the nurse started cleaning him up. They said the doctor was on the way. Rep and Mose were in the outer office when Rolley's mother and daddy came in. They both worked in the mill and were on the job when they were told Rolley had been shot. Rep quickly told them what happened

The doctor came in and he was quickly followed by Jim Hawke. Rep remembered Jim and told him what happened plus them knowing it was Sugar Boy Hogg that did the shooting. "I know Sugar Boy," he said. "He's one sorry piece of white trash." He looked at Rep. "What you gonna do bout it?"

"We gotta go after him."

"You ever been in that swamp where he lives?"

"I been in the swamp," said Mose.

Jim looked at Mose. "Then you know bout it. Sugar Boy's been there all his life and he knows it. Sho'nuff be a job findin' 'im without getting' shot."

"The sheriff ain't gonna go after him," said Rep. "So we gotta do it."

Jim nodded. "Gonna be mighty hard."

The ambulance came and carried Rolley to the hospital in Landon. His parents followed the ambulance. One of the men offered to take Rep and Mose back to the landing. When they got to the boat, they thanked the men for their help and headed up the river.

When they got to the Shoal Creek landing the sheriff was waiting.

Rep told him what had happened and about the trouble with Sugar Boy.

The sheriff wasted no time in telling Rep he had no interest in going after Sugar Boy. “He’s in the swamp now and I’m not gonna send my folks in there after him,” he said. “He ain’t worth fooling with. Just let him stay in the swamp. I’ll put out a warrant for his arrest but that’s all.”

“I can’t do that,” said Rep. “He’ll come out and shoot somebody else. I gotta go get him.”

The sheriff shook his head. “Damn foolish to do that. He knows that swamp and you don’t. Ain’t no sense in getting somebody else killed.”

“Don’t matter,” said Rep. “He can’t hurt our folks and just walk away.” He looked at Mose. “Lick said he had been in the swamp to Sugar Boy’s house. We need to go talk to him.”

6

May got to River Bluff, drove through the deserted town and parked on Pot Licker Lane. It was late, the middle of the night. She knew Star and Ruby were asleep and she didn't want to wake them, so she went to sleep in the car. She also didn't want to face Star tonight. The sun was up when Star tapped on the window and woke her up. "What are you doing sleeping in the car?" she asked.

"It was late, and I didn't want to wake you up."

Star looked at her but didn't say anything else. She opened the door and May climbed out. "I'm going to take a bath, change clothes and then I'm going to see Alva and ask her to let me come back and live with her," May said. "I need to be with Alva."

Star nodded. "I think that's a good idea."

May bathed, changed clothes and started walking up the road toward the stores. When she passed the Methodist Church, she saw Jim sitting on his bench.

He watched as she approached. "Hey, little girl," he said, "where you goin'?"

"I'm going to see Alva, Mr. Jim," she said as she turned and headed toward the dormitory.

. . .

Alva was sitting on the sofa when she heard a knock on the door. When she opened the door May was standing there. "Why, May. I'm so glad you came to see me. Come in."

"I wanted to tell you that I'm sorry, Alva, for the way I've acted," said May. "I would like to come back and live with you, if you'll let me," said May. Tears streamed down her face as she talked. "I still plan to be at the club for a while and I know you don't like that, but I need to be with you."

Alva nodded. "Of course, you can, dear. You know you're welcome to stay with me."

"If it's all right, I'll run home and get all my clothes." She hugged Alva again. "Thank you for letting me come back."

Alva smiled. "You go get your things and hurry back. Your room is just like it was when you left."

May ran out the door and headed out the road.

Rep remembered that Lick had said he had been to Sugar Boy's house in the swamp, so he decided to go talk to him about it. Saturday morning, he and Owen headed to Walnut Creek. He took Owen with him to expose him to as much of the area as he could. Since Rolley was in the hospital, Owen would have to shoulder the load of supplying fish to the farm.

When they landed Rep was looking for Lick. Owen didn't say anything, but he was looking for Sassy. He had been wanting to see her again. They got out, walked to the house and Rep yelled out. The door opened and Lick came out followed by Mattie.

"What ya'll doin' down here?" asked Lick.

Rep told him about Sugar Boy shooting Rolley.

"I told you, y'all oughta shot the bastard when you had the chance," said Lick.

Rep ignored his comment. "You said you had been to Sugar Boy's house in the swamp. What can you tell me about it?"

Owen was standing off to the side looking around.

"Where is Sassy?" Rep asked.

Lick looked around. "She's out feeding the chickens on the other side of the barn."

Rep looked at Owen. He knew he was anxious to see Sassy. "Why don't you go see Sassy while I'm talking to Lick."

Owen lit out for the barn.

Lick looked at Rep. "Why you want to know about Sugar Boy's house?"

"We gotta go after him."

Lick shook his head. "You gonna git yo'self kilt if you go in that swamp. He be waitin' for you and you won't never see 'im."

Rep shrugged. "We can't just let him go. He'll come back and shoot somebody else."

"That might be but I sho' wouldn't go straight in after 'im."

"What else could we do?" asked Rep.

"I been to his house more than once," said Lick. "That swamp feeds a creek that runs into the river bout a mile below here. You go up the creek in a boat to where the swamp starts. The house is way in the back, and you can't never get there unless you know the trail. The water is full of stumps and logs blockin' the way.

"How did you know the trail?" said Rep.

"Sugar Boy had it marked so folks comin' to buy whiskey could get to the house. Now he gonna take the markin' down and you'd never get there," said Lick. "Anyway, you wouldn't never go in there in a boat, he'd shoot you fo' you got started."

Rep understood what he was saying, but he didn't have any other thoughts. "What else could we do? We got to stop him."

Lick took his hat off and stared at the ground, then looked up at Rep. "The house is on a little spit of high ground in the middle of the water. You can't git nowhere close to the house. But you might can see the house from dry land with the leaves off the trees, but it'd be from a long way off, more than five-hundred yards. If you got there and could see the house, a man with a rifle, if he be a good shot, could hit 'im."

Rep shook his head. "Ain't no rifle I got gonna shoot that far and hit him."

Lick smiled. "I got one that will."

Rep was surprised. "You got such a rifle here?"

Lick nodded.

"Where'd you get it?"

"I brung it back from the war," said Lick.

"What war?"

"The war across the ocean in France."

"You were in the war?" asked Rep.

"I was in the army," said Lick. "I was a good shot with a rifle, and they trained me to be a sniper in them trenches in France. I killed Germans, some of 'im from so far off I could hardly see 'im. When I come home, I brought my rifle with me."

Rep was amazed. He'd never had any idea Lick had ever left Walnut Creek.

Lick got up and went in the house. He came out with a long rifle with a scope on it. "This is a 1903 Springfield rifle. This is what I used in the war."

Rep took the rifle and handled it. He pointed it toward the creek and looked in the scope. The bank on the far side of the creek looked like he could reach out and touch it. "That looks like a fine rifle."

"It is," said Lick. "I done good with it."

"If it be me," said Lick, "I'd walk in and get as close to the house as I could on dry land. I'd set up and wait for Sugar Boy to show up and then I'd kill im."

"Could you show me how to shoot this rifle," asked Rep.

Lick pursed his lips. "I ain't got time to do that fore you want to go after Sugar Boy." He scratched his head. "I'll go with you and kill the bastard myself."

Rep was startled at the offer. "When do you want to go?"

"We oughta go in later today and get set up," said Lick. "Ain't no way Sugar Boy will thank anybody gonna come after 'im early. We spend the night and bout daylight we'll kill 'im."

Rep thought Lick was talking about killing Sugar Boy like it wasn't nothing. "You killed men in the war?"

Lick nodded. "Killed plenty," he said. "You go to Shoal Creek and git yo' stuff and come back. We'll walk from here, it ain't but bout a mile. You might get Hattie Mae to send us some ham biscuits."

Rep got up, yelled for Owen and headed for the boat.

When Rep told Owen to go find Sassy, he had headed for the barn. She had been on his mind ever since he first met her. He didn't quite understand the attraction. He'd only seen her the one time and she wasn't very nice to him then. He had been around girls at school and they had never made him feel like he did about Sassy. He knew girls were different from boys -- they looked different, acted different, talked different and smelled different. He'd noticed that as they got older, they grew outward in some places that made them different from boys.

He'd never had much to do with any girl except talking. He was too shy. and they intimidated him. Sassy had talked smart to him, like she was making fun of him and he had decided he wasn't going to put up with that again.

When he walked around the barn, he saw her in the chicken pen scattering corn for the chickens that were all around her feet. He stood and watched her. She was wearing a thin dress, it fit tight against her body and he could tell she wasn't a little girl. He couldn't take his eyes off her.

After a minute she turned and looked at him. She stared and her nose turned up. "I done told you to not be lookin' at me like that." She opened the door to the pen, walked out and came toward him. "What be wrong with you, no how?"

Owen shook his head. "What are you yellin' bout? I just come out here to see you and you start screamin'."

"How come you be down here?"

"Rep be talkin' to yo' daddy about Sugar Boy shootin' Rolley."

Sassy's eyes widened and her face showed concern. "Rolley got shot?"

Owen nodded. "Me and 'im be in the boat and Sugar Boy shot 'im. Tried to shoot me too."

"Rolley be daid?"

"No, he be in the hospital." He looked at her. "You know Rolley?"

"I know 'im. He was my boyfriend, but he ain't no more."

"How come he ain't yo' boyfriend now?"

Sassy shrugged. "He didn't want to get married. I be done kissed 'im but he still run off."

Owen stared at her. "You ain't old enough to be married."

"Bess married Rep when she be sixteen. I be almost seventeen."

"Why are you tellin' me this?" Owen said.

"I done seen you starin' at me like you want to bed me. Mama done told me what you men want to do." She walked over to him and looked in his face. "Mama said any woman what let a man bed her and ain't got no paper, ain't nothin' but a whore." She shook her head. "I ain't gonna pay no attention to Mama. If I want a man to bed me, I don't need no paper. I'll just do it."

Owen had no idea how to reply to her. Then he heard Rep call him. Without another word he turned and ran to the house. He was relieved to be away from Sassy.

He got in the boat with Rep and they headed up the river. He looked at Rep. "You married Bess when she was sixteen?"

Rep nodded. "I did." He looked at Owen, he knew something was on his mind. "Did Sassy tell you that?"

Owen sat and stared at the water. "Sassy talks crazy. She say if she wants a man to bed her, she will do it."

Rep smiled. "I spect you need to stay away from Sassy. She might get you in trouble."

Owen nodded. That was what he intended to do, he thought. But as they rode up the river, he couldn't help but remember how she looked in that tight dress, poking out in several places.

When they got to the Shoal creek landing, Rep told Owen to bait up that evening and fish the hooks the next morning. He was going to the house, get his pack and rifle and go back to Lick's place. He stopped by the kitchen and asked Hattie Mae to fix some ham biscuits, then headed to the house. He knew Lila wasn't going to be happy with what he was about to do

Sunday morning Alva and May went to church. All the town was upset about Rolley Hill being shot on the river. Some people were blaming the whiskey people at Shoal Creek for the shooting, but Jim Hawke had said it was a man from downriver named Sugar Boy Hogg. Many of the men that fished and hunted on the river had heard of Sugar Boy. In fact, he was quite infamous for his illegal activities and lifestyle. Some wanted to know what was going to be done to him for shooting Rolley and demanded action. The men that knew Sugar Boy and knew he lived in Lost Man Swamp wanted no part in the hunt. They said it happened in Georgia and Georgia officials needed to take care of it.

All the churches in town had prayer for Rolley and his family. Everyone was thankful he was doing well and would recover. A couple of the more truthful church members said they needed to pray for whoever was going in the swamp looking for Sugar Boy.

7

As Rep expected, Lila was not happy that he was going in the swamp after Sugar Boy. He tried to explain that he wasn't actually going in the swamp, but he and Lick would be on dry land.

"You and Lick," she said, sarcastically. "Lick is sorry as hell; you've told me so yourself."

"I know I've said that" said Rep, "but I was talking about him being a sorry daddy. I didn't know he had been in the army and fought in the war. He said he was a sniper and can use a rifle. That's the safest way for us to get Sugar Boy."

Lila shook her head. "Just leave Sugar Boy in the swamp."

"I can't do that. He'd come out again and shoot somebody. We have to stop him now." He leaned over and kissed her. Then he walked over and kissed Rip, got his pack and rifle and headed to the landing. He stopped at the kitchen and Hattie Mae came out with a sack and a gallon of tea. Rep looked at her and shook his head. "Hattie Mae, we're just gonna be gone one night. You got enough here for a week."

She laughed. "I don't want y'all to git hungry."

Three of his guards with rifles met him at the landing. He instructed them to go downriver to the creek that came out of Lost

Man Swamp. They were to anchor in the mouth of the creek where it emptied into the river and make sure Sugar Boy didn't come out. He wanted to keep him locked up inside the swamp until they could get a shot at him.

Rep got in the boat, cranked the motor and headed down Back Slough. When he passed Sallie White and saw the new cabin, he thought that he'd not spent one night in it. He went on down the slough, went up Walnut Creek and landed at Lick's landing. Lick was sitting on the steps waiting for him. Rep took a few ham biscuits out of the sack for them to eat. He gave the other biscuits and the tea to Mattie.

Sassy was standing on the porch watching Rep. "You didn't brang that boy with you?"

Rep looked up at her. "You talkin' bout Owen?"

"Whatever his name be," she said.

"I don't thank he's comin' back down here anymore," said Rep, cutting his eyes at Sassy.

Sassy frowned. "How come he not be comin' back?"

Rep shrugged. "He said he didn't want to, wasn't nothin' for 'im down here."

Sassy turned and tossed her head back. "Don't matter to me what he ain't gonna do," she said as she walked in the house and slammed the door.

Rep laughed.

Lick handed him a pair of binoculars. "We always used to have two men together when we was goin' out shootin'. One man be the shooter and the other done the spottin'. You look through them and get 'im set for yo' eyes.

Rep put the binoculars up to his eyes and looked through them. "These are really good," he said, as the creek's far bank looked to be at his feet.

"We'll walk from here to the swamp," said Lick. "It ain't that far. We'll get as close as we can where we can see the house. With the leaves off the trees now we oughta be able to find a good place. Sugar Boy has dogs around his house. They won't come cross the water to us but if they smell us, they might get to barkin' and get him worried. We'll have to check the wind fore we go in."

Rep looked at Lick with a newfound respect he had never had before. He had never seen this side of him. They put on their packs and started through the woods.

Sugar Boy had taken all the signs and markings off the trees and logs that showed the trail through the swamp to the house. He didn't think anybody would be stupid enough to try to come up the creek and into the swamp after him, but he wasn't going to take a chance. He was in the lower part of the swamp when he heard a boat coming down the river. It was late in the afternoon and it got his interest. He paddled down to where he could see the mouth of the creek.

In a few minutes the boat slowed down and came to the creek mouth. He could see three men armed with rifles in the boat. The boat eased into the creek and landed on the upper bank. One of the men got out and moved into the trees. The boat backed out and went to the lower bank and another man got out and disappeared in the trees. The third man took the boat back in the river a few yards and anchored.

Sugar Boy watched. It was obvious they intended to keep him bottled up in the swamp and not allow him access to the river. That strategy didn't bother him. He had enough food and water to stay in his house forever. He figured that sooner or later they would get tired of blockading him and go away. His house was on a spit of dry land in the middle of the swamp. It was protected on all sides by water filled with stumps and logs, making it impossible for a boat to come across. The house was several hundred yards in every direction from dry land. There was no way anybody could get to him. He took one last look at the boat anchored in the mouth of the creek and paddled to the house.

Storm had spent Friday and Saturday nights in Atlanta. He had gone out each night with friends to parties. There were several women he knew at the parties; two he knew very well and had enjoyed their company in the past. They were glad to see him and both made it obvious they were open to anything he had in mind. When he had left River Bluff, he had thought finding a friendly companion would help ease the pain he felt, but when the opportunity presented itself, he backed away. On Friday and Saturday nights, all he had thought about was that May was half-naked on the stage in Phenix City. He had enjoyed getting away and being with his friends, but early Sunday morning he had enough. He got up, dressed and headed to River Bluff.

When he came into town the churches were letting out and people were walking up the streets toward their homes. He noticed that May's car was at the dormitory and he had thought that at least she got home safely. Then as he approached the stores and gymnasium, he saw Alva and May walking toward him. As he got closer, he saw that both had their eyes on him. He had no choice but to pass them if he kept going. He slowed down but hadn't decided if he should stop or wave and pass on by. When he got even with them, he stopped and rolled down the window. "Good morning, ladies," he said, keeping his eyes on Alva and avoiding looking at May.

"Good morning, Storm," Alva said.

Storm could feel May's eyes on him, but she didn't speak. He looked at her. She met his gaze without wavering. "Morning, May," he said, watching her face.

She stared at him for a minute, then smiled. "Morning, Storm," she said.

For a moment he thought she was going to say more. She didn't but kept her eyes on him. He was stunned by the look on her face and in her eyes. Her look seemed friendly and if he hadn't known better, he would have thought she was about to tear up. Then she turned her face away and the moment passed. He nodded to Alva and drove away, his mind confused.

. . .

Alva looked at May. "He was certainly friendly," she said.

May didn't answer but started walking away. Alva hurried and caught up with her. May stopped and looked at her. "I've been such a fool, Alva. I just went crazy."

"You made some bad choices," said Alva, "and sadly we must live with them." She smiled. "But hopefully everything will work out well from now on."

"But all the problems I created haven't gone away," said May.

The afternoon sun was fading as Lick stopped and knelt on one knee. Rep knelt beside him. "We be close now. I can smell the swamp," said Lick. "We gonna move real slow now." He slowly moved forward in a crouch. Rep followed. They moved through the pine trees into oaks and sweetgums, then they were within ten yards of the stagnant water. Along the water's edge were cypress trees mingled among dead trees and rotting stumps. Floating logs blocked any path into the swamp.

They were in a stand of waist high brush. Lick took the binoculars and moved around until he could see the house with a clear sight line. "This where we be," he said.

In a few minutes the sun dropped low and the shadows covered them. Lick found a small log and put it in front to use as a rest for the rifle. He got the rifle in position and sighted through the scope until he felt comfortable. "Now all we gotta do is wait for 'im to come out of the house," said Lick.

"How far do you say the house is from here?" asked Rep.

"I ain't got nothin' to go by on the ground," Lick said. "I say it be bout seven-hundred yards."

Darkness covered then as they laid out their tarps and settled down for the night. They ate Hattie Mae's ham biscuits and drank sweet tea. It had been a long day and they were tired. Soon both were asleep.

Sugar Boy woke up before daylight. What the Shoal Creek people might do or plan to do was on his mind. He slipped out the front door. He knew his way around even in the darkness and the half-moon provided a little light for him to get to the boat. He wanted to see if the men were still anchored at the mouth of the creek. If they were still there to keep him bottled up, then they had some kind of plan in place for either today or sometime soon. He didn't have to go far before he had the answer; there were fires on both sides of the creek at the mouth. Obviously, they weren't trying to hide their presence. He paddled back to the house wondering what they might be up to.

He had decided there was no way anybody would try to come straight up the swamp toward him. They couldn't wade through the muck and debris and it wasn't possible for a boat to get through. The house was surrounded by water in all directions and the distance from dry land was too far for anybody to take a shot at him. But they could be on dry land watching him and figuring what to do. He decided to check that out.

There weren't any houses for miles on the south side of the swamp. On the north side toward Walnut Creek were a lot of houses and a road to the river. If anyone came to spy on him, they would come from that direction.

He had four dogs, three Walker hounds and a bulldog. He used them to hunt wild pigs. He kept them in a pen behind the house. He slipped out the back of the house at daylight, got the dogs and carried them in the boat to dry land. The dogs were excited to be loose. He put them out and headed them toward the north side of the swamp.

. . .

Lick and Rep heard the dogs when Sugar boy opened the pen. "Damn," said Lick. "He's fixin' to turn his dogs loose." They started gathering up their gear. "He runs dogs after pigs," said Lick. "He'd have hounds and a bulldog. Don't worry bout the hounds, they'll run if you shoot at 'im but that bulldog be comin' after us. He's trained to be mean as hell." He got up. "Git yo gun out, find the biggest tree to git behind and git ready." About that time one of the hounds bayed and the others joined in and they heard them coming.

Rep got behind a tree, put his pistol in his belt and had his rifle ready. The dogs came out of the trees about a hundred yards away but in the brush, it was hard to see them to get a shot. One came across an open spot and both he and Lick hit it. When the shooting started both the other hounds stopped and started running away.

Rep stepped out from behind the tree and looked at Lick. The bulldog came out of the brush behind him and hit him in the back. The force of the blow knocked Rep on his face and the dog was on him, tearing at his shoulder. Rep tried to turn and knock him away, but he couldn't move him. He felt pain in his left shoulder as teeth bit into him. Then he heard a loud noise and the dog fell over to the side. Lick had killed him.

He was struggling to get up when Lick ran over to him. "Can you git up?" He grabbed Rep's arm and helped him get to his feet. "He done bit you good on the shoulder," he said as he pulled the shirt back. "We better git outta here." He looked toward the back of the swamp. "I don't reckon he'll come after us. I spect he's gone back in the swamp." Lick got Rep's pack. "Can you carry yo' rifle?"

Rep nodded and slung the rifle over his shoulder and started walking through the pines. He was exhausted by the time he got to Lick's house. Lick yelled for Mattie and she helped Rep get into the house where she washed the dog bite and poured alcohol over it. She then covered it with a salve they used for cuts and bandaged it.

"You better get to a doctor and get a tetanus shot," said Mattie. "This bite might git you full of poison."

"You want me to take you to Shoal Creek?" asked Lick.

Rep shook his head. "I'm going to River Bluff. They got a nurse and doctor up there." He got up and Lick went to the boat with him. "When I get to Shoal Creek, I'll send Mose back down here with food for the men at the creek. I want to keep Sugar Boy in the swamp till we can go get 'im."

"Don't you worry bout 'im," said Lick. "I'm going back tomorrow and get 'im. I'll let you know when I do,"

Mattie heard Lick make this statement and she immediately set him straight. "You damn well ain't goin' nowhere, Lick Shell. It ain't yo' fight. You let them Shoal Creek folks take care of Sugar Boy. You ain't got no dog in this here fight."

Lick looked at Rep and shook his head.

Rep got in the boat and started upriver. His shoulder was throbbing, and his vision was cloudy. He passed the mouth of Back Slough and stayed in the river until he got to the landing at River Bluff. As he had expected there were several men there with trucks. He yelled and they met him at the riverbank. He quickly told them he had been after the man that shot Rolley and a dog bit him. They got him to the truck and one of the men carried him to the nurse's office at the mill. Miss Neal, the mill nurse, took him in, took off the bandage and treated and redressed the wound. She gave him a tetanus shot and told him to come back the next day and let her look at it again.

Rep thanked her and the man took him back to the landing. He thanked all the men and went upriver to Shoal Creek. He headed directly to the barn and found Mose. He told him what had happened and told him to take food to the men at the creek and set them up to stay.

Then he went to the house and faced Lila.

Sugar boy let the dogs loose and they headed up the north side of the swamp. It wasn't long before he heard them strike the trail and soon after that he heard shooting. In a few minutes two of the hounds returned. He sat with his rifle ready and waited. After an hour he figured whoever the dogs had found were gone. He slipped through the trees in the direction the dogs had gone. Several hundred yards up the swamp he found the hound, and a little further on he found the bulldog. Beneath the bulldog was a bloody piece of a shirt, so he knew somebody had been hurt.

Not far away he saw where two people had been. Papers were scattered about where they had eaten, and parts of biscuits were on the ground. From what he saw it was obvious they had spent the night and were watching his house. He was not sure what their purpose had been other than to see what he was doing. The distance from where they were to the house was a long way, certainly too far for a rifle to be effective. He walked away still unsure as to what their purpose was. He got the two hounds and went back to the house.

8

Lila was not happy with Rep. "I told you not to go in that swamp after him," she said, her face crimson, she was so mad. "You keep doing stuff like this and get yourself killed and little Rip will grow up without a daddy." She glared at him. "Have you thought about that?"

"I got bit by a dog," he said. "That's all it was."

"That dog would have torn you apart if Lick hadn't killed him." She shook her head. "Don't try to tell me that crap."

He smiled. "You are really pretty when you're all red-faced."

She wheeled about and walked away. "You're going to think pretty when you sleep by yourself for the next week. You might as well go to the shed and sleep with Owen."

"You don't mean that" he said.

"Watch me," she yelled back.

~

Sugar Boy was mad. The killing of his bulldog upset him more than anything, a good bulldog was hard to find. He decided he wasn't going to let it go without reprisal. Just before dark he paddled down the swamp toward the mouth of the creek. He eased behind a dead tree and rested his rifle on the stump. The boat was still anchored in the river. He could see one man in it, and he knew there were men on each bank, he had seen them before. He didn't want to kill anybody, although the man in the boat was an easy target. Killing somebody would get a posse after him and he didn't want that. He wanted them to leave so he could get out, go downriver and hit the various beer joints along the bank.

He opened fire, not trying to hit the boat but hitting all around it. He let the man in the boat know he had him targeted. After several rounds he stopped and yelled, "Y'all got five minutes to get the hell out of here and then I'm gonna start shootin' again and I ain't gonna miss."

In a minute, the man in the boat slowly stood up, cranked the motor and headed to the bank. He picked up the other two men and headed upriver. Sugar Boy listened as the sound of the motor faded. He paddled out into the creek, cranked up and headed down river.

The three men didn't stop until they got to the Shoal Creek landing. They got out and headed to the barn to find Mose. He listened to their story, then went to see Rep. They agreed Sugar Boy would be a problem until he was stopped, but Rep would have to wait until his shoulder healed to go after him. In the meantime, he hoped Sugar Boy stayed out of Back Slough.

It was late afternoon. May and Alva were in their rooms. "I'm going to talk to Star," said May as she opened the door and went out. She walked up to the road and instead of getting in the car, she decided to walk to Pot Licker Lane. Halfway to the stores she saw Jim sitting on his bench. Then she saw Storm's car come around the Methodist Church, pull over in front of the gym and park. He got out and walked over to Jim.

She had not wanted to see Storm but with him standing with Jim looking at her, she had no choice but to keep going. "Hey, Mr. Jim," she said as she walked up to them. "Hey, Storm," she added. "I'm going down to see Star." She walked on past; she didn't want to get into a conversation with Jim with Storm standing there. She was hardly five steps past them when she heard Storm call her.

"Wait up, May," he said.

She stopped; she could hear him walking up behind her. Then he was beside her. She looked up at him.

"Will you talk with me?" he asked. "I haven't talked to you in several days."

"I've been busy."

"Yes, I have too. When I talked to you and Alva Sunday, I was just getting back from Atlanta."

She didn't know what to say so she started walking out the road. He walked beside her

He stepped in front of her.

She stopped and looked up at him.

"You don't have to worry, May. I'm not going through all I said before." He looked in her eyes, looking deep. "I'm just asking you if you will go out with me?"

She returned his look, seeing that he was serious. She smiled. "Yes, I will go out with you." She took a deep breath and looked deep in his eyes. "This will be regular dates, Storm." She smiled. "I will not spend the night with you."

He nodded and laughed. "I wouldn't ask you to." He stepped aside. "You're going to see Star?"

"Yes, I am."

"I'll call you."

"Okay," she said as she started out the road.

Owen went down Back Slough fishing his hooks. Meeting Sugar Boy and the shooting had made him cautious. Before he went around a bend in the slough he would slow down, ease around to look and make sure nobody was waiting for him. As he

fished the last trotline he sat and thought about what to do next. Normally he would go back to the landing, dress the fish and take them to the kitchen. But today something else was pulling on him. He couldn't get over the memory of Sassy in that tight dress. Finally, he could stand it no longer. He put the fish in a live cage and tied them out on a limb next to the trotline. He kept out five nice channel cats and left them in the boat. He cranked the motor and started down the river.

He went up Walnut Creek and landed. He didn't see anybody at the house, so he walked to the porch and yelled. The door opened and Lick came out. "What you doin' down here?" he said.

"I brung you some fish," said Owen.

"They be dressed?"

"They will be," said Owen. He looked around. "Where is Sassy?"

Lick turned around and yelled. "Sassy, git yo' ass out here."

Sassy walked out on the porch and looked down at Owen. "Rep say you weren't comin' back no more."

Owen frowned. "I ain't never said that."

"Why you be here?"

"Brought you some fish. I gotta go clean 'em." He started walking back toward the boat.

Sassy came down the steps. "I help you clean 'em." She looked at him as they walked. "How come you be brangin' us fish?"

"I come to see you."

Sassy stopped. "Why you do that?"

They got to the boat. Owen didn't answer. He put the fish in a bucket and went to the well and cleaned them. Sassy dressed as many as he did. He was impressed.

"How old you be?" Sassy asked.

"I done told you I be eighteen."

"I forgot. I be bout seventeen. Bess be married when she be sixteen."

"Damn, girl, you done told me that a hundred times."

Sassy laughed. She took him by the hand. "Let's go to the barn. I gonna see if you ever kissed a girl." They went in the barn and she took him to the feed sacks. In a few minutes she had taught Owen all she had learned from Rolley about kissing.

Owen liked kissing her and the feel of her body pressed against him aroused feelings unlike anything he had ever felt before. He took over the action, although he wasn't sure what he was doing.

She pushed him away, pulled her dress down and looked in his face. "You done bout enough." She stood up. "You say you fish up at Shoal Creek," she said. "When Rep fished, he lived in a cabin on Sallie White. When Bess married 'im, they went to live in his cabin. Do you have a cabin?"

Owen shook his head. "I live in the shed."

Sassy frowned. "I ain't never heard of no shed." Then she remembered she had been to the landing. "You talkin' bout that little place at the landin'?"

Owen nodded.

Sassy snorted. "That place ain't fit for no dog to stay in." She stared down at him. "You cook down there?"

"I ain't got no stove. I go to the kitchen and Hattie Mae feeds me."

Sassy looked disgusted. "Where's yo' outhouse?"

"I ain't got one. I just go in the woods."

Sassy started walking away. "Ain't no way I gonna marry no boy what ain't got no fit place to live."

Owen started after her. "I ain't said nothin' bout gettin' married," he said. "How come you say that?"

Tightlipped, Sassy stared at him. "You done felt me all over. You sho' must wanta bed me."

Owen stood and stared at her. He didn't answer.

"You ain't bedding me till we git married and I ain't marrying you till you got a decent place to live." She wheeled about, walked to the house, went up the steps and went inside.

Owen stood and thought about what had happened since he got here. He didn't remember saying one word to Sassy about getting married. He walked to the boat shaking his head. He got in the boat, cranked up and headed up the river. As he went, the memory of kissing Sassy and how soft she felt kept getting in his head. The taste he'd had of her body had whetted his appetite for more. He needed to talk to Rep.

When he got to the landing he got out and headed to the barn. Rep was inside talking to Mose when Owen walked in. "I need to talk to you, Rep," he said, sitting down in a chair at the desk.

Rep looked at him, thinking this seemed out of character for Owen. He had never approached him with such a question while appearing to be so anxious. "About what?"

"I been living in the shed ever since I come here, and I thank I need a better place to stay."

Rep looked at Mose and then back at Owen. "What else do you need exactly?"

"I ain't got no place to cook and there ain't really much room."

Rep chuckled. "Hattie Mae feeds you ever day. What would you want to cook?"

Owen didn't answer. He looked at Mose and then at Rep, unable to think of a suitable answer.

"What brought this up, Owen?" Rep said. He'd ever seen him so uncomfortable.

"Sassy said she ain't gonna have nothin' to do with me if I don't have a decent place to live."

Rep leaned toward Owen and smiled. "Is she gonna move in with you?"

Owen frowned and shook his head. "No," he said. "I didn't say nothin' bout it, but Sassy be talkin' bout us getting' married. She said you had a cabin when you married Bess and she ain't gonna marry me if I don't have a cabin."

Rep leaned back in the chair. "Did you ask Sassy to marry you?"

"I didn't ask her nothin'. We was just kissin' and all of a sudden she started talkin' bout getting' married."

"So, you was kissing Sassy."

Owen nodded.

"Anything else?"

Owen shook his head.

Rep looked at Mose. "On Big Island right below Sallie White

there's a little ridge that's pretty flat and big enough for a cabin. There's plenty of trees there for logs so it wouldn't be much trouble."

Mose nodded. "Wouldn't take long to do one like you had on Sallie White."

"Why don't you put some men down there and get it started," said Rep. Then he looked at Owen. "You can tell Sassy you gonna have a cabin, but don't you let her talk you into getting' married unless you want to." He stared at Owen. "She'll get to kissin' on you and get you all stirred up and next thang you know, she'll have you married. You better be careful."

"I will," said Owen. "Thank you." He jumped up and ran out the door.

"That po' boy sho' got it bad," said Mose.

9

Rep's shoulder was sore, and he felt so foolish for allowing the dog to maul him. He got up Wednesday morning to go to the mill nurse in River Bluff and let her check his shoulder. He went to the landing and got Owen to take him across the river. When they get to the River Bluff landing, he told Owen to stay with the boat and he walked up the hill to the mill.

Miss Neal took off his bandage, looked at the wound and told him he was doing well. She dressed his shoulder and as he was about to leave, Storm Gill walked in. He asked Rep how he was doing, and Rep told him what happened to him, about Sugar Boy and the bulldog.

Storm shook his head. "Seems like y'all folks across the river have a lot of trouble."

Rep looked at him. "A good bit of the trouble we've had come from this side of the river, as I remember."

Storm laughed. "You are right. If I remember right, the Hobbs invaded y'all."

"Yes, they did." Rep thought for a minute. "I wanted to check on Rolley Hill. Do you know how he's doing?"

"Rolley is at home and is doing well," said Storm. "If you want, I'll go with you. I haven't seen him since he came home from the hospital. He lives just a little piece up the road. I'll walk up there with you."

They left the mill and went to the Hill house. Rolley's mother met them at the door, they went in, saw Rolley and talked for a while. He was doing well and thanked them for coming to see him. He told Rep that he was starting to college right away, would be working in the mill and didn't plan to fish anymore for Shoal Creek. Rep thanked him for all he had done, and they left.

"We're having a big Thanksgiving dinner for all our people at the farm next Saturday. It's a big deal and I'd like for you to come," said Rep as they walked to the mill. "We're gonna hunt birds that morning, eat and then shoot doves that afternoon. You said you like to hunt so I thought you would enjoy that."

"I'd like to do that," said Storm. "Sounds like a good day."

"I'll pick you up bout seven Saturday morning at the landing," said Rep.

"Sounds good to me," said Storm. They shook hands. Storm went in the mill and Rep headed to the landing.

Rep told Owen that it looked like he would be doing the fishing now since Rolley wasn't coming back.

That suited Owen. He had seen the work on his cabin started on Big Island and he was ready to tell Sassy he was going to have a place to live. If he was fishing full time for Shoal Creek and also had a cabin, he would be in the same situation Rep had been in when he married Bess. When the cabin was ready, he planned to go get Sassy.

When May got out of school on Wednesday, she went to see Star. When Star opened the door, May said, "We have to talk."

Star walked to the sofa and stared at her.

"I slept with Walt the other night," said May.

Star's face showed her surprise. "What the hell did you do that for? Did he force you?"

"No, but I thought it was best under the circumstances." May told her of their conversation and the promises Walt had made. "I don't want him all over me all the time."

Star was skeptical. "Walt ain't never been very good about keeping promises. Do you believe him?"

"Not really, but if he acts bad, we'll deal with it."

Star nodded. "I'll kill the bastard."

May smiled. "You'd have to beat me to it."

"Let me know how it turns out," said Star.

May left Star and walked toward the stores. When she passed the church, she saw Storm in front of the gym talking to Jim Hawke. She was going to talk to him, and this seemed to be as good a time to do it. She walked on and she could see both were watching her.

"Hey, little girl," said Jim as she approached.

"Hey, Jim," she said, as she turned to Storm. "Can I talk to you?" she said. She started walking toward the gym steps.

Storm followed her to the steps. She sat down and he sat beside her. He looked at her, wondering what she was about, her face looked too serious.

"I want to talk to you, Storm," said May. "What I'm going to tell you won't make any sense to you, but I'm going to tell you the truth."

He frowned, trying to understand what she was saying or about to say.

She took a deep breath and looked at him. "You asked about going out with me and I said I would. And I still will but I wanted to make sure you understood everything. I am still going to be at the club in Phenix City"

He nodded. "I think I understood that."

"I wanted to make sure you knew. I will still be at the club on Friday and Saturday nights."

"On the stage?" he asked.

"Yes."

"Half naked?"

"Yes."

Storm leaned back and looked at her. "You like doing this?"

"I plan to stay till the end of the school year and then go to college."

"What about us?"

May shook her head. "There is no us, Storm. I like you very much but there is no us. I had agreed to date you, that's all. I just wanted you to know the truth about what I'm going to do."

Storm took a deep breath. "You have a way with words, May. With a few words you can cut a man's heart out of his chest, throw it on the ground and stomp on it." He got up and started walking toward his car.

May jumped up, ran after him, and caught his arm. "Storm, I know you don't like this, but I would still like to spend time with you."

He shook his head. "Maybe on Friday night I'll be standing at the edge of the stage holding some money and we can spend some time together while I run my hands over you." He turned and walked away.

She watched him go. When she turned around, Jim Hawke was looking at her. She walked past him without speaking and headed to the dormitory.

~

Karen Hogan arrived at Shoal Creek for Thanksgiving. She and her mother, Miss Sara, as everybody called her, came Thursday afternoon and announced they would stay until Sunday. Rep decided that if Miss Sara was going to be in the house he would head to the river.

Lila told Karen that Rep had been to River Bluff and visited Rolley and he was doing well. Karen showed little interest in Rolley's condition. "I thought you were all in love with him," said Lila.

Karen shook her head. "You know that was just a summer fling," she said. "Rolley was really too young for me."

"Have you found anybody else?"

"No," said Karen, "nobody else."

Lila smiled. "Then I have somebody for you to meet. He is coming to bird hunt with Rep on Saturday and will be here for the dinner." Lila then told Karen about Storm Gill. "He is handsome, already graduated from college and his father owns the mill across the river in River Bluff. His family is wealthy, and he will run the mill after his father retires."

Karen was definitely interested in meeting Storm and was looking forward to Saturday.

Rep walked to the landing where Owen was dressing the morning's catch. "You been down by Big Island where the men are buildin' yo' cabin?" he asked.

"Walked up there this morning," said Owen. "They're putting the tin on the roof. Ought not to be long fore it be ready for me to move in."

"You said anything to Sassy about it?"

Owen shook his head. "I ain't been down to see her yet. I ain't gonna tell her nothin' till it be ready."

"We're havin' the dinner Saturday for everybody. Why don't you bring her up here? On the way you could stop and show her the cabin. That ought to impress her about yo' intentions, if you have intentions."

Owen smiled. "I'll sho' do that. She'll have to believe me after she sees the cabin."

"That would be good," said Rep. He turned and went back up the hill.

Owen finished the fish, took them to the kitchen and when he got back to the landing, he got in his boat and started to Willow Creek. When he landed, he walked to the house and hollered. One of the younger sisters opened the door and walked out on the porch. She looked down at Owen. "What you be doin' down here?" she asked, staring at him.

"Where is Sassy?"

"She be at the dog pen." The sister grinned down at him. "Sassy say you live in a shed and use the bathroom in the woods."

Owen ignored her and started walking toward the barn. He walked around to the dog pen and saw Sassy watering the dogs. He stood and watched her.

Finally, she turned, put the bucket down and looked at him. She did not look friendly. "Why you be here?"

"I come to see you."

"I ain't talkin' to you."

"I gonna ask you to come to Shoal Creek Saturday and eat with me at the big Thanksgiving dinner. Rep said I could ask you."

She turned up her nose. "Why would I want to go with you?"

"If you go, I'll show you my cabin."

"You ain't got no cabin."

"Yes, I do. It be on Big Island. Rep's men be building it fir me."

She walked over to him. "You better not be lyin' to me."

"I ain't lying."

"It gonna be like Rep's cabin?"

He smiled. "It gonna be bigger. It gonna have two rooms."

She walked over and put her arm around him. "I go with you, but you better not be lyin' to me," she said as she pulled him into the barn. She led him over to the feed sacks. "I gonna see if you remember what we done last time."

Owen sat down beside her and put his arm around her. He remembered everything from last time and had thought about other things he wanted to do with her. When they left the barn, he was familiar with all parts of Sassy's body as she was with him. As they walked to the house he wondered when his cabin would be ready. He hoped it would be soon.

Lick was on the porch when Owen and Sassy came to the house. "Folks be tellin' me that Sugar Boy is at them beer joints downriver tellin' everbody that he gonna git them Shoal Creek people what kilt his bull dog." He looked at Owen. "You tell Rep he ain't gonna stop till he come back up here and cause some more trouble. He gonna have to do somethin' bout 'im."

Owen nodded and then walked to the boat with Sassy. "I'll be back Saturday mornin' to git you," he said as he got in the boat.

"We go and see yo' cabin," she said.

He nodded, cranked the motor and headed upriver. When he landed, he went straight to the barn and found Rep. He was with Mose and he told them what Lick had said about Sugar Boy.

"We can't let 'im go on doin' all this," said Mose.

"I know that," said Rep. "As soon as my shoulder gets right, we gonna have to go after 'im."

"We can't wait too long," said Mose. "That boy ain't got no sense, we gonna have to kill 'im."

"I know that," said Rep. "Sayin' it and doin' it be two different thangs." He thought for a minute. "I'm gonna have to get that long rifle from Lick and git him to show me how to shoot it. If Sugar Boy is in them beer joints downriver, then we gotta get 'im when he's out of the swamp."

"That be right," said Mose.

10

Thursday night May walked in from school and Alva was sitting on the sofa waiting for her. "I want to talk to you about something, May," she said.

May sat down and waited.

Tomorrow night is when you go to the club, isn't it?"

May nodded. "I go Friday and Saturday nights."

"You know that I'm not in favor of you doing this," said Alva, "but we've already talked about that."

May watched her, wondering where she was going with this.

"You told me what you do, and I talked to Jim Hawke about it." She paused. "However, I will never completely understand about it until I watch you on stage." She looked at May.

Wide-eyed, May stared at Alva. "You want to go with me tomorrow night and watch me on stage?"

Alva nodded. "Yes, that is what I want to do."

"I don't know I want you to see me, Alva. Knowing you were there would embarrass me."

Alva smiled. "I would embarrass you but standing in front of a crowd of men doesn't?"

May smiled. "I guess that is kind of silly. Are you sure about this?"

"Yes, I am. I am your friend, although I don't like what you are doing, but I want to understand it."

May shrugged. "If that's what you want to do, I can't say no."

Alva reached over and hugged her.

Friday afternoon May and Alva got to the dormitory from school about the same time. Alva was nervous and May was somewhere between nervous and excited. Anticipating being on stage always excited her. She was trying to keep her feelings under control.

"Are you sure about doing this?" asked Alva as they dressed.

"We've already talked enough about it," said May. "I've already told you how I feel."

"All right," said Alva. "I won't ask you again."

They got in May's car and headed to Phenix City. Little was said, both were dealing with their own thoughts. May looked at Alva as they pulled into the parking lot and stopped. "Walt has a private room, Alva. I'll ask Walt about you staying there. You can see the stage, but the people can't see you. You might want to go straight there and not go to the dressing room. I'll have to dress for the show as will everybody else and people will be naked. Nobody thinks anything about it, but it might bother you."

Alva smiled. "It won't bother me as long as I don't have to get naked."

May chuckled. "Sometimes you surprise me, Alva."

Alva laughed. "Sometimes I surprise myself."

When they walked in the back-door Walt was waiting for them. He went over, hugged May and kissed her on the cheek. He turned and looked at Alva.

"This is my friend, Alva Tinney, Walt. She came with me today," said May.

Walt offered his hand. "I'm really glad that you came with her, Miss Alva."

Alva smiled and shook his hand. "Thank you, Walt.

"Walt, I was wondering if Alva could sit in your private room instead of out in the crowd?"

Walt smiled and looked at Alva. "Certainly, she can. In fact, if she doesn't mind, I would join her."

"That would be very nice," said Alva

Walt cocked his head and looked at Alva. *This is a beautiful and classy lady,* he thought. *Damn, she would be something else to get to know.*

Josie came out and she and May headed for the dressing room.

Walt took Alva's arm and walked behind them. "They are going to dress for the show," he said. "If you want, we can go straight to the room. I will have some food and drinks brought in."

"First, I'd like to see May get dressed and then I'll go with you," said Alva. "I want to see everything she does."

Walt nodded and led her into the dressing room. As May had told her there were women in all states of dress and undress in the room. Men workers were walking through the room seemingly paying no attention. May and Josie were standing in front of Alva and Walt with nothing on. Walt admired them both and they paid him no mind. Alva glanced at Walt; his eyes were watching May.

When May finished dressing, she and Josie walked out of the room and stood at the curtain. Alva could see other girls on the stage dancing and shedding their clothes. She followed Walt down a hallway and into a small room. There was a window across the front of the room. She could see the entire stage and the crowd out front.

"We can see out the stage, but they can't see us," said Walt as he pulled out a chair for her.

Alva sat down and Walt sat beside her. The door behind them opened and a waitress came in carrying trays of food and drinks.

"I didn't know what you liked to eat," said Walt. "I prefer seafood, we have it brought in fresh daily, so we have shrimp and lobster prepared. We also have steak if you prefer that or the kitchen can prepare anything else you would like."

Alva looked at all the food laid out before her. "This is fine," she said. "You have prepared too much."

"I just wanted you to be pleased," said Walt.

Alva took a shrimp cocktail and ate it, while Walt ate a lobster tail. She watched four of the women on stage as they danced and undressed. Walt was eating and never looked up. Alva was waiting for May to come out.

"You said that you teach school," said Walt as he pushed his plate away and turned to her.

"Yes, I have for five years now."

"My mother was a schoolteacher," said Walt.

Alva looked at him, surprised by his statement. "Where did she teach?"

"She taught in college in Birmingham. She's retired now," he said. "My father was a lawyer."

"It sounds like you had a good upbringing."

Walt nodded. "I did. Went to college and wanted to be a writer but that didn't work out." He looked at Alva. "You're probably wondering how I ended up in this business. I suspect you don't approve of what I'm doing here, and I understand your negative feelings about it." He smiled. "My folks would certainly agree with you. But I'm a businessman and this is my business, although it's somewhat different from most."

"I don't approve of this business," said Alva, staring in Walt's face, "it's sinful and wrong. You strike me as a man who is smart, very capable and could be successful in other businesses, but you chose this."

Walt nodded. "I wouldn't argue with anything you said." He looked in her eyes. "You're a very beautiful woman, Alva and smart. I get to talk to few women in this business that can carry on a meaningful conversation. I would like to get to know you better."

Alva shook her head. "Let me be honest with you, Walt. I'm here because of May; I'm concerned about her. If not for that, I would never be in the same room with you under any circumstances. I don't like any part of you, who you are and what you do. People fear you because you have the power to do harm to them. That is wrong."

As she said that the band got louder, the curtain opened, and Josie came out on stage and the crowd noise overrode the band. Alva watched as Josie went into her act and the crowd responded. After a few minutes the band picked up the volume again, the curtain opened, and May walked out. The crowd erupted and Alva could see why Walt wanted May on stage. She was the star of the show. Alva watched as May took over the crowd. Josie was good but she didn't compare to May's presence on stage. In spite of herself, Alva caught herself, like the crowd, being mesmerized by May's performance. May was in her element.

Alva watched as May moved to the edge of the stage. She faced the men gathered there, all were holding up money and she allowed them to tuck the money in her G-string as they rubbed their hands over her. May was enjoying it, standing there almost naked, teasing the crowd and laughing at their futile attempts to grab her.

Alva's face was hot, her palms were sweaty, and she was breathing faster as she watched May perform. She was so engrossed and caught up in what May was doing that she felt like she was on stage. She hadn't been aware that Walt was watching her until out of the corner of her eye she noticed him looking intently at her and smiling.

He leaned over toward her. "Gets you all stirred up, don't it?"

She looked at him. "Yes, it does." She smiled. "May got the crowd and me all excited."

"You're a lady, Miss Alva and I've known few like you," said Walt, staring deep into her eyes. "But underneath you are still a woman and have a woman's baser feelings, although you may try to ignore them. You don't like me but for you I could be a much different person. You might find that you could like me."

As he was talking May and Josie exited the stage. Alva got up from the table. "I thank you for the meal, Walt," she said. "I do have feelings, Walt, like a normal woman." She turned and started toward the door, stopped and looked back at him. "I understand where you hope to go with me, Walt. You're accustomed to having your way with women. I've been wined and dined before by men and I'm not lily pure." His eyes were on her. "I've been in bed with a man, Walt, more than once. It was always my choice to do so and I can tell you now, you will never have me in your bed." She walked out the door and went to the dressing room.

Walt watched her leave. He sat and thought about what she had said for a moment. Damn, he thought, that is one hell of a woman. He jumped up and ran out the door toward the dressing room.

May was almost dressed when Alva got to the dressing room. Walt came rushing in, congratulated May and Josie on a great job. He kissed May on the cheek and handed her an envelope. "This is a little bonus for you, May, for doing a great job." he said.

May had never been handed an envelope before, She opened it and looked at the money inside, then looked at Josie. "You take all the tips, Josie. I've got enough."

Josie hugged her and thanked her.

Walt turned and offered his hand to Alva. "It has been a pleasure being with you, Alva." She took his hand, he held her hand, bowed and kissed the back of her hand. Then he looked up at her, still holding her hand. "Don't ever judge a book by its cover, Alva."

Alva pulled her hand away and smiled at him. "That's true, Walt, I never do. But remember, I've already read the first chapter." She smiled at him, took May by the arm and they went out the back door to the car.

When they were in the car, May turned to Alva. "What do you think?"

"Walt did as he had promised. He was a perfect gentleman around me."

"You saw me on stage?"

"Yes, you did very well. If that is what you want to do, you are very good at it."

"But you don't approve?"

"You know I don't approve, May. But you and I are different."

May started the car and headed toward River Bluff. "You said Walt acted well. What did he say to you?"

"Walt can be very charming, and he was in every way. I can see why women could be impressed with him. But underneath that façade is another person," said Alva. "There is a very dark person somewhere in there and he is scary."

May nodded. "You're right." She looked at Alva. "There's no need for you to come back tomorrow night. I think Walt will act right at least for a while. If I see him changing and getting to be a problem, I'll tell you."

"All right, I agree," said Alva. "Maybe next week I'll come one night without telling him. Maybe that will keep him honest."

May laughed. "Sometimes you have a sneaky mind."

It was late when they got home. They were tired and went to bed.

When Storm left the mill, he rode up the road and when he passed the dormitory, he saw that May's car was gone. He knew she had gone to Phenix City and would be on stage tonight. He knew he had to get over her and get her out of his mind. That was easier said than done but the best way to do it was not to sit around and mope but to find somebody else. That was what he needed to do, but that was also easier said than done. He decided to start looking for someone else tomorrow.

Rep left the Shoal Creek landing right after daylight and headed across the river. When he got in sight of the landing at River Bluff landing, he saw Storm standing on the bank. He had a gun case and a pack on his back. His hunting clothes were new and looked just out of the box.

Rep looked at him when he landed. "You gonna put all us to shame, Storm, with yo' fancy hunting clothes."

Storm laughed as he put his pack in the boat and stepped in. "I didn't think about it when you asked me to come, but I've been gone five years and I outgrew all my hunting clothes. I had to scramble to get something to wear." He sat down in the front of the boat.

Rep cranked the motor and headed upriver. As they went by Big Island and turned into Back Slough, Storm thought of all the time as a boy he'd spent on the river with Jim Hawke. He loved the river, and he was glad to be back in River Bluff. He'd missed this life when he was away at college and now, he was back for good.

They landed at the Shoal Creek landing, unloaded and went up the hill past the kitchen. They stopped and when Rep knocked, Hattie Mae came out with ham biscuits and coffee. I didn't know if you'd had breakfast or not," said Rep, "but these are good."

Storm thanked Hattie Mae and they sat on the bench outside and ate.

"We'll go to the barn and meet Mose, he'll hunt with us. Then we'll get the dogs and head to the fields. We have a bunch of coveys we can hunt before we eat. Then after we eat dinner with all the folks, we'll shoot doves till late. Then we'll eat the birds we killed for supper."

"Sounds like my kind of day," said Storm.

They finished eating the ham biscuits and went to the barn. Mose already had the dogs ready and they headed out into the fields.

Owen was up before daylight and had finished fishing all his hooks soon after the sun was up. He went back to the landing, dressed the fish and took them to the kitchen. He went back to the landing, got a rag and soap and washed off the smell of fish the best he could and headed for Walnut Creek. He was looking forward to taking Sassy to see the cabin.

When he went up Walnut Creek and landed, he didn't see anybody at the house. He walked to the steps and yelled. The door opened and one of the sisters looked out.

"I come to get Sassy to go to the dinner," he said.

"She be gittin' dressed, She be there in a minute."

Owen stood at the bottom of the steps and when Sassy walked out on the porch he stood and stared at her. She looked totally different with her hair combed and wearing a pretty dress. He'd never seen her look like this; she was a beautiful young woman. "You sho' do look pretty in that dress," he said as she walked down the steps.

"I thank you," she said. She took his hand and they walked to the boat. When she got in, she wrapped a scarf around her head. "Bess told me when you ride in a boat to always wear a scarf cause the wind will mess up yo' hair up somethin' awful," she said.

Owen stared at her in awe at her beauty and her understanding about things. He was impressed with her even more than he had been. She was not a little girl.

He cranked the motor, and they went upriver. He turned into the mouth of Back Slough. In a few minutes he cut across the slough to the Big Island bank and went in the narrow cut between Sallie White and Big Island. He pulled into the bank, tied the boat to a tree, got out and helped Sassy get out of the boat.

When they walked up the bank, they were right in front of the cabin. Sassy looked up and stood there wide eyed. She looked at Owen. "That be yo' cabin?"

"It be mine."

"It sho' is pretty," she said as she walked up on the steps, pushed the door open and went in. The stove and table were at the far end of the room. She walked over and touched each one. "All this be yo' stuff?"

"Rep done put in most ever thang," said Owen. "He say I need a place to live cause I be fishing for Shoal Creek."

Sassy walked out of the big room into the smaller room and stared at the large bed. She glanced at Owen. "That sho' is a big bed."

Owen grinned. "Sho is. You want to see how it feels?"

She looked at him and walked back in the big room. "Right now you ain't livin' in this cabin. When you be livin' in it, I git in that bed." She walked out the door and headed for the boat.

~

Storm loved to see the dogs work as they ran back and forth across the field. They hadn't gone far before the lead dog pointed and the other dog backed her. They walked up three abreast and the covey exploded out of the sedge brush beneath their feet. Storm had forgotten how much noise came with a covey rise and he was initially startled. He recovered, shot twice, was late and missed.

He shot better as the morning passed but he wasn't satisfied with how he had done. He knew he needed practice and repetition shooting at live birds. They had a good hunt, both Mose and Rep were excellent shots and made up for his misses. They had plenty of birds by the time they got back to the barn. Mose gave the birds to one of the women to be cleaned for supper.

When they walked in the barn several tables were set up and many of the farm's people were already seated and eating. There were platters of food on the tables and gallons of tea, Storm was hungry and followed Rep and Mose to a table on the end of the line. There were three women at the table. One was Lila and as soon as he saw her, he was again struck at how beautiful she was. The older woman sitting by her was introduced as Miss Sara, Lila's mother. Then he turned as the other woman stood up and he almost gasped. She was a younger, taller version of Lila and just as striking. He stared at her. She was introduced as Karen; Lila's sister and he could see the resemblance.

He sat down. Karen was seated directly across from him and he had a hard time keeping his mind on what he was doing. Suddenly he realized she was speaking to him and waiting for a reply.

"What did you say?" he asked.

She smiled. "I was asking if you enjoyed the hunt?"

He finally got control of his feelings. "Yes, I did, but I didn't shoot very well. Mose and Rep had to cover for me." After that exchange he handled himself well and acted like he had good sense. In the first few minutes together, they had both decided they were interested in the other. They both kept glancing at each other. At times their eyes would meet, and they would glance away.

Lila watched the exchange with interest. She had hoped Karen would like Storm and her wishes seemed to have come true. Miss Sara had been told that Storm's family was well off, so she had already given her blessings to the potential match.

Rep saw Owen and Sassy walk in the door. He jumped up, ran over to them and brought them to the table. "This is my brother, Owen and this is his friend, Sassy Shell," he said. Then he introduced Karen and Miss Sara and lastly Storm. Lila moved over in her seat and Rep put Owen and Sassy between them. Sassy was sitting next to Lila.

"You certainly look pretty, Sassy," said Lila. "I haven't seen you in some time. You certainly have grown into a beautiful young woman."

"I thank you," said Sassy. "This was Bess's dress. Rep give it to me."

Lila smiled. "It is a pretty dress. I remember Bess wearing it. You look a lot like her."

"That be what everybody say bout me."

Lila nodded and looked at Rep. "Bess was a very pretty woman."

Rep listened to the exchange and nodded to Lila. He had never been prouder of her.

Rep looked at Owen. "Did y'all go by the cabin?"

Owen nodded. "I showed it to Sassy. We went inside and she liked it."

Rep looked at Sassy. "What did you think about the cabin?"

"I liked it," she said. She looked at Owen. "I be glad he got it. I done told 'im that I ain't gonna marry 'im while he be livin' in that shed down by the landing. That ain't no fit place for no woman." She looked at Rep. "I told 'im I wasn't gonna git in his bed till he had a decent place to live."

Rep smiled. "Well, it's good he's gonna have a cabin then, Sassy."

Miss Sara looked at Sassy, rolled her eyes, then looked at Lila. It was obvious she didn't know what to think about Sassy.

Karen looked at Sassy. "I think every man should have a good cabin before he asks a woman to marry him. I agree with you, Sassy." Karen cut her eyes at Storm as she spoke.

Sassy nodded. "That be what I say. I sho wasn't gonna live in that shed and use the bathroom in the woods."

Owen looked at Rep. "I ain't never asked her to marry me. This is all her talkin' bout gittin' married."

Rep looked at Storm. "Do you have a good cabin, Storm?"

Storm nodded. "It's pretty good. The roof don't leak." Everybody laughed and Storm looked at Karen. Their eyes met and she smiled.

They finished eating and Rep said the men were going to the dove field. He said that any women that wanted to come were welcomed to go also. Sassy immediately said she was coming with Owen. Karen told Rep she would also like to go. Storm quickly volunteered, telling her he would be glad for her to go with him. They walked out the door together.

"I understand you live in Atlanta," said Storm as they walked to the field.

"Yes, I do. I lived here at Shoal Creek until I went to college. I always loved it here but when Daddy was killed, I went with Mother to Atlanta. I've told Lila I want to come back here." She looked at Storm. "You live across the river in River Bluff?"

"Yes, I grew up there. My family owns the mill in town. I've been away for five years except for short visits during school. I'm back now and glad to be back."

"You work in the mill?"

Storm nodded. "I do. I'm learning about the business, so I'll be ready when Daddy retires."

"Sounds like you'll have a big responsibility."

"It will be. The entire town depends on the mill for jobs, so it needs to do good."

"I've been to River Bluff," she said.

This surprised him. "You have?"

"Yes, I went over with Rolley Hill. He was fishing for Shoal Creek and I went over with him." She looked at him. "Do you know the Hobbs from River Bluff?"

He looked at her, wondering where this question came from. "Yes, I know the Hobbs."

Karen shook her head. "My trip to River Bluff was very strange. Rolley was taking a girl, Josie was her name, across the river to see the Hobbs. I never understood it all, but Josie worked in a club in Phenix City and the owner of the club had problems with a Hobb girl. He sent Josie to talk to her about straightening out their problems. I went with Rolley and he showed me the town."

Storm also knew Josie, but he didn't say anything about it. He decided not to talk about the Hobbs any longer. "Maybe sometimes you can go with me and I'll show you the town."

She put her hand on his arm. "I would like that. Maybe I could see your cabin."

Storm was aware that her hand was on his arm. "I'll make it happen," he said, smiling.

The afternoon passed quickly. There were a lot of doves on the field and the shooting was constant. Karen had never shot at a bird before and Storm helped her by getting behind her with his arms around her and helping her hold the gun. He liked the feel of her in his arms. She welcomed his help.

Rep finally walked out in the field and said it was time to quit. Everybody started walking back to the barn. When they got there, the tables were already set. The quail they killed that morning had been prepared with all the trimmings. The hunters from the field got seated and Lila and Miss Sara joined them. Lila had Rip with her, now six months old. This was the first time she had brought him to one of their gatherings.

There was the usual talking and bragging and ribbing about the hunt, as to who killed what and who missed the most birds. "I'll tell you one thing," said Rep, "you better not sit close to Sassy on the field. If you do you won't get much shooting, cause she don't miss." He looked at Sassy. "How did you learn to shoot like that?"

"Lick trains bird dogs and we be huntin' all the time," said Sassy. "Ain't nothing to shootin' them doves. They just come floatin' in and they be easy to hit."

Some of the others didn't agree with her statement about being easy to hit.

Everybody enjoyed the meal and again congratulated Hattie Mae on her cooking. It had been a long day; everybody had eaten too much and were tired. Owen got up and said he had to get Sassy back down the river before dark, so they had to leave. Everybody had fallen in love with Sassy. She was so direct and plain in her talking and nobody knew what was going to come out of her mouth next. Lila and Karen hugged her, Storm shook hands with Owen, and they left.

Miss Sara took Rip and walked back to the house. She had taken up with him and wanted to have him with her all the time. Lila was glad to see her mother involved with the family. "I'll walk back to the house with Mother," said Lila as she got up and went out the door.

Rep looked at Storm. "I'll take you back across the river when you get ready. There ain't no hurry. I've got to go see Mose." He got up and followed Lila.

Storm and Karen were left alone for the first time. They were both hesitant to speak first.

"It seems," said Karen, "that my sister has schemed to leave us alone together."

Storm grinned. "It would seem so. I don't have a problem with that. I've been wanting to have a chance to talk to you. How long will you be here?" he asked.

"I'm supposed to leave tomorrow afternoon. Mother has to go back to Atlanta."

"I wish you had more time."

"So, do I," said Karen as she smiled. "I think poor Owen has got hold of more than he can handle with Sassy."

Storm laughed. "Sassy is a sight and I think you are right; she has her eye on marrying him. She flat said as much."

"I like her," said Karen. "She says what she feels and thinks."

Storm looked at her. "Most people don't do that. Do you say what you feel and think?"

Karen stared at him. "Sometimes, depending on who I'm talking to."

Storm returned her stare. "What about right now? What do you think and feel?"

Karen smiled, looked up at the ceiling for a moment and then her eyes returned to his face. "I was wondering if you had someone waiting for you across the river tonight?"

He shook his head. "Nobody is waiting for me across the river. What else might you be thinking."

"If nobody is waiting for you across the river, why do you have to go back across the river tonight?"

"That's a good question," said Storm, his eyes never leaving her face. He thought back to what he had thought about earlier. He had to get his mind off May and the best way was find someone else to replace her. As he looked at Karen, he thought fate has put that person right in his path. He nodded. "I'm a grown man, so if I don't want to go across the river, I don't have to. I could stay." He pursed his lips. "But where would I sleep?"

Karen smiled. "That's not a problem," she said. She got up, took his hand and led him across the barn to the back room and opened the door. She pointed to the bed that Rep had brought in. "Here's a bed you can use for the night if you decide to stay." She looked at him. "Rep had this bed put in after he and Lila were married. He said sometimes when he and Lila are working down here, they got tired and need a place to rest together."

Storm nodded. "Very convenient. I like Rep's thinking. This should work for me."

"I bet you like Rep's thinking," she said as she punched him and walked out. "Let's go up and see Lila. You need to tell Rep you won't be going back tonight if that's what you want to do." They headed up the hill to the big house. Lila and Rep were in their room and Karen told them about Storm's plans to stay the night.

Karen ran in the bathroom and asked Lila to come with her. "Don't say anything to Mother," said Karen, "but I am going to stay with him and talk for a while tonight."

Lila shook her head. "Karen, you just met him today. What is he going to think about you? Did he ask you to stay with him?"

"He didn't ask me; he doesn't know I'm staying with him. I've got to go back to Atlanta tomorrow, so we have little time. I'm not going to do anything with him except talk, that's all. But I want him to remember me."

Lila smiled. "I tried that with Rep at his cabin. I made it through the first night, but the second night I got pregnant."

Karen smiled. "It's good then that I only have to last one night. Don't say anything to Mother." She ran out of the room, got Storm's hand and they headed down the hill.

Rep watched them leave. He looked at Lila. "Storm's not leaving. What was that all about?

"Nothing," said Lila.

~

Owen and Sassy left the barn and headed to the landing. "I had a good time," said Sassy. "I thank you for lettin' me come. All of them people be mighty nice to me." They got in the boat and headed down Back Slough.

When they got out at Willow Creek Owen took Sassy's hand as

they walked to the house. "Now you know that cabin be mine," said Owen. "You heard Rep say so."

Sassy hugged him. "You got a place to live now. I be ready to marry you and go live with you, if you be ready."

"I don't know bout doin' all that marryin' stuff," said Owen. "You talk to Mattie and tell me what to do."

Sassy kissed him. "When you move in the cabin, we git married. You tell me when that be."

Owen shook his head. "I be lettin' you know." He kissed her and headed back to the boat.

Karen and Storm got back to the barn. "I had brought a change of clothes," said Storm. "I didn't know if I would have to change after hunting for supper or not. So, anyway I have something to wear tomorrow."

"Why don't we go in the back room where it's more comfortable," said Karen. "There's a couch in there where we can sit that's more comfortable than these chairs.

They got up, Storm grabbed his pack and gun and followed Karen into the room. Karen sat on the couch while he put his gear in the back. He walked over and sat down beside her. He looked at her.

Karen smiled and took his hand. "I want to tell you a story," she said. "We're both adults, so I think you'll understand this."

He leaned back on the sofa and watched her face.

"Lila said that when she met Rep, she was so attracted to him that she acted foolishly. Daddy told her she acted like a bitch dog in heat. She invited herself to his cabin and told him she was going to spend two nights with him. But she told him she would sleep with him if he would just hold her, nothing more than hold her. Rep finally agreed." Karen looked in Storm's eyes. She had his full attention.

"The first night went fine. Rep did as she had requested, he just held her. The second night didn't go as planned. Lila forgot about their agreement and she ended up pregnant." She watched Storm's face for his reaction.

Storm's brow furrowed. "I'm sure there's a point to this."

She nodded. "There is. I just meet you today and I'm attracted to you, Storm, but I'm not going to be as foolish as Lila was. I don't know how you feel but I'd like to sit here on this sofa and talk to you for as long as you want." She paused and looked at him.

"That sounds good to me," said Storm. "I stayed tonight because I think I would like to spend time with you."

May was getting ready to go to the club Saturday afternoon. Alva was sitting on the sofa when she came out of her room. Alva looked up at her. "Are you sure you don't want me to go with you."

"No," said May. "I have to go alone today and see how Walt is going to act. I feel sure he will do right today."

"You know I would go with you if you wanted me to," said Alva.

"I know that, but I'll be all right." She hugged Alva and went out the door, got in the car and headed to Phenix City. She pulled into the parking lot, got out and went in the back door. Walt was waiting for her. He walked over, put his arm around her and kissed her on the cheek. "Miss Alva didn't come with you?"

May shook her head. "No, she didn't come. I'm all by myself."

Walt seemed disappointed. "I was hoping she would come. I enjoyed being with her last night. She is a beautiful and classy lady." He looked at May. "You tell her that I asked about her. I hope she will come back."

May was surprised by his comment. He sounded as if he truly missed Alva. "I'll tell her what you said." She walked into the dressing room where Josie was already getting ready. She looked back and Walt was going up the stairs to his office. She didn't see him again while she dressed. This was the first time she had ever undressed without him standing there watching her every move. It seemed going to bed with him had settled him down. It was a relief not having him watching and touching her.

She went on with Josie. They had a good night. The crowd was large and boisterous, and she enjoyed her time on stage. When she came off the stage Walt hugged her, told her what a great job she did and handed her an envelope. Then he took Josie's hand, and they went up the stairs to the office.

May went in the dressing room, put on her clothes and went to River Bluff. Alva was in bed when she went in. She was tired so she went to bed. She would get up early and go to church with Alva.

It was late when Karen kissed Storm and reluctantly told him that she had to leave. "I don't want Mother to think I'm a complete tramp," she said, "so I need to be in my bed at daylight."

Storm got up with her and kissed her. "I've been thinking about what you said last night about sleeping with you and just holding you." He smiled. "I would have done that."

Karen stepped away from him and shook her head. "I wasn't worried about you. I don't think I could have lasted." She turned and started for the door. She looked back. "When you get dressed come up and eat breakfast with us."

Storm watched her leave and smiled.

Owen was fishing his hooks the next morning. He had no fish on the first set hooks and that wasn't normal. When he got to the tree where the first trotline was tied, the trotline was gone. It was obvious it had been cut. Owen went on down to the last trotline and it too had been cut. Owen cranked the motor and headed up the slough to the landing. He beached the boat, jumped out and ran up the hill. When he got to the barn there was nobody there, so he headed to the big house. He went in the back door to the kitchen.

Lila, Rep, Karen, Storm and Miss Sara were at the table eating. Owen walked in and told Rep what he had found.

"There was no fish on the set hooks and two trotlines was cut?" said Rep, looking at Owen.

"Both lines was cut right at the tree. They didn't break, they was cut with a knife."

Lila was concerned about Owen's news, but she didn't want to start anything in front of her mother and Storm. She looked at Rep.

"I've got to go see Mose," he said as he got up from the table. "We'll have to see about this." He motioned to Owen. "You come with me." They went out the door.

Lila looked at her mother. "Mother," she said, "will you please go see after Rip. I need to go talk to Rep and Mose."

Her mother nodded, got up and left the room.

Karen and Storm were looking at Lila, not understanding what was happening. "Sugar Boy Hogg, the man that shot Rolley Hill and owned the dog that hurt Rep did this." Said Lila. "Now Rep and Mose will have to go after him. He is a dangerous and mean person. I'm afraid for Rep."

"Won't the law do anything about this Sugar Boy?" asked Storm.

Lila shook her head. "They won't. He lives way back in a swamp and they won't go in after him. Everybody is afraid of him." She looked at Karen. "I have to go talk to Rep."

Karen looked at Storm. "We'll go with you."

When they started toward the barn, Rep, Mose and two guards, all armed with rifles, were walking up the hill toward the kitchen. When Rep saw them, he stopped. "I'm going to Licks," he said to Lila. "I'll be back later." Rep looked at Storm. "Owen is at the landing. I told him to take you back across the river when you get ready to go."

Storm nodded. He didn't know what else to say. These people were armed like they were in a war and going to meet the enemy. Then he thought of all the shootings and killings that had happened at Shoal Creek in the last year and it was like a war zone.

"Be careful, Rep," said Lila. "I've already talked to you about this."

Rep walked over and kissed her. "I'll be back." He turned and walked up the hill toward the kitchen. Mose and the two guards followed him.

"I'm sorry about all this trouble," said Lila to Karen and Storm. "You do whatever ya'll want to do. I have to go see about Rip and get Mother ready to go." She looked at Karen. "Mother said she wanted to leave right after lunch." Lila walked back toward the house.

Karen watched Lila walk away. "This was not the way I wanted things to work out," she said.

"This is not good," said Storm. "If they're going after this man with rifles, this is serious business."

"Welcome to Shoal Creek," said Karen, shaking her head. "My Daddy and brother were killed in the past year and Rep's wife, Bess was killed too. We don't need any more killings."

Storm walked over and put his arm around Karen. "You have a lot to do, maybe I should leave."

"I don't want you to leave." She put her head on his shoulder and hugged him. "We haven't had much time, but I enjoyed last night and getting to know you."

He looked at her. "I want this to just be the start with us, Karen. When can you come back, or I will come to Atlanta?"

"I'll come back next weekend and plan to stay for a while. That would give me time to get Mother settled. I'll do that if that would suit you?"

"I'll plan to be here next Saturday morning. What about I take you across the river to see my cabin?

Karen smiled. "I'd like that. I remember what Sassy said to Owen." She laughed. "Sassy said 'I told 'im I ain't gittin in his bed till he has a decent place to live.'"

Storm smiled. "Then I hope my place is decent."

"I do too," said Karen. She took his hand. "Come on. Let's go get your stuff and I'll walk with you to the landing."

They walked to the barn, got his pack and gun and went to the landing where Owen was waiting. They stood on the bank and kissed and held each other. Neither wanted to turn loose but finally Storm stepped back. "I'll see you next Saturday." He said as he walked to the boat.

Karen stood on the bank and watched until the boat was out of sight.

11

Rep and Mose and the two guards went to the landing. Rep told the two guards to go downriver, hit the beer joints where Sugar Boy had been hanging out and see if he was there today or if anybody had seen him recently. If they found him or knew where he was, they were to come to Lick's house, that's where Rep and Mose would be.

The two men got in the boat and left. Rep and Mose got in the other boat and headed down Back Slough to Willow Creek. When they landed, Lick was standing on the porch. He saw them and came walking across the yard to the landing.

"What y'all be doin' down here?" he asked.

Rep told him what had happened with Sugar Boy. "I want to borrow yo' long rifle and get you to show me how to shoot it," he said.

Lick shook his head. "There ain't nough time to do that. It sho' take too long to learn you bout the rifle. You couldn't never hit 'im from dry land."

Rep frowned. "I can't hit 'im with my rifle from that far off."

"Tell you what I do," said Lick. "Y'all wait till yo' folks git back from looking for Sugar Boy. If he be in the swamp, I'll go with you and we kill 'im."

They walked to the porch and sat on the steps while they were waiting. They looked up as Sassy came walking from the barn. She walked up to Rep. "Where be Owen?" she asked.

"He took Storm to River Bluff. I spect he's back at the farm by now."

Sassy nodded. "When he be gonna move in his cabin?"

"The men said they be finished with everthang in two weeks," said Rep, watching her face.

She cut her eyes at him. "Did he tell you he gonna be marrying me?"

Rep shook his head. "He ain't said nothin' to me bout it. I heard you say y'all was getting' married but I don't know what he thanks bout it."

Sassy grunted. "It don't matter what he be thankin'. He be knowin' we gonna git married. He better git ready." She turned and walked in the house.

Rep smiled. "If Owen marries that gal, he better be ready for a wild ride, in more ways than one."

Two hours later Rep's two men came back to the landing. They hadn't seen Sugar Boy and nobody in the joints on the river had seen him in two days. They figured he was in the swamp.

"All y'all go git yo' stuff and come back 'fore dark," said Lick. "We'll go in like we done before and set up. With five of us we won't have to be worried with 'im slippin' up on us."

Rep agreed with Lick's plan. They loaded in the boats and headed to Shoal Creek. When they landed, Rep told Mose and the men to be back in an hour. He went by the kitchen, told Hattie Mae to fix a bunch of ham biscuits, then went to the house. He got his pack and told Lila what he was going to do.

"You about got killed the last time you tried this," she said. "You and Mose don't have the sense of a Billy goat. And Lick Shell has less than either of you."

Rep walked over and kissed her. "I'll be back sometime tomorrow."

Lila stared at him as he walked out the door.

. . .

Lick was sitting on the steps waiting when they landed. "The last time we was there," he said, "Sugar Boy come out the back of his house and got in his boat. This time I'll set up in the back." He looked at Mose. "You take one of the men and you set up looking at the front of the house. The other man can come with us and set up below us." Everybody nodded that they knew what they were to do.

It took them over an hour to get to the edge of the swamp. They split up as they had planned. The sun was fading behind the trees in the west and soon the dark shadows covered them. They could see lights in the house. They ate a ham biscuit and then settled down. They had agreed that one would stay awake and watch. Rep took the first hours. The others went to sleep.

~

Storm rode back to the River Bluff landing with Owen. They landed, he thanked Owen for bringing him over and got out. To get to his car he had to walk by the group hanging around at the landing. There were fewer here since it was Sunday. At least some had gone to church. Storm had known all of them since he was a boy.

"Hey Storm," said one of the men. "Yo' car's been here all night. You must have shacked up with one of 'im Georgia women."

"There's plenty of 'im over there, Rick. One's waiting for you," Storm said as he walked past."

"Hell," another man said. "She'll sho' be disappointed."

All the men laughed. Storm got in his car and started up the hill. He went to his house, took a shower and dressed. He thought of Karen. He couldn't have asked for a more beautiful woman to turn up in his life at just the right time. She was everything any man could ask for and she seemed to like him. She had promised to return next weekend and then he would have time with her to see if she was what he wanted. Also, she would have time to look at him.

He also thought of Rep and the other men he'd just left. Four men, all armed with rifles, were going down the river looking for some man named Sugar Boy because he had cut their trotlines. Then he thought, Sugar Boy did more than that, he had also tried to kill Rolley Hill, so there was some justification for the hunt. Across the river was some rough people and their response to trouble was different. But he also thought, River Bluff had the Hobbs.

Thinking of the Hobbs made him realize this was the first time he'd thought of May. Suddenly, in spite of not wanting to think of her, she was back in his mind. He realized then that she was in more than his mind, there was a desire for her deep inside him. Someone had once told him that once you have that special magic with a person of the opposite sex, it will never be forgotten, no matter what you do. You may never see the person again or have any more dealings with them, but that feeling will always be there. A song might trigger the memory or a place or another person could bring it up. He tried to concentrate on Karen and being with her last night, but to no avail. Right now, May was in his mind.

He thought about riding up the road but then he thought he might run into her, so he dropped that thought. Instead, he rode to the house and decided to walk over to the mill. It was Sunday, the mill was shut down and the clean-up crews would be there. It had always been the custom that young boys from the town made up the cleaning crew. It was their introduction to the mill, their first job. He had been part of that group before he went away to college.

The mill was covered with cotton lint while operating during the week. The crew would come in, blow off all the machinery with compressed air and sweep up wagon loads of cotton waste. It was a hot and dirty job. The air was filled with lint that stopped up your nose and matted up your eyes. But it was necessary.

Storm left the house and walked over to the mill. He hoped spending time in the mill would help clear his mind.

~

May and Alva left church and walked to the dormitory. "I haven't really had a chance to talk to you about last night," said Alva. "You haven't said anything, so I assume everything went well."

"It was a strange night," said May. "Walt met me at the door and was a perfect gentleman. The first thing he asked me was if you were coming. When I told him you weren't, he really seemed disappointed."

Alva looked at her, her face questioning. "That is strange after all I said to him about not liking him."

May smiled. "Whatever you said must have got him interested. He said you were a beautiful and classy lady. He hoped you would come back again. He said to be sure and tell you that he said it."

Alva shook her head. "I told him I knew why he was being so nice; I'd been wined and dined before. I said I'd been in bed with a man before, more than once, but it was always my choice. And he was wasting his time with me, because I'd never be in his bed."

"You told him that?" said May. She chuckled. "What did he say then?"

"I went to your dressing room after I said that. He followed me and kissed my hand," said Alva. "He was very nice."

May smiled. "He has the hots for you."

Alva stared at her. "Sometimes you need a good whipping." She turned and walked in her room. She knew Walt was a terrible and dangerous man, but he was also attractive, both in looks and manners. She went to the mirror and looked at herself. "Alva," she said to the woman staring back at her, "you have better sense than to feel like this."

Rep and Lick were awake at first light. The woods were noisy in the mornings. Birds were moving and squirrels were loose in the trees jumping from limb to limb. A flock of Wood Ducks swooped in and landed in the water right below them. Noisy crows were all over the trees, seeming to fuss at everything.

Lick was sighted in on the back door, some seven or eight hundred yards away, or so he thought. Rep had the binoculars and was watching the house. Nobody stirred. Then a dog in the back yard started barking and the back door opened, A woman walked out, went down the steps to the dog pen and fed the dogs. They were jumping and barking. She went back up the steps and in the house.

"Who is the woman?" asked Rep.

"That's Lizzie, Sugar Boy's mama."

"Do you know her?"

"I know her. She's a tough woman. There was a man livin' with her for years but I don't thank he was Sugar Boy's daddy. Ain't nobody seen him in years. Some folks say she kilt 'im but don't nobody know that. She was raised up over in Alabama somewhere. She run away when she was a young girl. Hung around the beer joints waitressing till she found out men would pay her for sex. After then she was a whore. Then she got pregnant and went to the swamp with the man and Sugar Boy was born."

"Does she stay in the swamp all the time?"

"Naw, she comes out sometimes and goes to the beer joints and gits her a man. She ain't a bad lookin' woman. She'll shack up for three or four days and then go back in the swamp."

"She sounds like a tough woman."

Lick grunted. "She sho be that. She knows about that swamp good as Sugar Boy. Goes in and out when she wants to."

And hour later they saw the back door crack open and they could see somebody looking out. Then the door swung open and a man ran out, went down the steps past the dog pen to the edge of the water. "Sugar Boy," said Lick.

He was in the edge of the trees and it was difficult to see him clearly. He pushed his boat into the water and jumped in. The boat drifted into a clearing and Lick fired. The bullet hit Sugar Boy in the left leg and knocked him into the bottom of the boat. He struggled up and was halfway sitting when the second bullet hit him in the back and knocked him out of the boat into the water. Rep could see him lying face down in the bloody water. He wasn't moving.

Suddenly, the back door swung open and the woman ran down the steps, across the yard and waded into the water. She grabbed Sugar Boy and held him, screaming and crying. "You bastards killed my boy!" she screamed.

Rep and Lick sat and watched for a few minutes till it was clear Sugar Boy was dead. They gathered up their gear and headed out. The guard from below them came running up. They could still hear the woman screaming. When they got to the pines, Mose and the other guard was waiting. Mose looked at Rep. Rep nodded. They all started walking toward Lick's house.

Nobody said a word all the way back. At the landing Rep told the two guards not to say a word about what happened to anybody. They understood. Rep shook hands with Lick and thanked him for what he did. They headed upriver.

When Rep walked in the house Lila looked at him. "It's done," he said. She ran over and hugged him.

~

Lizzie was on her knees in the water holding Sugar Boy. How had this happened? She looked across the water toward the trees on the far bank that were on dry land. It was a long way to those trees from where she was. Sugar Boy said they were safe; nobody could harm them from that far away. He had been wrong; some bastard could do harm and he had.

His body was wet and heavy. It took her a while to hoist him over into the boat. Afterward she had to sit for a while to get her breath and strength back. She crawled out of the muck, went in the house and washed off. She put on clean clothes and went back outside to the boat. She carried a clean sheet and covered Sugar Boy's body. Then she cranked the motor and left the swamp.

She had thought about what to do. She knew there was no need to go to the sheriff in Shoal County, they wouldn't do anything about him being killed. All Sugar Boy had ever had with the sheriff was trouble. Going downriver to the beer joints wouldn't accomplish anything either. She came out of the swamp and headed upriver.

The old men at the River Bluff landing heard the boat coming from downriver. When it got in sight, they watched it approach and wondered who it was. They didn't recognize the boat. When the boat got closer, they could see the driver. "Damn," said one of the men. "That's a woman driving."

The boat beached and the woman stood up and stepped out on the bank. Several of the men walked toward her. A woman on the river in a boat was unusual and they wanted to see her. "Y'all got a sheriff here?" she asked as they got closer.

"Ain't got no sheriff," said one of the men, "but Jim Hawke is the constable. What's yo' trouble?"

Lizzie bent over and pulled back the sheet on Sugar Boy's body. "Them bastards over at Shoal Creek killed my boy. They shot him in the swamp."

The men came forward and looked at the body. "Who is it?" asked one man.

"It's Sugar Boy," said another.

"I'll go get Jim," said one of the men. He turned and ran to his truck.

Storm had thought about his trip to Shoal Creek and the men going after Sugar Boy. He left the mill and went to see Jim. He wanted to talk to him about what he had seen and what the men were planning to do. He had just pulled up to the gym and got out when a truck came speeding up from the direction of the river.

Jim was sitting on his bench when the truck stopped in front of him and the man yelled out the window. "Hey, Jim. There's a dead man at the landing. A woman brought him there in a boat."

Storm's first thought was they had killed Sugar Boy. He decided he wasn't going to say a word about what he knew.

Jim jumped up and ran to his car. The man in the truck turned around and headed back toward the river. Jim was right behind him and Storm brought up the rear.

Jim stopped at the boat ramp, got out and walked to the boat. He recognized Lizzie Hogg. "Hey Lizzie," he said as he walked up. He'd had no idea who the man in the truck was talking about and was surprised to see Lizzie. He'd known her for years, back to the time he was fishing on the river. He knew her and her reputation. Even in his younger hell raising years, he'd stayed away from her. She was bad news.

"I'm Jim Hawke, the constable here. You remember me?"

Lizzie nodded. "I remember you, Jim. They must be bad off for law here if you be the constable. The damn game wardens was always chasin' after you."

Some of the men laughed.

Jim glanced at them and then looked back at Lizzie. "What happened?"

"Them bastards from Shoal Creek killed my boy."

Jim walked over and looked at the body. "Where did this happen?"

"In the swamp where we be livin'."

"Did you see 'em? Did you see the people what shot 'im.""

"Hell no, I didn't see 'em. Sugar Boy come out the back door, got in his boat and the bastard shot 'im from dry land. They weren't nowhere close in the swamp."

Jim looked at her. "You sure bout that, Lizzie? From yo' house to dry land is a long ways."

Lizzie nodded. "I be tellin' you they be on dry land. They tried one time before and Sugar Boy put the dogs on 'em. They kilt his bulldog. He found where they be on dry land."

Jim looked at her. "What is it you want me to do?"

"I want you to go over to Shoal Creek and lock the bastards up."

Jim shook his head. "I can't do that. He was killed in Georgia and

I'm in Alabama. I don't have no authority over there. You go see the sheriff over there."

"Ain't no need to go see 'im. Them folks never did like Sugar Boy. They won't do nothin'."

Jim shrugged. "I can't do nothin' neither. I don't have jurisdiction cross the river."

Lizzie looked up at him. "Then I reckon I'll have to kill the bastards myself."

Jim shook his head and looked at her. "You better stop that talk, Lizzie. Sugar Boy shot one of our boys from River Bluff not long ago. Lots of people over here could have shot Sugar Boy, he had a lot of enemies." He stared down at her. "Sugar Boy weren't worth a damn, Lizzie. It's a wonder somebody didn't kill 'im long ago."

"Damn right," said one of the men in the crowd. "Sugar Boy fished my hooks all the time. If I'd caught 'im, I'd have killed the son'abitch myself."

Several of the men standing around agreed. "Bastard never was worth a damn."

Lizzie heard the talk. She looked at the unfriendly faces of the men surrounding her and saw she wasn't going to get any help here. She looked at all the men. "Y'all all can go to hell, for all I care." She got in the boat.

"What you gonna do with the body?" asked Jim.

"What the hell do you care?" She pushed the boat off. "I'm going to the swamp and bury 'im." She walked to the back of the boat, cranked the motor and headed downriver.

Jim watched her go. He walked to his car. The river was rid of one problem, he thought.

Storm was standing on the edge of the crowd and heard every word of the conversation with Lizzie. He decided to keep quiet. He did intend to go to Shoal Creek and tell Rep what he had heard. He got in his car and drove to the store. He had to pick up a package from the Post Office for the mill. He went in, saw Mrs. Williams and got the package. When he walked out the door, he was staring straight in May Hobb's face. If she had been a snake it wouldn't have startled him anymore.

May saw the surprise in his face and it tickled her. "Hey, Storm," she said, "how are you?" She knew she bothered him and decided to push him further.

"I'm fine," he said, but he wasn't. Her standing in front of him looking in his eyes wiped out all the intentions he'd had to forget her. He decided to get on the offensive and not allow her to fluster him. "Did you go to the club Friday and Saturday nights?" he asked.

She smiled and moved closer to him. "I did," she said. "I was on the stage both nights almost naked." She moved and was almost touching him. "But you know about that, don't you because you've seen me naked." She reached up and patted him on the cheek.

He stood there and looked down at her. He smiled. "You are such a bitch," he whispered. Her lips were inches away from his face as he spoke.

She nodded. "Yes, I'm a Hobb bitch," she whispered back, smiling up at him.

He laughed and pushed her away. "What are you doing here?"

"I was picking up a package for Alva." She looked at him. "I'm disappointed," she said. "In the past when I ran into you out here you tried to get me to ride to the river with you." She was pushing him.

Storm decided he wasn't going to let her make a fool of him. "I was about to ask you to do that. You want to go to the river with me?"

She smiled at him. "Let me get Alva's package and I'll go with you." She stepped past him and went in the store.

Storm stood there surprised. She was going with him to the river. How did this happen and why did he let it happen?

In a minute she came out with a small package, grabbed his hand and walked to the car. He opened the door and she got in. He ran around and got in, cranked up and started toward the river. She slid over against him; her hip was against his side. His mind was completely messed up.

They got to the river and parked in the regular place. She moved away from him. "I want to talk to you," she said. "All right?"

He looked at her and nodded.

"I'm going to tell you the truth about what I'm doing," she said. She then told him everything. The only exception was she didn't tell him all Walt had done. She told him about Walt's agreement to let her be on stage and he would leave her alone, about Alva going down with her and Walt having the hots for Alva and how much money she was making.

"You are making more in one night than I make in a week," he said.

She laughed. She told him how much she enjoyed being on stage, even though she knew most people thought what she did was wrong. She told him it was her plan to do this until she graduated and then go to college. She stopped, leaned back and asked him if he had any questions.

"You know I never imagined I'd be here with you tonight," he said. "I thank you for being honest and telling me all this."

She nodded. "I know you didn't plan to be here and neither did I."

"Tell me the truth," he said, his eyes looking at her, "why are you here?"

She slid over against him. "I like you, Storm. There's nobody here in town that I want to be with or be around except you, so here I am. I'm making no promises long term but right now I'm yours. However you want me. I'll be your girl if that's what you want." She stopped and looked at him, waiting for him to reply.

"You are still planning to go to the club as you do now?"

"Yes, I explained that to you."

"And you have your plans all set and you are willing to be with me as long as it lasts."

She nodded. "That's what I said.

"But nothing long term. When you decide it's over, it's over."

She frowned. "When you say it like that, it makes me sound like a terrible person. I don't mean to be that bad."

"If I agreed to this, what are the ground rules?"

"There are no ground rules. Remember, I'm a Hobb, I have no shame."

He looked at her. "Why do you keep saying that to me, May? That bothers me when you do that. You know that doesn't matter to me."

"I know," she said. "I won't say it again."

"Thank you," said Storm. "All right. You've told me the truth, so I must tell you the truth before I talk about us. I've met someone recently," he said. "She's someone that could be special but there's been no commitment, I hardly know her."

"You like her?"

"Yes, I do like her."

"She's maybe the marrying kind?"

"Yes. I think she would be a great wife."

"Then obviously she's not dancing on stage in a club."

He smiled. "Not at the moment." He paused. "She lives in Atlanta and will probably be with me here this weekend."

"Staying in your house?"

"Possibly, but I don't think so. Anyway, you'll be at the club, so it won't matter with you."

May nodded. "That's true." She looked up at him. "So, what do we do now?"

"You said there are no ground rules. Would you go to the house with me right now and go to bed with me?" he asked.

She slid over against him. "If you ask me to go with you I will, if you're really serious." She stared at him. When she had agreed to come with him to the river, she had been teasing him, but now she was serious.

Storm pulled her to him and kissed her. She returned his kiss. They held each other for a long time. Then he started the car and drove toward town. He passed the road to his house and went on to the dormitory. He stopped in the driveway. "Maybe another time, May, when we both know what we're doing." He smiled at her. "The other night with you at my house was very special to me. I think too much of you and that night to ever cheapen it. Good night, May."

She leaned over, hugged him and kissed him. "Good night, Storm. Thank you." She got out and walked inside.

~

Owen was fishing the last trotline when he heard a boat coming up the slough. He was surprised, rarely did he ever see a boat while fishing on Back Slough. He waited and watched, a little nervous not knowing who it might be.

The boat came around the bend and headed straight at him. When it got closer, he saw that a woman was driving. She was alone in the boat. Now he was really surprised, he'd never seen a lone woman driving a boat. The boat pulled up alongside and stopped. The woman, wearing overalls and a flannel shirt, stared at him. He could tell she had a dip of snuff in her lower lip. "Who the hell are you?" she said, then turned and spat in the water.

Her question and manner of speaking startled Owen, "I'm Owen Doe." He looked in the boat. A double-barreled shotgun was lying on the seat beside her.

"What are you doing here?"

"I'm fishing my trotline."

She wiped her hand across her mouth. "Where you be livin'?"

"I live up at Shoal Creek landin'." He wondered who she was and what she wanted.

"You work for 'em?"

Owen nodded. "I fish for 'em."

"Who be the head man up thar?"

This questioning seemed strange to Owen and he didn't like telling her anything else. "Why do you want to know?"

He lips tightened and she put her hand on the shotgun. "You listen to me, you little shit. Who be the head man?"

"He be Rep Doe."

"You know 'im?"

"He be my brother."

She nodded. "You take me to see yo' brother. I be right behind you with this shotgun. You hear me boy?"

Owen nodded. "I hear you." He cranked the motor and started toward the landing. She was right behind him.

They both landed and tied up the boats. The woman got out with the shotgun cradled in her left arm. She looked at Owen. "You take me to yo' brother. Where do he stay?"

"I spect he be at the barn," said Owen as he started up the hill. The woman followed him.

They passed the kitchen and started down the road toward the barn. Owen saw Lila walking from the big house toward the barn. She saw him, smiled and waved. Owen didn't answer, just kept walking, the woman right behind him.

Lila stood for a moment, then started walking fast toward the barn. Owen watched her go inside.

Rep and Mose were in the barn with one of the guards when Lila came rushing in. "Owen is coming down the hill and there's a woman with him carrying a shotgun."

"Lizzie Hogg," said Rep as he and Mose got up. Rep looked at Mose. "Y'all go outside and come around the end of the barn and cover her. I'll go out on the porch and see what's on her mind."

"You better not go out there," said Lila. "Those people are crazy."

Rep shook his head. "You stay in here; I'll take care of this." He walked to the door, opened it and walked out on the porch. He saw Owen and the woman about fifty yards away coming straight at him. Lila walked out on the porch behind him.

When they were about ten yards away Rep held up his hand. "That's close enough. What can I do for you?"

"You bastards killed my boy," she said. "I want to know who done it."

"Mose," said Rep, in a loud voice. Mose and the guard stepped out from the end of the barn and walked toward the woman, rifles pointed at her. "You put the shotgun down and I'll talk to you," said Rep. "You make a move with that shotgun and they will kill you." Rep stared at her. "You give Owen the gun."

She looked at Rep and then at Mose. Then her shoulders slumped, and she lowered the gun. Owen stepped toward her, took the gun and walked toward Rep.

"Who are you and what are you talking about?" said Rep.

"I be Lizzie Hogg and you know damn well what I be talkin' bout. Y'all killed my boy, Sugar Boy."

Rep nodded. "I heard Sugar Boy was killed but he had lots of enemies that didn't like 'im. He shot a boy named Rolley Hill from across the river and them people didn't like it neither. You don't know who killed 'im."

"He told me that if he got kilt, it would be y'all Shoal Creek people." She turned and spat. "You know I be tellin' the truth."

Rep walked off the porch and walked over to her. "I'm sorry about yo' boy, Lizzie. He was always causin' trouble and had lots of enemies. Finally, somebody shot 'im cause of the way he done, but it wasn't me or anybody here at Shoal Creek."

She stared at Rep. "You be tellin' me sho'nuff the truth?"

Rep nodded. "It be the truth. I didn't shoot 'im and nobody here at Shoal Creek shot 'im."

Lizzie looked at Lila standing on the porch. She nodded toward Rep and then looked back at Lila. "He be yo' man?"

Lila nodded. "He be my man."

Lizzie walked toward Lila. "He be tellin' me the truth?"

"Yes," said Lila, "he be tellin' the truth. Nobody here at Shoal Creek shot yo' boy."

Rep handed her the shotgun. "Best you don't come back up here with a gun, Lizzie."

She nodded and looked at Mose and the guard. "If I didn't give you my gun, you be done had them shoot me."

Rep nodded. "Yes, I would."

Lizzie laughed. "I seed it in yo' eyes. You woulda sho' kilt me standin' right here." She looked at Lila. "I sho' wouldn't never believe yo' man, but I believe you." She turned and started walking up the hill toward the landing.

Rep looked at Owen. "You go with her and make sure she gets off all right." He looked at Lila.

"We did tell her the truth, didn't we, Rep?" Lila asked.

"Yes, we did. Lick don't live or work at Shoal Creek."

Lila stared at her walking up the hill. "I feel sorry for her. Now she's all alone."

12

The next few days were quiet, and then it was Friday. As always, May was excited about going to the stage Friday night. She thought about Storm and their conversation. She knew he still had feelings for her but for the moment he had been strong enough to turn down just a physical involvement. She knew he wanted her to commit to something long term and she wasn't willing to do that now. If she had, even with her continuing to go to the club, she felt he would still be with her. She thought of him saying he had met someone. If that involvement got serious, she could lose him. For now, she had made her choice.

Storm was anxious to see Karen Saturday morning. He had not seen May since Monday and had not wanted to see her. When she had told him that she would be his girl and would go to his house, her offer was tempting. He had walked away, but if he saw her again, he didn't know if he was strong enough to do it again. He needed to see Karen and spend time with her without any more complications from May.

~

When May got home from school Alva was sitting on the sofa reading. "Do you want me to go with you to the club tonight?" she asked.

"No," said May. "I don't see any need for you to go. Walt hasn't been a problem the last week."

"You know I'd go if it would help. I don't think you can always trust Walt."

May laughed. "I never said I trust him, Alva. I just said he hadn't been a problem lately. If you go you might be the one in trouble, I know he has his eyes on you."

Alva looked at her. "Sometimes I worry more about what comes out of your mouth than I do about you being on stage in that club."

May laughed and ran in her room to get dressed. She came out in a few minutes, hugged Alva and went to her car. She drove to Phenix City, pulled into the club parking lot and went inside. Josie was waiting for her in the dressing room. She was undressing when Walt walked in.

"Did you bring Alva with you?" he asked. He walked over, kissed her on the cheek and patted her on the rear.

"No, she had something else to do tonight."

"You tell her that I asked about her and I hope she will come with you soon. I enjoyed talking to her."

"I'll tell her," said May. She was surprised at his interest. She wasn't going to tell him, but he was wasting his time chasing after Alva, if that was what he was doing. He could keep on thinking whatever he was thinking about her.

She undressed with him standing beside her, but he made no move to touch her, just watched.

"You look good tonight," he said. He turned and walked out.

She watched him leave, wondering what he had on his mind. At least he had acted good.

She and Josie went on stage and had a good night. Walt met them after the show, hugged May and gave her the envelope. He walked out and May didn't see him again. She left the club and drove back to

River Bluff. It seemed the time in bed with Walt had settled him down.

~

Saturday morning Storm went to the mill, went in the mechanical shop and got the keys to the boat the mill kept in the river. He walked to the tailrace behind the mill, unlocked the boat, got in and headed to Shoal Creek landing. When he got to the landing, he didn't see anybody there, so he walked up the hill past the kitchen and on to the barn. When he walked in Rep and Mose were sitting at the desk. They got up, shook hands with him and he asked about Karen. Rep told him she was at the house with Lila and she had been waiting for him.

Storm started to tell them about seeing Lizzie Hogg at the River Bluff landing earlier and the threats she had made.

Rep laughed. "She's already been here." He told Storm about Lizzie's visit.

"She was mad when she left the landing," said Storm.

"She was mad when she came here too," said Rep. "She was carrying a shotgun when she showed up. I hope we got her settled down." He looked at Storm. "Karen is with Lila. You better get on up there if you want to see her. Come on, I'll walk with you."

When they walked in the house, Lila and Karen were in Rip's room. Karen was holding the baby, but when she saw Storm, she handed the baby to Lila, walked over to him and took his arm. Storm spoke to Lila. Then he took Karen's hand and they walked down the hall to her room. They walked in, she shut the door and they grabbed each other and kissed for a long time. They finally turned loose.

"It's been a long week," said Karen. "I thought Saturday would never come."

"I thought so too," said Storm as he kissed her again. They stood and held each other. Storm was so glad to see her. He wanted to get any thoughts of May out of his head. "I had thought that we would go to River Bluff today. I want to show you my house and show you the town."

Karen smiled. "I certainly want to see your cabin." She hugged him. "You know us Shoal Creek women ain't never gonna marry no man unless he's got a fit cabin to live in."

He laughed. "You paid too much attention to Sassy."

"I would like to go across the river with you," Karen said. "Let me go tell Lila." She came back out shortly carrying a small bag.

They walked to the landing, got in the boat and headed across the river to the River Bluff landing. As usual, Storm saw several men gathered around the trucks at the boat ramp. He looked at Karen. "These men are going to say things when they see me with you. Just keep walking and don't pay any attention to them. They like to give me a hard time."

"Why would they do that? Do you know them?" asked Karen.

"Known them all my life," Storm said as he helped her get on the bank. "They love to try to embarrass any man that brings a girl here. Some of the things they say can be rough." They started walking toward the car, Storm held her hand.

"Hey, Storm," said one man, "That ain't the same gal you was with yesterday."

"Storm has to go cross the river to get one them Georgia women what don't know bout 'im," said another.

The men all laughed and other comments were made.

Storm and Karen were in front of the group when she stopped, put both arms around Storm and looked at the men. "Ain't he bout the sweetest thang ya'll ever did see?" She reached up and kissed Storm on the cheek, turned, waved to the men and started walking toward the car.

Her actions got the entire crowd stirred up and when they got in the car, they could still hear the men yelling.

Storm started the car and looked at her. "You really started something. I won't ever hear the last of that."

Karen laughed. "Do they always talk to you like that?"

"Yes, they do," said Storm. "They really get on you when you're with a girl."

Karen cut her eyes at him. "They said I wasn't the one you were with the last time."

He shook his head. "I told you not to listen to them."

She smiled. "I think they like you."

He chuckled. "If they didn't say anything to me, I would think they were mad with me."

She looked up at the houses lining the ridge. "That looks so pretty, all the little white houses in a row on the hill.

They rode past the mill and went to his house. He pulled into the driveway. "Is this your cabin?" she asked. "It's nice. I like it."

They got out and went inside. She walked through each room; Storm followed her. They ended up in the bathroom. "You have a shower," she said. "Over at Shoal Creek we only have tubs."

"You can take a shower when you wish," said Storm. "I'll be glad to help you soap off."

She smiled, walked over and kissed him. "All in due time," she said and walked out.

"Let's walk up in town," he said. "I have somebody I want you to meet."

May slept later than usual, took a bath, dressed and decided to go see Star and tell her about her experience with Walt. Alva had already gone, she had said she would be gone for the weekend, so May was alone. She left the dormitory and started walking toward the stores.

Storm and Karen walked up the hill past the Methodist church. Storm was telling her about different parts of the town and what went on at various places. "I want you to meet Jim Hawke," he said as they got in sight of the gym and the stores. "He's the constable for the town and helped raise me as I grew up. He sits on a bench up here and watches and knows everything going on in town."

"Is that all he does?" asked Karen.

Storm laughed. "No, sometimes somebody might get in trouble and he has to see about it. But we don't have much for him to do in River Bluff."

They walked on as Storm had expected, Jim was on his bench. He was watching them approach.

"Morning, Jim," Storm said as they walked up. "I want you to meet Karen Hogan. Karen lives over at Shoal Creek."

Jim nodded. "Good to meet you, Karen." He looked at her. "You kin to Red Hogan?"

"Yes sir," said Karen. "He was my daddy."

"Thought so," said Jim. He looked at Storm. "She's mighty pretty, Storm. Maybe you better hold on to her."

"I plan to," said Storm. As he said this, he looked up the road and saw May walking toward them. Her eyes were on him. He glanced at Jim. Jim saw May too and he was watching Storm and smiling. He knew fireworks might be about to happen.

As May got closer to the stores, she saw someone walk up to Jim who was sitting on the bench. Then she recognized Storm. A girl was with him and she remembered he had said a girl would be with him this weekend. They all were watching her as she got near so she had no choice but to keep walking.

"Morning, May," said Jim as she walked up.

"Good morning," she said. She looked at Storm. "Good morning, Storm," she said, with a half-smile on her face.

"Good morning, May," said Storm. He saw her smile and the devilment in her eyes as she looked at him. "This is Karen Hogan, May. She's my friend."

May turned to Karen. "Nice to meet you, Karen," she said. "It's good Storm has a friend. Sometimes he has a hard time keeping them."

Karen immediately sensed that there was something going on here between May and Storm by what she said and the way she looked at him. May was a beautiful woman in every way and when she looked at Storm's face, she knew she was right. "I'm glad to meet you, May," she said, as she took Storm's hand and moved against him. She intended to let May know that Storm was with her.

May saw Karen take Storm's hand and she knew what she was doing.

Jim sat on the bench and watched. He saw both women's eyes and knew what both were thinking. There was one man here and they both had their eyes on him. Storm looked like he was caught between two wild cats.

Storm heard May's comment and knew she was going to be bitchy, so he decided to take the offensive. "Last night was Friday, May, did you go to the club?"

May looked at him and smiled. "You know I go every Friday night, Storm. That's my job and I love it."

"I guess you'll be there tonight too," said Storm.

May nodded. "Yes, I'll be on stage tonight as usual, doing what I do. You know what I do, Storm. You've seen me on stage before."

Karen knew there was something going on here, but the conversation had lost her. She looked at Storm, her face questioning.

"May works in Phenix City, Karen. That's what we were talking about," said Storm. He felt like this had gone far enough and it was best to let it drop.

May had no intention of dropping it. "I'll be on stage tonight, Storm, like I said. Why don't you bring Karen to the show tonight? She might enjoy it; I know you do." She looked at Karen and smiled. "Karen might like to come on stage with me, she has the body for it."

"I don't understand," said Karen. She looked at May. "What do you do?"

May smiled at her and looked at Storm. "Storm didn't tell you, but I work in a strip club in Phenix City. I get on stage and take my clothes off in front of a crowd of men. He's seen me before, on the stage and other places too." She looked at Jim. "See you later Jim. Bye, Storm," she said as she walked on out the road.

They watched May walk away. Karen looked at Jim. "It was nice to meet you, Mr. Jim." She took Storm's hand and started walking away. Storm followed her. She looked up at him. "Obviously, I have a lot to learn about you, Storm. You want to tell me about May?" She turned his hand loose and walked on.

He caught up with her and stopped her. "Both of us have a history, Karen. I'm sure you've been with other men in Atlanta as I've been with other women. All that is in the past before we met and should be left in the past. What is important is what we do from now on." He talked as they walked back toward his house. "May is from here. She's young, eighteen or nineteen. Her sister has quite a history, including being a stripper among other things. I dated May and I've seen her one time on the stage. She's the star of the show at the club. That's about it."

Karen didn't say anything for a while. "You've seen her on the stage?"

"Yes, I said I had."

"Does she take off everything?"

"Not quite. Everything except a G-string around her hips."

"She is a good-looking woman."

"Yes, she is." Storm smiled. "She invited you to come on stage with her. She said you had the body for it." He put his arm around her. "I think you do too."

She pushed his arm away. "I think there's more to this than you've told me. Are you sure that's all that happened?"

"I swear I've never done any more with May than I've done with you." Storm didn't think Karen would react well if he told the truth here.

She stared at him. "I'm not sure that I believe you."

They walked in the house. She walked over and sat on the sofa. Storm sat down beside her. "I've never been to a club like that. May said she will be on tonight. Would you take me to see her?"

Storm was surprised. "Are you serious?

"I'm serious. I think it would be fun." Karen had seen the way May looked at Storm. Regardless of what Storm thought, May had feelings for him. Karen had already decided she wanted Storm for her own and she was ready to do whatever it took to get him. She leaned against him. "How much time do we have before we have to leave?"

~

Lizzie Hogg left Shoal Creek and went downriver. She didn't know if the Shoal Creek people had told her the truth or not about killing Sugar Boy, but there was nothing to gain by her causing more trouble. As she rode down the river she thought of her situation. She was alone and living in the middle of a large swamp. She and Sugar Boy had been getting by with him catching fish and making whiskey. She didn't look forward to doing that in the future by herself. It wasn't much of a life anyway. She had to come up with something better.

She took stock of what she had. She had a house in the swamp, and she had herself. That wasn't very much. She was forty years old now, not old but not a young woman either. She knew, based on what she had done in the past, she could go to the beer joints on the river and get a man to use for a while. She had done that in the past but that was a short-term fix. She wanted something more permanent, but she didn't want to find somebody to marry and have to put up with a husband.

She rode up the swamp and thought of her two assets, the house and herself. When she landed, she had decided on a tentative plan of action. She went in the house, took a tub bath, washed her hair and put on the best dress she had. She looked at herself in the mirror, she didn't look bad.

She went across the river to see a man she had shacked up with in the past that was a carpenter. In a few minutes she had worked out a barter agreement with him where he would come to the house and remodel part of the house in exchange for sharing her bed.

She went downriver to a beer joint where two young women she knew were waiting on tables and getting by the best way they could. It only took her a few minutes to talk then into coming with her to the swamp. The carpenter came to the house, fixed up two rooms for the two girls and within a week Lizzie was in business. She spread the word in all the joints and stores along the river that her establishment was open. She marked the path through the swamp to the house and soon there was a steady stream of boats coming in.

She quickly found out she not only needed the girls, but she also needed food and drinks available for the men. She went across the river and hired an older black woman as a cook.

Lila and Rep were at the desk in the barn when the door opened. They looked up and Lizzie Hogg walked in. They both got up and stared at her. Her hair was combed, and she was dressed in a nice dress. They had never seen her cleaned up. She was not unattractive. Rep could see that she wasn't armed, so he was relieved. "What can we do for you, Lizzie?" he asked. He had no idea why she would be here. "You want to come and have a seat?"

Lizzie shook her head. "I can talk good right here," she said. "I want to do some business with you."

Rep was surprised. He looked at Lila and then back at Lizzie. "What is it you need?"

"You heard bout me having some girls at my house in the swamp?"

Rep nodded. "I did hear about that." Lick had told him earlier and he hadn't even mentioned it to Lila.

Lila looked at him, her face questioning.

"Sugar Boy had a still but I ain't got time to fool with it. I need to buy some whiskey, some of the men want a drank after they do their business. I'm told y'all make the best." She looked at him. "Y'all got a boy fishing. Y'all have enough fish you could sell me some."

"We can get you fixed up," said Rep. He glanced at Lila. "Mose is over at the warehouse. I'll take you over there and he'll get you what you need." He walked to the door, opened it for her and followed her out. "Is your business good?" he asked as they walked to the warehouse.

"We doin' good," she said. "I might have to git another girl." She looked at him. "You tell all yo' folks here on the farm they can come see us."

Rep smiled and kept walking. They walked in the warehouse and when Mose saw Lizzie, he looked at Rep.

"Lizzie wants to buy some whiskey for her business, Mose. She also wants some fish. I told her you would fix her up."

Mose was relieved. "We sho' can do that."

"You can tell Mose anything else you need, Lizzie." said Rep.

Lizzie nodded her head.

Rep walked out and went to the barn. Lila was waiting for him. "What was all that about?"

He laughed. "I forgot to tell you, but Lick told me that Lizzie has brought in some girls and she's operating a whorehouse in the swamp."

"Are you serious?"

"She said business is so good she might have to bring in another girl."

Lila shook her head. "I can't believe that."

Rep smiled at her. "Every man is not as lucky as I am to have a woman like you in his bed."

Lila got up and started toward the door. She stared back at Rep. "Sometimes you men make me sick," she said as she went out the door.

Walt pulled into the driveway at the club. He parked in his special place and was about to get out when the passenger door opened. He looked around as Star slid into the seat. She was holding a pistol and it was pointed at him. Her eyes were on him.

He was surprised but quickly got his feelings under control.

"Well, Star, I wondered when I would see you. With May here, I knew you would show up sooner or later." He looked at the pistol. "Do you intend to use that?"

Star smile. "Don't temp me, Walt. You're about a sorry bastard and I would love to shoot you right now. You surely deserve it."

"If you were going to do that, we wouldn't be talking, Star. You would have already shot me." He got out a cigarette and lit it. "I know you want something. What is it?"

Star stared at him. "Damn," she said, "You make me want to shoot you right between the eyes when you act like this. You're such as ass."

Walt laughed. He reached over and patted her on the shoulder. "We had some good times Star, you know that. You didn't always hate me."

Star shrugged. "I was young and stupid, Walt. You used me and took advantage of me."

Walt nodded. "I did, but you used me too. I took you in when you had nothing." He looked at her. "I'm sure you didn't come here to talk about old times. What do you want?"

"May likes being on stage. Don't ask me why, she just does. I've tried to talk her out of it, but I've had no luck." She pointed the pistol in his face. "She's the star of your show but you keep bothering her and she don't like it."

"I know that, but we've worked everything out." He puffed on the cigarette. "You girls are good at killing people, especially men you don't like. You killed Red Hogan, May killed Marvin and both of you are running around free."

"That's right," said Star, "and you'll be next if you don't treat May right."

He smiled. "Why don't you come tonight and go on stage with May? Y'all would be the biggest hit ever if you would. People still remember you."

She shook her head. "I've already done it. All that stuff I did that I'm ashamed of is way behind me now. I don't want any part of you or what you're selling."

Walt smiled. "You were the best, Star, on the stage and especially off the stage."

"The part off the stage is what I'm really ashamed of. Especially the time I spent with you," she said.

Walt stared at her and shook his head. "One thing about you Star, you always told the truth. If you say you didn't enjoy being with me, you are lying. We had a good time."

"You're not as smart as you think you are, Walt, if you think that." She opened the door. "You've heard me about May. She don't know I'm here and you better not tell her. Finally, if I hear of one of your people nosing around River Bluff again, I'll kill you. You can count on it."

Walt smiled. "It's been a pleasure talking to you, Star. You come back to see me anytime."

Star slammed the door and walked away.

Walt said there for several minutes before getting out and going in the club.

Owen was at the landing dressing fish when he saw Rep coming down the hill. "Owen," said Rep as he walked up. "The men say they have your cabin finished and everything is ready down there. Lila sent you some sheets, blankets and towels to the cabin. You can move out of the shed when you want to."

Owen didn't move or reply. He stood behind the table and stared at Rep.

Rep cocked his head and looked at him. "What's the matter?" he asked.

"I can move in now?" Owen seemed to be hesitant.

Rep nodded. "That's what I said. Is there a problem? I thought you'd be happy."

"I be glad the cabin be ready," said Owen. He paused. "But now I have to go tell Sassy." He looked at Rep. "Sassy say when the cabin be ready, we gonna git married."

"I heard her say that" said Rep. He looked at Owen's face and it was obvious he was worried. "Didn't you ask her to marry you?"

Owen shook his head. "It weren't no matter of me askin' Sassy nothin'. She just said we gonna git married. I didn't never have much to say bout it."

It took all Rep could do to keep from smiling. "You don't want to get married?"

"It ain't that, Sassy just wants to run everthang."

"That's up to you, Owen, to tell her what you want. You better do it now when you go see her." Rep walked over to him. "You tell her it be yo' cabin and you be supporting her cause you have a job. If she wants to come with you and be yo' wife, then you have to be in charge."

Owen shook his head. "Sassy sho'nuff be a strong-willed woman, Rep."

"You don't have to get married if you don't want to, Owen. She can't force you to marry her," said Rep. "If you don't want to marry her now, just don't go down to Walnut Creek."

Owen stared at Rep. "I like Sassy and I want her to be with me."

"You need to move in the cabin, get everything all set up and then go see her," said Rep. "That way you can show her you're in charge."

"That be what I'll do," said Owen.

Two days later Owen had moved and was set up in the cabin. The next morning, after he had fished the hooks and dressed the fish, he got in the boat and headed down Back Slough. He landed at Willow Creek, got out and walked to the house. He didn't see anybody, so he walked to the steps and hollered. The door opened and one of the sisters came out on the porch. "What you be wantin'?" she said.

"Where be Sassy?"

The sister pointed at the barn. "She be feedin' the chickens."

Owen headed toward the barn. He walked around back. Sassy was in the pen throwing corn to a flock of chickens around her feet.

He stood and watched her. She turned and looked at him. "What you be doing, standin' there lookin' at me?"

"I be livin' in my cabin. I done been there two days."

She walked to the gate, opened it and came out towards him. "You done been livin' in the cabin?"

"That's what I say."

She looked at him. "What you be doin' here?"

"I come to ask you if'n you want to come live with me."

She stared at him for a moment. "I ain't comin' cept we be married."

"That's what I be askin' you."

Sassy was surprised. Owen had never talked to her like this. "You be ready now?"

Owen nodded. "I be ready." He looked at Sassy. "Can you cook?"

Sassy frowned. "Why you be askin' me that?"

"Hattie Mae feeds me ever day now," said Owen. "If we live down on Big Island in my cabin you gonna have to cook ever day. I sho' ain't gonna do it."

Sassy took his hand and led hm toward the house. "If I be yo' woman, you don't worry bout cookin' or nothin' else." She reached over and kissed him. "I gonna take care of you, cookin' and everthang else. Let's go talk to Mattie. Then we go see Preacher Snow."

Owen didn't say another word as they went to the house. Mattie was in the kitchen when they walked in. "Owen done moved in his cabin and we be gonna git married," said Sassy.

Mattie cut her eyes at Owen. "Yo' cabin be ready?"

"I done moved in," said Owen.

"Sassy ain't goin' off with you cept you be able to take care of her."

Owen stared at her. "I be fishin' for Shoal Creek and I got a cabin with a stove. Got a bed too with sheets and blankets."

"That be good," said Mattie. "You ever been with a woman?"

Owen just stared at her.

Mattie shook her head. "Never mind, I done talked to Sassy. She knows what to do."

"We gonna go see Preacher Snow," said Sassy. "He married Bess and he gonna marry me and Owen."

Mattie frowned. "I ain't gonna talk to 'im much. All he do is fuss at me and Lick bout drankin'. He oughta mind his own business."

"I like 'im," said Sassy. "He be a good man." She took Owen's hand. "We gonna go see 'im now. We be ready to be married and ain't no need to be waitin." They went out the door and headed to the boat.

13

Karen sat on the sofa with Storm. She still had the meeting with May on her mind, she knew more had gone on between May and Storm than he had admitted. "I don't think you've told me all the truth about you and May," she said.

Storm shook his head. "I told you we dated some but that was back some time ago."

"You saw her at the club."

"I did," said Storm. "We were dating, and she kept leaving town on Friday and Saturday nights and wouldn't tell me what she was doing, so I had her followed. That's how I found out she was going to Phenix City to the club. So, I went to the club and saw her on stage."

"That's the only time you saw her on stage?"

"Yes."

"What did you think?"

"Think about what?"

"What did you think about her being on stage and taking off her clothes?"

"I thought she had a good body." He smiled.

Karen punched him. "You know that's not what I meant, silly."

She glared at him. "I'm sure you enjoyed seeing her naked. I meant what was your reaction to her doing that?"

"I was surprised and disappointed in her. I told her that."

"What was her response?"

"She said that was what she was going to do. She enjoyed it."

"So, you stopped dating her?"

"Yes."

Karen looked at him. "Will you take me to see her tonight?"

"If you want to go, I'll take you." He thought for a minute. "It will be late when we get back and we'll have to go across the river in the dark."

"I don't plan to go across the river in the dark tonight," she said, her eyes on his face.

He nodded and looked at her. "Are you planning to stay here?"

"Yes, I am."

"Did you tell your folks you weren't coming home?"

"I'm a grown woman, Storm. I don't always report as to what I'm doing."

He smiled. "I guess we'll work this out as the night goes on."

"How it works out will depend on you." said Karen.

"What does that mean?"

"It depends on how honest you are with me tonight."

Storm was puzzled. "Honest about what?"

"After we see the show tonight, how honest you are with me about your relationship with May," said Karen. "I saw her look at you today and I saw how you looked at her." She shook her head. "I don't intend to waste my time with someone that is in love with someone else."

Storm shook his head. "You have this all wrong. I'm not in love with May."

She half smiled. "We'll see."

"You've been asking all these questions of me," said Storm. "It's my time ask you some. Why do you want to go see May on stage?"

She cut her eyes at him. "She's going to be naked, so I'll know how you want a woman to be."

Storm smiled. "I've already seen her on stage. Take off your clothes and I'll tell you how you compare."

Karen shook her head. "You think you're so smart. I had planned to have my clothes off by now, but after I saw you look at May, you may never see me without them." She got up. "I'd like to get something to eat and then go to the club." She looked at him. "What happens when we get back will depend on how you do." She walked out the door.

Storm followed her. His afternoon hadn't turned out as he had planned.

May got in her car and headed toward Phenix City. The meeting with Storm had upset her. She'd had no intention of seeing him, but it had happened. The girl, Karen from Atlanta, had made the meeting more disturbing. Storm had said he'd met someone, and she was special, but Karen was more than she'd expected. She was beautiful, smart and handled herself very well.

As she rode, she tried to convince herself that she wasn't jealous, but she wasn't having any success. She had made the decision that if she was on stage, she knew she couldn't have Storm and she was staying with that decision. Inside, there was a part of her that told her she was stupid. Storm had offered himself in marriage and she had turned him down. Why would anybody do that?"

She pulled into the parking lot at the club with the same discussion still going on in her mind. She got out and went inside. Josie was dressing and Walt was with her. He came over, hugged her, kissed her on the cheek and walked out. May got dressed. It was nice to get through dressing without Walt standing beside her or having his hands on her.

Storm and Karen drove to Columbus, went to a restaurant and ate supper, then went across the river to Phenix City. The parking lot at the club was almost full when they arrived. They walked to the front, got tickets and went in. Storm intended to sit in the very back out of the way, but Karen insisted they sit closer to the front. She wanted to see everything, especially May.

They ordered a drink and sat down. There were four girls on the stage. Karen watched them move about and take off their clothes, but she was not impressed. She looked around at the crowd. Some men were watching, a few were at the edge of the stage with money trying to get the girls to come closer. Most of the crowd were either talking or drinking and showed little interest in the stage.

A couple of the men had made comments to Karen as she walked in and even now some were eyeing her. There were only a few women scattered about in the crowd and most of them looked like they may have been there on business. Storm had heard the comments made to Karen and hoped they got out of the club without a fight. He knew that as the evening went on and more drinks were served, the crowd would get rougher. It was always that way in these type places.

A little later Storm could feel the noise level in the room rev up and the band got louder. The anticipation level in the room picked up. He knew the main show was about to begin. The curtain parted and Josie came out and the crowd woke up. Josie, unlike the other girls, played to and moved the crowd and the crowd responded.

Karen turned and looked at Storm. "That's Josie. She's from Shoal Creek."

Storm nodded. "I know Josie."

Karen shook her head. "I didn't know she was at this club." She watched as Josie danced and shed her clothes. She was good and soon men were at the stage with money. Josie allowed them to slip the money in her G-string and some grabbed at her, but she was quick to move away. Karen was impressed with her.

Then the mood in the room revved up even more. The music was louder, the curtain parted, and May walked out on the stage. The crowd exploded and Karen immediately saw that May was the star and she deserved to be. While Josie had been good on stage, May was at another level and the crowd knew it. Karen watched her as she moved over near Josie and they went into their act of alternating taking off pieces of clothing. When they got to the final part and Josie unfastened May's top, it was bedlam. May walked over to the edge of the stage where the men were holding up money. She worked the crowd, smiling and talking and teasing them. She was having a good time.

The man Josie had said was Harry Rinkley the third or fourth was in the crowd. May had not seen him since he had offered her money to come sit with him. He looked nice, wearing slacks, a tie and a sport coat. When she got near where he was sitting, he came to the stage and made the offer again. May smiled at him and walked on.

When May was at the edge of the stage directly in front of Karen and Storm, Karen stood up and waved to her. She was the only woman in that part of the crowd and when May looked up and saw her, she stopped and stared. In a moment she caught herself, laughed and waved. Then she saw Storm sitting with her and her demeanor immediately changed. She stopped smiling and stared at him. She stepped away from the edge of the stage, ignoring the men at her feet yelling for her, and walked back to where Harry Rinkley was standing. She knelt on the edge of the stage and motioned to him.

He walked to her.

She smiled and leaned over. "Do you want to see me?" she asked.

"Yes, I do." he replied.

"Go around to the door at the end of the stage and I'll be there in a minute," she said. "Do you hear me?"

He nodded and started walking around the stage.

May took a couple of steps back, then turned and ran through the curtain and off the stage.

Storm grabbed Karen's arm and pulled her down in her chair. "What the devil are you doing?" he said.

Karen looked at him and laughed. "I wanted her to see us here. She asked us to come."

"She saw us as did everybody else in the place." He looked around at several of the men looking at him and talking. He stood up. "Come on, let's get out of here."

They went out the door and went to the car. He was relieved to get away. When they were inside, he looked at her. “Well, you saw May. What did you think?”

“I liked it. It was fun.” She slid over next to him. “Thank you for bringing me.”

He started the car and pulled out of the parking lot. “Well, you saw the show and you saw May naked. That’s what you said you wanted to do.”

Karen nodded. “Yes, I did. I was impressed with May. She is good at what she does, if that is what she wants to do.”

May ran off the stage to the dressing room. She grabbed a wrap, put it on and ran out to the door at the end of the stage. When she opened the door, Harry Rinkley was standing there looking at her. She grabbed his arm and pulled him in. “You wanted to talk to me?” said May, staring up at him.

He was younger than she had thought and was nice looking up close.

He smiled and nodded. “I did.” He stuck out his hand. “I’m Harry Rinkley, everybody calls me Rink.”

“I’m May,” she said as she shook his hand.

He shook his head as he stared at her. “I’m surprised to be here. They told me you never talked to anybody.”

May smiled. He was so friendly and nice that she was taken with him. “I usually don’t. In fact I never have till today,” she said.

“Well, I’m really glad you’re talking to me,” he said.

May had only gone back and talked to him on stage because of Storm having Karen there. But now that she had met Rink, she decided to talk more.

“If you want, we can go in here and talk.” She led him to Walt’s private room, opened the door and went in. Rink followed her. She sat on the couch and he sat down beside her. “You’ll have to excuse me,” she said, “I just threw this on.”

"You're the prettiest woman I've ever seen," he said.

May smiled. "Alright, we're here now. Why did you want to talk to me?" She paused. "You don't look like the regular folks I see in the crowd here; you're dressed much nicer and you look younger."

"This is the second time I've ever been here. I came one time before and tried to get you to talk to me, but everybody told me I was wasting my time. They said you wouldn't have anything to do with anybody in the crowd. After seeing some of the men out there, I don't blame you."

May laughed. "So why were you here the first time?"

"My friend brought me. He said he was coming out here to see the most beautiful woman he'd ever seen and asked me to come." He smiled. "When I saw you, I knew he was right, and I wanted to meet you."

"That's very nice," said May, "but I'm afraid you'll be disappointed. I'm just a regular girl and most people aren't impressed with what I'm doing."

"I'm impressed," he said. "The fact that you stay away from mixing with this drinking crowd says a lot about you."

"I appreciate you saying all these nice things about me and I'm glad that I got to talk to you," said May as she started to get up.

Rink shook his head and put his hand on her arm. "You don't know me, but I don't want this to be the end. I don't know exactly how to say this, but I want to get to know you. You can ask anybody about me and my family, we're good people." He looked in her eyes. "My intentions toward you are honorable."

May sat back down and looked at him. "What are you saying?"

"I would like to go out with you and get to know you."

She put her hand on his arm and looked in his face. "You just saw me naked on the stage. Is that somebody you would want to take home and introduce to your parents?"

He smiled. "I don't have a problem with that. Tomorrow afternoon my parents are having a gathering at our house in Columbus. Daddy wants me to be there and he has been on me because I don't have a girlfriend. I would like for you to go with me."

May got up and walked to the window. She could see three girls on the stage. She thought about his request. Why shouldn't she go? He seemed to be a nice young man. Also, the picture of Storm with Karen in the audience was in her mind. She turned and looked at Rink. "Are you serious?"

"I'm serious."

"How would we do this, if I were to go with you?"

"However, you want to do it. I could pick you up at home."

May shook her head. "I live up in Alabama. It would be best if I met you here."

He nodded. "That would work. It starts at three tomorrow afternoon. I could meet you here at two."

"What should I wear?"

"A nice dress, sorta fancy," he said. "The women that will be at the house will be dressed up."

May stared for a moment looking at the girls on the stage. She turned around. "I don't know if this is smart or not, but I'll be here at two." She walked over, opened the door and went out. He followed her.

"You can go out the back door to the parking lot," she said.

"I'll be here at two," he said, his face still questioning.

She smiled. "I'll be here."

Rink went out the door and when she turned around Walt was standing across the room watching her.

"Who the hell was that and what was he doing back here," he asked as he walked over to her.

"His name is Harry Rinkley and I asked him to come back."

"Rinkley?" he asked. "Is he one of the Rinkleys from Columbus?"

"I don't know," said May. "He said his folks lived in Columbus."

"You better be careful who you bring back here." Walt shook his head and walked away.

When May walked in the dressing room Josie came running over. "I saw you with that Rinkley boy. I told you his folks own half of Georgia and are rich. What did he want?"

"He asked me to go to something at his house tomorrow."

"Damn," said Josie. "Ask him if he has a brother."

May laughed, dressed and headed to River Bluff.

Sassy and Owen got in the boat, went up the creek to the bridge and landed. They got out, walked up the hill and across the road to Preacher Snow's house. He opened the door as soon as they knocked. "Why, Sassy," he said, hugging her. "It's good to see you." He looked at Owen.

"This be Owen Doe, Preacher Snow. Me and Owen be gonna git married."

Preacher Snow looked at Sassy and then at Owen, his brow furrowed. "Married, you say? This seem to be sudden, Sassy. I've never even heard you mention Owen's name."

"Owen be fishin' up to Shoal Creek and he has a cabin," said Sassy. "He asked me to marry 'im."

Preacher Snow turned to Owen. "I remember Bess married a young man named Doe. Is he your folks?"

"He be my brother."

Preacher Snow nodded. "How old are you, Owen?"

"I be almost nineteen."

Preacher Snow looked at Sassy. "Sassy is sixteen, so you are very young to be getting married."

"Bess, she be sixteen when she got married. I be as old as she was," said Sassy.

"I understand that, Sassy. Do your parents know about this?"

Both Sassy and Owen nodded.

"When do you plan to have the wedding?" Preacher Snow asked.

"It be next Saturday," said Sassy.

Preacher Snow looked back at Owen. "Are you a church going man, Owen?"

"No, suh," said Owen.

Preacher Snow frowned and looked at Sassy. "You need to bring him to church with you, Sassy. Both of you will need guidance if you are going to get married at such a young age."

"Yes, suh," said Sassy, "I be sho' branging 'im with me."

"You tell your folks the ceremony will be here at eleven in the morning on Saturday," said Preacher Snow. "I'll pray for you both."

"I thank you," said Sassy. She took Owen's hand and they headed to the boat.

Owen took Sassy to the house. When they landed, Owen helped Sassy out. "I've got to go tell Rep that we gonna be married. I want him to come."

Sassy wrapped her arm around him and kissed him. "I'm gonna go tell Mattie." She turned and ran toward the house.

Owen watched her until she ran up the steps and into the house. He headed to Shoal Creek. When he landed he went straight to the barn. Rep and Lila were inside. "Me and Sassy gonna git married," he said.

Rep stood up and looked at him. "Y'all already decided about it."

"We done gone and talked to Preacher Snow. He say it be Saturday at eleven in the morning."

"That's good, Owen," said Rep. "Did you tell Sassy bout it bein' yo' cabin and you bein' in charge?"

Owen shook his head. "I told her bout me fishin' and havin' the cabin, but it be hard to git Sassy to listen much. Fore I say much she done grabbed me and we done gone to see Preacher Snow."

Rep smiled and looked at Lila. "Sometimes it's hard to get women to listen to what you say."

Lila looked at him, shook her head and got up and hugged Owen. "I'm glad for you, Owen. Sassy is a good girl. I know you will be happy."

Owen looked at Rep. "I need to talk to you bout this being married, Rep. Sassy be talking bout bedding her and I ain't sure bout all this."

Rep smiled. "I'm sure y'all will work it out." He walked over and put his arm around Owen. "I think Sassy will look after you." He looked at Lila. "Lila and I will be there Saturday morning."

14

Karen and Storm drove back to River Bluff. She had sat next to him all the way, so he took that as a good sign. She had said before they left that how he acted would determine her actions when they came home. He parked in the driveway, they got out and walked to the door. He unlocked it and they went in.

"Do you remember the story I told you the other night about Lila and Rep?" said Karen.

"Where Lila asked Rep to hold her all night?"

"Yes, that one."

"Tough story."

"Yes, it is. As I remember, you claimed you could do that," said Karen.

Storm shook his head. "I don't remember saying that."

Karen laughed and punched him. "Regardless, that is what I'm asking you to do if I sleep with you. Otherwise, I go to the guest room."

Storm took a deep breath. "I will do that if you insist."

"I insist." She started walking toward the bathroom. "I have to take a shower." She looked around. "You said something about soaping me. You still interested?"

He nodded and followed her into the bathroom. He turned the water on.

She slowly unbuttoned her blouse as he watched. Then she slowly took off the blouse, her eyes on his eyes the entire time. He knew what she was doing, she was doing May's act, and doing it very well. She proceeded to take off each article of clothing the same way, slowly and deliberately. Her eyes never left his face. He watched every move, fascinated, until she was naked before him.

She looked at him and smiled. "You can't get in the shower with your clothes on." She turned and got in the shower.

He quickly stripped off his clothes and joined her. She handed him the soap. They bathed, got out, dried off and then went in the bedroom. They got in the bed and she wrapped her arms and legs around him. "You remember what you promised," she said.

"I remember," he said. "But this is not fair."

She smiled, kissed him and turned her back to him. "Good night."

He pulled her tight against him. "Now I've seen you and May. She doesn't have a thing on you. Good night."

Karen smiled.

Rep was up early Saturday morning. He walked in the bedroom. Lila was lying in bed with Rip. "Karen didn't come back last night," he said, looking at Lila.

"She told me she wasn't coming back so I didn't expect her."

"She stayed with Storm?"

"That was her plan."

"Reckon where she slept?"

Lila laughed. "I imagine she slept with Storm." She looked up at him. "As I remember you didn't hesitate to sleep with me."

"That was all yo' doings," he said as he walked out the door.

Lila laughed. "I hope Karen is more careful than I was."

~

Storm slipped out of bed, went in the kitchen and put coffee on. Then he cooked bacon and eggs with grits and toast. When he walked back in the bedroom Karen was awake and looking at him. He sat on the bed and leaned over and kissed her. "Breakfast is ready."

"I smell the coffee," she said as she crawled out of the bed and put on a robe. She walked in the kitchen and looked at the table. "You are going to make somebody a good wife."

He poured the coffee and they sat down and ate. "What do you want to do today?" he asked.

"You have to work tomorrow so I'll go back to Shoal Creek whenever you're ready."

"When are you going back to Atlanta?"

"Since you're working, I may as well go back tomorrow. I'll stay with Lila tonight."

"If you can come back next Friday, I'll take the day off and we'll have the entire weekend," said Storm.

"Sounds good to me," said Karen. She got up. "I don't want to get in that bed with you again. I don't think I have the courage. Come sit with me on the sofa and we'll get to know each other better."

Storm followed her to the couch. In a few minutes they were both asleep; neither had slept much during the night. It was mid-afternoon when Karen got her bag and they headed to the landing. When they drove up, she saw the old men gathered at the boat ramp.

"You're going to have to walk past them," said Storm. "You got them all stirred up last time."

They got out and walked toward the boat. Karen's eyes were on the old men, she was waiting for them to say something.

"Hey, Storm," said one of the men. "You takin' her back? She musta not worked out." All the men laughed.

Karen walked straight to the man, put her arm around him and kissed him on the cheek. "I want you to go to Georgia with me," she said and then walked on to the boat.

Her target was red-faced, and the other men were giving him hell.

"They won't ever forget you, Karen," said Storm. "You have made their day." They got in the boat and headed across the river. They landed at Shoal Creek, got out and walked up the hill. They got to the house and stood holding each other. Neither wanted to leave.

I'll be over here early next Friday," said Storm.

Karen looked at him. "I'll be here." She kissed him. "If everything goes right, I'll be in your bed Friday night."

He kissed her. "I'll be here early. He smiled and headed toward the boat landing.

Alva was asleep when May got home Saturday night, so she had to wait until Sunday morning to tell her about Harry Rinkley. "He seemed very nice," said May, "and Josie said his family was rich."

"He invited you to come to his house this afternoon?" asked Alva. "He asked you after he had seen you on the stage?"

May nodded. "He did. He said they were having a gathering of some sort. He told me to wear a nice dress, but I don't know anything else about it."

"I have a dress you can wear," said Alva. "When we get home from church, we'll get you all dressed up. I have a necklace and bracelet you can wear."

"I thank you for that," May said as she glanced at Alva. "I have no idea what I'm about to get into."

Alva laughed. "Just behave yourself."

They left the dormitory, went to church and when they came back Alva got out the dress for May, fixed her hair and put the necklace and bracelets on her. She stepped back and looked at May. "You look beautiful, May. Any man would be proud to be seen with you."

May looked in the mirror. The woman looking back at her was different from what she'd seen in the past. She got up, hugged Alva and went to her car. She went to see Star. When she pulled up to the house Star was sitting on the front porch. She stared at May. "What in the world are you doing so dressed up? Where are you going?"

"I'm going to Columbus," May said. Then she told Star about Storm bringing Karen to the show and Rink coming backstage and talking to her.

"You met him yesterday and you're going to his house today and meet his parents," said Star. "Is that what you're saying?"

May nodded. "That's what he said."

"His name is Harry Rinkley and Josie said he's of the Columbus Rinkleys?"

"That's what Josie said," replied May

"If he is, then the Columbus Rinkleys are rich. I never met any of them, but I heard about them." Star frowned. "These people are Columbus society. What are you going to tell them when they ask you questions?"

"What kind of questions?"

"Like where you're from and who are your parents and how did their son meet you? Are you going to tell them you work in a strip club?" Star shook her head. "Somebody is going to ask you questions so you'd better be ready."

"I hadn't thought about that?"

"Well, you'd better think about it," said Star. "He's gonna meet you at the club?"

"I thought that would be easier since I had no idea where they lived."

Star thought for a moment. "You better clear up some of the questions with him before you get to the house. You better talk about what y'all will say when the questions come or you gonna look mighty foolish."

May chuckled. "I think you're right." She hugged Star and went to the car. All the way to Phenix City she thought about what Star had said and she knew she was right. She was going to have to talk to Rink before they went to the house.

When she pulled into the parking lot, she saw a fancy car already waiting. The car was bright red with black fenders. Rink was standing beside the car waiting for her. She parked and got out. She looked at the car. "That is a pretty car," she said as she walked up to him.

He laughed. "It's a new 1931 Ford A-Model coupe with a rumble seat. I just bought it. You like it?"

"Yes, I do." She looked at him. "We need to talk, Rink, before we go to your house. I didn't think of this yesterday but there could be problems if people ask me questions."

"Like what questions?"

"Where did I meet you?"

Rink nodded. "A friend introduced me to you."

"Do you know where I live and what my parents do?" She stared at him. "Did you know I'm eighteen and a senior in high school?"

He smiled. "Are you really in high school? I thought you were my age at least, I'm twenty-four."

"Yes, I am a senior and I live in a cotton mill town up the river." She pursed her lips. "Sooner or later, somebody will find out I work in the club and ask you about it. Are you sure you want to take me to your house?"

He walked over, took her hand and led her to the car. He opened the door and motioned for her to get in. She looked at him and got in. He ran around to the driver's side and got in. He turned to her. "I don't know why you're working at that club, but I know you're very good at it. I can see you're a beautiful girl, you are very smart, and you have moral standards. I know that because you don't act like the other girls that work there, that's your reputation. The people you work with know that and that's good enough for me." He started the car.

May glanced at him. "We're headed to your house?"

"Yes, we are. You stay close to me and we'll handle whatever comes up." He grinned at her. You stay real close to me."

May shook her head. "I've impressed with you to this point, Rink. Don't mess it up."

He laughed and drove on. They went across the river bridge, through downtown and on into the town. They turned through a gate and went up a long winding drive lined with tall oak trees. Then they were in front of a huge two-story house, with white columns across a long porch. Rink jumped out, came around and opened her door.

When they walked up the steps, Rink opened the door and they walked into a large hallway. To the left May saw a huge room with a number of people standing around. Rink took her by the arm and led her into the room. As soon as they walked in a man and woman came toward them. They were both smiling.

"I'm Martha," said the woman as she offered her hand. "I'm Rink's mother, we're so glad to have you with us."

"This is May Hobb, Mother," said Rink. He turned to the gray-haired man. "Dad, this is May."

"I'm Tap," he said. "It's nice to meet you." He looked at Rink. "I'm impressed, son. I don't know where you found her, but you did well." He looked at May and smiled.

Martha took May's arm. "Come with me, dear and I'll show you around." She led May to a group of women and introduced her. She had no idea who they were but May had never seen so much gold and so many diamonds. They walked through several rooms, all furnished with furniture like May had never seen. Finally, they walked back to the room where Rink and three young men were standing.

He came over, took her arm and introduced her to the young men. They all three looked May up and down. Rink saw the looks and guided her away. "I don't know why they have these things," he said. "They all know each other and talk about the same things. I hope you don't mind. Daddy asked me to come so I did. I'm glad you came with me. My folks are impressed with you. We'll get out of here as soon as I can."

Rink's daddy came toward them and took Rink's arm. "Excuse me, May. I need to steal him for a minute. I'll bring him right back." He and Rink walked away.

May looked up and one of the young men Rink had introduced her to was coming toward her. May looked at him as he walked up. "I'm Jock, May," he said. He leaned over and in a low voice said, "I brought Rink to the club to see you, I saw you first. I didn't ever think he would ever get you to go out with him. You don't have to worry; I'm not going to tell anybody you're a stripper."

May looked at him. She had the feeling he was about to ruin her day.

"I wanted to talk to you at the club, but he beat me to it. I tell you this, whatever he's paying you, I'll top it. I guarantee you'll be happier with me than Rink, I know how to please a woman."

May stared at him, waiting for the rest.

He looked across the room at Rink and his daddy. "It would be a shame for Rink's folks to find out what you do at the club."

May looked at him. "Rink is not paying me anything, he's getting me free." She shook her head. "You won't ever have enough money to have me." She stared in his eyes. "You don't know me, Jock, but I killed a man not long ago that was a bastard like you." She stepped away and looked back at him. "If I ever see you at the club again, I'll have my folks put a rock around your neck and put you in the river." She stepped back toward him. "You son of a bitch, I may have them do it anyway." She walked away.

A pale-faced Jock watched her walk toward Rink. He had seen May's eyes and he knew he had made a mistake. Then he turned and headed for the door.

May knew she was with the wrong people and in the wrong place. Rink seemed like a nice person but if he had anything in his mind, she hadn't seen it. Regardless, she knew this wasn't going to work. She saw Rink and his daddy talking to another man. She walked toward them.

When Rink saw her face, he knew something was wrong. He met her in the middle of the room. "What is it?" he said. His eyes searching her face.

"Your friend Jock just offered to top whatever you're paying me if I would go to bed with him. If I did, he wouldn't tell everybody that I'm a stripper." She looked in his face.

He looked around the room, looking for Jock. "That bastard," he said.

May shook her head. "Don't blame him, Rink. I don't know what you had in mind, maybe nothing, but You brought me here and I am a stripper. Jock knows that most strippers are whores too, so, he assumed you had paid me." She started walking away. "I'll be at the car. You can take me to my car, or I'll walk. It's up to you." She went out the front door.

Rink's daddy saw the discussion and came toward him. "What's going on, son?" he asked as Rink started after May

"I'll tell you later, Dad," Rink said as he went out the door after May.

May was at the car when Rink ran up. "Let me talk to you, May. You have me all wrong."

"I'm not blaming you, Rink. It's my fault, I never should have come. Take me to my car."

He opened the door and she got in. He went around and got in, looked at her and started the car. "I know you're upset," he said as they rode through Columbus, "but all I wanted was to meet you and get to know you. I told you that."

"I don't doubt that," said May, "but I am what I am. That's a fact and I can't be with you."

They rode across the river in silence. He got to the club and pulled into the parking lot. "I wish you'd talk to me and we could work something out."

She smiled and shook her head. "I'm sorry, Rink. There is nothing to work out." She opened the door, got out and went to her car. She got in and headed to River Bluff. She had learned a lesson today. She had wanted to escape the stigma of being a Hobb. But you can't escape from being one bad thing by becoming something worse.

May parked at the dormitory and went in the room. Alva was reading when she walked in. She could look at May's face and see something was wrong. "What happened?" she asked.

"I'm a stripper, Alva. I take off my clothes and stand naked on a stage. I get paid to do that." She shook her head. "Since I'm a stripper, everybody assumes I'm a whore too." She turned, walked in her room and shut the door.

Alva sat on the sofa and bowed her head.

. . .

An hour later the door opened and May walked out of her room. Alva was still sitting on the couch. May walked over and sat by her. She stared at the floor. "I can't do what I'm doing and lead a normal life, can I Alva?"

"No, you can't," said Alva. "What you are doing is not what the normal person does so it will never be accepted."

May told her what happened at Rink's house.

"It's good it happened now instead of later when you'd have gotten involved with that family."

May nodded. "I think you're right."

"So, what are you going to do?"

"If I want to have a normal life, I can't work at the club," said May, looking at Alva.

"Yes," said Alva, "I think that's the choice."

May got up. "I'll sleep on this tonight. I don't want to make a decision when I'm so upset at what happened today."

"I think that's wise," said Alva. She got up and hugged May. "I would also pray about it."

May nodded. "I'm going to see Star." She had to talk to her, tell her what happened and decide what to do. She left the dormitory and headed down to Pot Licker Lane.

Star opened the door when May knocked. "I need to talk to you," said May as she walked in, went to the sofa and sat down. She told Star what had happened at the Rinkley house.

"That's the way it's gonna be from now on," said Star. "Because the men see you naked on the stage, they think you're an easy mark if you do that."

"I don't want to be thought of like that," said May.

Star shook her head. "You can't have it both ways. It won't work, I know that."

"If I want to have a normal life, I can't do this."

Star nodded. "That's right, but you've already in it and it won't be easy to get out."

May shrugged. "I'll just quit and not go anymore."

"That would be stupid," said Star. "You're Walt's star, his main attraction. He's not gonna want to lose you, but not showing up would really cause problems."

"So, what do I do?"

"We'll have to go talk to him. Tell him you're quitting and not coming back and it's final. He can't force you to stay, but he will threaten you."

"What do we do when he threatens me?"

Star shook her head. "We have to figure out a way to kill him and not get caught. I'll have to think on that. We'll need to go tomorrow."

May left Star and went to the dormitory. Alva was on the sofa when she walked in. "Star and I are going to see Walt tomorrow after school. I'm going to tell him I quit."

"I don't know if it's good Star is going with you, May. She hates Walt and they'll probably end up in a fight."

May laughed. "That's probably right but I can't go by myself, there's no telling what he would do to me."

"You can't go by yourself," said Alva. "I'll go with you."

May shook her head. "Alva, you can't do that. Walt is mean."

Alva smiled. "May, I'm not as sweet and innocent as everybody thinks. One good thing is that I already know Walt and I can talk to him without any bad feelings between us. Also, if he is going to pitch a fit, we need some other help. I have a friend, a lawyer, that lives in Montgomery and he has some influence in politics. I can get him to represent you and that could have an influence on Walt."

"You have a friend that's a lawyer?"

"Yes, he is."

"Why would he help me? He doesn't know me."

Alva smiled. "That's true, but he knows me." She walked over to the couch and sat down. "Come sit with me and let me tell you a story." May sat down beside her.

"When I was sixteen years old," said Alva, "I met Win Street, twenty-two years old and just graduated from college. He was home for the summer before starting law school. I was impressed with him and I fell in love with him and we had an affair."

"I never would have thought that" said May.

Alva grunted. "Well, it did happen. It lasted all summer and then he went to school. I had a couple of letters but after Christmas I heard nothing. He came home in the summer and asked me to marry him. I was going to college in the Fall and he was in law school, so I told him no. I finished college and he finished law school. I've been teaching and he has done well in law."

"Do you ever see him? Is he married?"

Alva smiled. "He's not married, and I do see him. Twice a year I go down and spend the weekend with him."

"You surprise me, Alva," said May. "Did he ask you to marry him again?"

"Every time I see Him."

"Will you ever marry him?"

Alva frowned. "I might. I'll like to have children before I'm too old."

"You're going to ask him to help me?"

Alva got up. "I'll call him now." She walked to her room.

Owen fished all his hooks, dressed the fish and took them to the kitchen. He got in his boat and headed to see Sassy. It was Monday and he was supposed to get married on Saturday. Sassy had told him she wanted to see the cabin again before they got married so he was going to get her.

He landed at Walnut Creek and walked up to the house. He didn't see anybody, so he got to the steps and hollered. The door opened and one of the sisters came out. She stood on the porch and stared down at him.

"Where's Sassy?"

"She be gettin' her clothes to take to the cabin. She say she be out in a minute." Owen sat down on the steps. He heard the door open and Sassy came out carrying a box. Owen jumped up and ran up the stairs to get the box.

"These be my clothes what Bess had that Rep give me. I gonna take 'em to the cabin," said Sassy. Owen headed to the boat and she followed him. He got in the boat and set the box down. Sassy stepped in the boat, hugged and kissed him. "I be glad you done come to see me."

He turned her loose, cranked the motor and went up the river. He was excited to be with her and taking her to see the finished cabin. They landed, he took the box and walked to the cabin. She opened the door, and they went in. He set the box down on the kitchen table. Sassy walked around the room looking at the stove and table and in the cabinets.

"Hattie Mae sent down what she said you would need in the kitchen," said Owen. "I reckon you be havin' what you need."

Sassy looked at everything in the cabinets. "You done good, Owen," she said, walking over and hugging him. "Git the box and I'll put my clothes in the closet."

She walked into the bedroom. Owen came in, set the box down on the floor and sat on the bed. He watched her every move as she hung her clothes up. She finished with the clothes and looked around at him. "This be our home now, Owen. I done got my clothes here. I ain't never had much what be my own."

"Me neither," said Owen.

Sassy walked over and sat down by him. "We be here all by ourselves, Owen. Ain't nobody else gonna say nothin' bout what we do." She kissed him. "You be bedding me after we be married come Saturday, but ain't no reason we can't get to know each other some more." She pushed him back on the bed and wrapped her arms around him.

The sun was low in the west when they headed back to Walnut Creek. Owen was excited about Saturday.

15

Monday afternoon May called Star and told her Alva was going with her to see Walt. They discussed Alva going and Star agreed that would be better.

They drove to Phenix city and parked at the club. Both were nervous. They didn't know what to expect from Walt, but they knew it wouldn't be good. They walked inside and went up the stairs to Walt's office. He was sitting at his desk and was surprised to see them when they walked in. He got up. "Miss Alva, it's so good to see you," he said as he shook her hand. He walked over and hugged May. "Ya'll have a seat. What can I do for you ladies?" he said as he went behind the desk and sat down.

May didn't waste any time. "Walt, I've decided I don't want to be on the stage anymore, so I'm quitting," she said, her eyes on his face.

Walt reared up in his chair and stared at her. "Quitting!" he yelled. "What the hell are you talking about? You can't just quit. I've invested a lot of money in you. There's no way you can quit."

May shook her head. "Whatever you say don't matter. I've made up my mind and I quit."

Walt stood up. "Damned if you are. You better have your ass here Friday like you're supposed to, or I'll come get you."

Alva interrupted. "Do you have a contract with May stating she has to work here?"

Walt looked around at her. "You stay the hell out of this, Alva. This is between me and May."

Alva stood up and handed him a card.

Surprised by her move, he took the card. "What the hell in this?"

"That's the business card for Win Street from Montgomery. He's May's lawyer.

"What the hell has she got a lawyer for?"

"If you cause May trouble about not working here," said Alva, "he will have you in court. He says without a written contract, you have no basis to force her to be here."

"That's bullshit," said Walt. "May knows we had an agreement."

"That doesn't matter," said Alva. "May doesn't want to be here and you can't require her to be here."

Walt looked at May. "You better be here Friday night, or I'll come get your ass." He looked at Alva. "I've tried to be nice to you, Alva, but you're messing in something that's not your business. You better get your prissy ass back to wherever you came from or you'll be sorry you ever met me."

Alva stood up. "Walt, I'm already sorry I met you." She turned toward May. "Come on, May. We're wasting our time here."

May had been sitting in the chair with her purse in her lap. When Walt threatened Alva, she put her hand in the purse and grasped the pistol. When Alva stood up, she stood up and pointed the pistol at Walt. "You bastard," she said. "I knew I'd have to kill you sooner or later." She stepped toward Walt, who was starting to fall back, his eyes wide open.

Alva grabbed May's arm and pulled it down. "You can't do this, May. He's not worth it. They'd arrest you for murder."

May dropped her arm to her side. She stared at Walt; her eyes filled with hatred. "If you send any of your people to River Bluff, I'll find you and kill you," she said.

Walt didn't reply. He looked at May and then at Alva. He realized it was best he remain quiet; he knew that he had already stared death in the face.

Alva took May's arm and led her out of the office, down the stairs and to the car. They rode back to River Bluff, both silent.

Walt sat in his office for an hour. His heart was pounding. After a while he settled down and then thought about what his situation would be if he lost May. His partners had been proud of him for getting her on the stage, the business she had brought in and the money they had made. He had promised them that he would have her tied up long term and now, if she quit, that wouldn't be possible.

The people he worked for didn't care about anything but results and wouldn't listen to excuses. He got up and walked to his car. He was worried. As he drove away it dawned on him that Star and Alva were the two people influencing May to quit the club. If they were gone, then he could get May back. He thought about that as he went to his house.

That evening when Josie came to the club Walt was waiting for her. He told her about his meeting with May and Alva and that May had said she was quitting. Josie listened but wasn't sure that it had anything to do with her.

"Tomorrow I want you to go see May and tell her I'll pay her well if she will come back," said Walt. He hugged Josie. "If you get her to come back, I'll pay you well too."

Josie stared at him. "I'll go talk to her, but I don't thank it's gonna do no good."

"You go anyway. You tell her that if she don't come back, she's damn well going to regret it. Star and Alva will regret it too." He grabbed Josie's arm. "You tell her that it's going to be bad for her and her friends."

"I'll go tomorrow and tell her," said Josie. She walked to the curtain thinking about what Walt had said. She was sorry May had quit; they had done well together. She was worried about May because Walt was mad, and she knew how mean he could be when he was mad. She would talk to May but didn't think it would do any good.

The curtain parted and she went out on stage. The first person she saw was Harry Rinkley. He was standing at the edge of the stage and was holding up money. She walked over to him. "I need to talk to you, and I'll pay you," he said.

Josie nodded. "Go to the door at the side of the stage and when I get through, I'll talk to you." He turned and started toward the door. She went through her act, went through the curtain and went to the side door and opened it. Harry was at the door waiting. Josie stepped out with him. She had nothing on except a G-string. She didn't know what he wanted but in case he wanted her, she was going to let him see the merchandise. "What do you want?" she asked.

He handed her some money as he looked her up and down. "I know you know May. Will you tell me where she lives?"

She shook her head. "I'm not gonna tell you where she lives. I wouldn't do that." Josie stared at him. "Why are you asking me this? You were with her yesterday."

Rink frowned. "I was with her, but it didn't work out. I need to talk to her." He quickly told Josie what had gone on at his house. "When will she be back here?"

Josie shook her head. "She ain't coming back. She quit."

He was surprised. "She quit?"

"That's what they told me today."

He looked back at her. "If you won't tell me where she lives, I'll pay you to take me there. I won't get out of the car; you go in and ask her if she would talk to me. If she won't, I'll leave and won't bother her." He took out more money and looked at her, his face questioning.

Josie looked at the money. *I've got to go see May tomorrow afternoon anyway* she thought. *I could ride with him, tell May what Walt said and then ask her about talking to Rink. If she don't want to, then we come home.* Josie didn't see any harm in doing this and she would make money. She took the money. "You pick me up here at two tomorrow and I'll take you. I'll ask May if she wants to talk to you, but if she don't, we come home. All right?"

Rink was having a hard time keeping his eyes on her face, his eye kept wandering. "All right," he said. "I'll be here at two."

Josie took his hand. "I have a room inside. If you want, we can go inside and talk or whatever else you want to do."

Rink stared at her. "I have to go." He turned and almost sprinted away from her.

Josie laughed.

~

Rep and Mose were in the barn when Lila walked in. "I had a call from Mother. She said the states are voting to repeal prohibition and soon it will be legal to make whiskey again. When that happens, people won't need us if they can buy whiskey legally."

Rep looked at her. "We been wanting to get out of this business. Maybe this will give us a chance."

"That's what I'm thinking," said Lila. "We can get by with just the farming all right if we shut the stills down."

"Them people in Phenix City ain't gonna like that," said Mose. "You shut down the stills and they sho' be comin' to see us."

Rep agreed. "Well, we haven't had a talk with them lately. Let's send them word that we're going to shut down in two weeks and see what they do." He looked at Lila. "Does that suit you?"

She nodded. "All this whiskey business has done is bring us trouble and sorrow. The trouble and sorrow are still with us and will never go away unless we stop it." She looked at Rep and Mose. "How do we tell them we're going to shut down in two weeks?"

"We be shippin' a truck today," said Mose. "I be tellin' 'em we be stoppin'."

"Do that," said Rep, "and we'll see what they do."

"We'll hear from Walt Wend," said Lila. "He is a despicable man."

"You're right," said Rep. "We haven't seen him in a while, but I bet he comes."

Mose got up. "That truck be loadin' now. I go tell 'em." He walked out the door.

"I hope Walt doesn't come up here and start a lot of trouble," said Lila.

Rep shrugged. "The last time Walt was here and threatened us, I told him if he came back looking for trouble again, I would give it to him." He stared at Lila. "I still mean it."

The next afternoon May left school and headed to see Jim Hawke. He was, as she expected, on his bench. "How you doin', little girl," he said as she walked up.

She sat on the bench beside him. "Jim," she said, "I wanted to tell you I have quit the club in Phenix City. I told them yesterday."

Jim looked at her and nodded. "That's good, May. That wasn't a good place for you to be."

May smiled. "Yes, I remember you telling me that." She glanced at him. "You talked pretty mean to me about it, as I remember."

Jim chuckled. "Didn't mean to be mean to you, but I meant what I said."

"I know you did, and you were right."

Jim rocked back and looked at her. "That was some meetin' you had with Storm and his new girlfriend the other day."

May knew Jim was pushing her about Storm. "What he does is his business. Don't matter to me."

"Did something happen at the club to make you quit?" asked Jim, his eyes on her face. "I figure somethin' had to happen."

May nodded. "Storm brought that girl to the show Saturday Night, for one thing. I didn't like her seeing me on stage while she was sitting with Storm."

Jim frowned. "I don't believe just that made you quit. What else happened?"

May took a deep breath. Then she told him about her experience with Harry Rinkley.

"You be right about all that," Jim said. "Folks know you work in that club; they thank all sort of bad things about you."

"I realize that now," said May. "I don't want to be thought of like that."

"It be best you quit now before it sho' git bad," said Jim.

"I need to tell you one more thing," she said. She told him about the meeting she and Alva had with Walt. "Walt didn't like me quitting and said he's gonna come after me. I wanted you to know so you could watch out for his people."

"I'll sho' watch out for 'em," said Jim. "You better be careful too." He cut his eyes at her. "What you gonna do about Storm? Now he be runnin' round with a new woman, a sho'nuff pretty one too."

May stood up. "Jim, every time I think you're my friend, you start messing in my personal affairs again." She walked away toward the dormitory. She could hear Jim laughing behind her.

Storm left the mill and headed to see Jim Hawke. He parked in front of the gym, got out and walked over and sat on the bench beside Jim.

"If you had been here a few minutes earlier you could have seen May," said Jim. "She was here talking to me."

"What makes you think I'd want to see her," asked Storm. "I know she doesn't want to see me."

"She said you brought yo' new girlfriend to see the show Saturday night."

"I did. What did she say about that?"

"She didn't say anything about that." Jim paused. "But she did tell me she has quit the club and ain't goin' back no more."

That got Storm's attention. "Why did she do that?"

"I'm not sure," said Jim, "but she said that people thought she was a bad person. She said she wasn't like the other strippers." Jim watched Storm's face.

"I think it's good she quit," said Storm. He shrugged. "It doesn't really matter to me what she does."

Jim smiled.

"Jim," said Storm, "You remember when the woman came to the landing with her son, Sugar Boy."

Jim nodded. "I remember, I knew her."

"I was over at Shoal Creek right before then and I saw several armed men leave there going to look for Sugar Boy."

"I figured that," said Jim. "Sugar Boy had shot Rolley Hill, so they were going after him. That is their way, an eye for an eye." He took a breath. "When the Shoal Creek people brought Rolley here and told me Sugar Boy shot him, I knew Sugar Boy was a dead man. Killing him was their way of keeping order in their territory."

"They said he lived in a big swamp and they were afraid to go in and get him," said Storm.

Jim nodded. "I wouldn't have gone in there neither, cause he had the advantage."

"I don't understand," said Storm. "They shot and killed him."

"Sugar Boy lived on a piece of dry land in the middle of the swamp," said Jim. "His house was several hundred yards from any dry land, so he felt safe. They wouldn't come in the swamp after him and it was too long a shot for any rifle we have. He wasn't afraid."

Storm shook his head. "How did they do it?"

"There is a rifle the army has that a trained sniper can use that will kill at a great distance. That's what they used," said Jim.

"I saw the men when they left," said Storm. "I didn't see any special rifle."

"They didn't have the rifle but the man they were going to get had it," said Jim. "He killed Sugar Boy." Jim looked at him. "One night I was with this man, we was both drinking, and he told me he had been a sniper in the army. He fought in the war and still had his rifle."

Storm nodded. "So, you know him."

"Yes," said Jim, "but it be best I don't tell you his name."

Storm shook his head, "I don't need to know."

Jim rubbed his hand across his face. "What you gonna do about May?"

Storm got up. "I'm not going to do anything about May, and I don't know why you keep bringing her name up." He walked to his car and drove away.

Jim, chuckling, watched him leave.

May left Jim and walked back toward the dormitory. She was about to turn in the driveway when she saw a car coming down the road. She hesitated for a moment, then saw the car was red with black fenders. Rink's car she thought, as she ran down the hill. She ran in the door and to her room.

She rushed in; Alva was standing by the bathroom. "Alva," she said, "Rink's car just drove up. I don't know how he found me. If he comes to the door, tell him I'm not here." She ran to her room and slammed the door.

A surprised and confused Alva stood there and then there was a knock on the door. She hesitantly walked to the door and opened it. When she saw Josie, she was really surprised.

"Hey, Alva," Josie said, "is May here?"

Alva nodded. "Come in, I'll get her." She walked over and knocked on May's door. "May, Josie is here to see you."

The door opened and May peeped out. "Josie is here?" Then she opened the door more and saw Josie. "What are you doing here?" She walked out of the room. "I thought I saw Rink's car."

Josie grabbed her arm. "Let me tell you, May. Walt sent me but Rink brought me up here."

"What are you talking about?" said May. "Why are you with Rink? Why did you bring him up here?"

Alva was standing to the side watching this develop. She walked over to May and took her arm. "Sit down, May," she said. "Let Josie explain what she's trying to tell you." May sat down on the sofa and Alva got Josie in a chair. "Now Josie, you tell May what is going on."

"Walt told me you had quit, and he told me to come talk to you," said Josie. Then she told May what Walt had said and the threats he had made if she didn't come back to the club.

May and Alva listened, asked a few questions but it was clear to them that Walt intended to try to force May to come back. They were both concerned about the threats to Alva and Star.

"All right," said May. "What is Rink doing here?"

'He saw me at the club and asked me to tell him where you lived. I told him you had quit, and he asked me to bring him up here. He said if you wouldn't talk to him, he would leave and not bother you again. I had to come tell you what Walt said, so I got him to bring me." She looked at May.

"He's waiting in the car?"

"Yes."

May looked at Alva. "What do you think?"

"It's up to you."

May looked at Josie. "You stay with Alva." She got up, walked out the door and then outside. She walked up to the driveway. She could see Rink in the car, he had seen her, and his eyes were on her. May walked to the passenger door, opened it and got in.

Rink looked at her. "Thank you for seeing me."

"What do you want?"

"I regret what happened at the house the other day," said Rink. "My folks asked me what happened, and I told them the truth. I told them about you working at the club and what Jock had said to you. They thought it was terrible how you had been treated in their house and they wanted you to know that they apologize. I went to the club wanting to tell you that and I found out you had quit. So, I asked Josie to bring me here today." He watched her face and waited.

May stared out the window, Rink's words in her mind. "I thank you for your concern and tell your folks that I appreciate their thoughts," she said. "You seem like a nice person, but you don't know me, and I don't see any reason to start a relationship with you. Your world and my world are too far apart."

"You won't even give me a chance to change your mind?"

She shook her head. "No, it wouldn't work, Rink. I'm in love with somebody else."

She opened the door and got out. "I'll send Josie up." She closed the door and went inside. She opened the door to the room. Josie and Alva looked up when she came in. "Rink is waiting for you, Josie. When you get back you tell Walt that if I hear one more word from him or see any of his people here, I will come after him." She walked in her room and slammed the door.

Josie looked at Alva.

Alva shook her head. "I'll try to talk to her, but I think she's had enough."

Josie shrugged and walked out the door.

Owen's schedule each day was to check his hooks, clean the fish and go see Sassy. She would be waiting for him with items to take back to the camp for her. Mattie gave her an iron skillet, large and small cookie sheets and two pots. Lila had already given Owen enough knives, forks and spoons to do them. The other items she sent, and there wasn't much, were mostly girl's stuff she had collected and saved.

After loading the boat, Owen would help Sassy with whatever chores she had to do and then she would take him to the barn. She had said that when they got married on Saturday, they wouldn't have to waste time getting to know each other, that would already be done. After days in the barn, Owen was praying that Saturday would hurry where he could bed Sassy and get some relief.

Lick had given them a bird dog and a beagle. There were several coveys of quail on Big Island plus rabbits and squirrels, so they should have meat. He gave them a milk cow with a calf, along with a rooster and six hens. Owen felt they were set up well

Wednesday after school Alva asked May to walk to the store with her. They were halfway way there when May saw Storm's car come past the Christian church and park in front of the gym. Storm got out, walked to the gym steps and sat down.

Jim Hawke wasn't on his bench and May thought that odd. She hadn't seen Storm since the show Saturday night and hadn't wanted to, she didn't feel ready to face him. If she hadn't been with Alva, she would have turned around and gone back to the dormitory. She followed Alva to the store. Alva went in to see Mrs. Williams and she waited on the porch.

She was aware that Storm was sitting on the gym steps watching her. She had decided to go in the store and get away from his view when he got up and started walking toward her. She didn't want to look as though she was running away from him, so she stood and waited. He crossed the street and stepped up on the porch.

"I haven't seen you in a few days," he said.

May stared at him. "You haven't seen me since you and your girlfriend saw me naked on the stage. I guess y'all had a time laughing about that."

Storm shook his head. "I've never laughed at you, May. You know better than that."

"You were sitting on the steps, Storm, all by yourself," she said. "I didn't call you. Why did you come over here?"

"Jim told me that you had quit the club. I wanted to tell you that I'm glad you did."

May continued to stare hard eyed at him. "I don't want any pity from you, Storm."

Storm frowned. "Why would you say that May? I've never thought you needed pity." He looked at her, his face troubled, "Don't you know how I feel about you?"

May nodded. "I know how you feel, sitting there with another woman watching me take off my clothes."

Storm stepped closer to her and dropped his voice. "What the hell are you talking about? I asked you to marry me. I was in love with you, but you told me you didn't want anything to do with me." He took a deep breath. "What was I supposed to do, sit and mope? When you love somebody like I loved you, it don't ever die." He shook his head. "I still love you." He turned and walked across the street, got in his car and drove away.

May watched his car go up the street until it was out of sight.

Alva came out of the store. "Was that Storm you were talking to?" she asked.

"Yes, it was Storm."

Alva stared at her. "You look upset. What did he say?"

"He was glad I had quit the club."

"That was nice of him," said Alva. "But Storm is a nice man."

May nodded and smiled. "Yes, he is a nice man."

Storm drove away from the store and away from May. He couldn't believe that he had told her he loved her again. It looked like he would learn after she had told him repeatedly that she didn't want him. Now he had Karen coming back Friday and she expected them to now be a couple. He had promised her the weekend, beginning with him picking her up Friday. He remembered what she said when she left, "I'll be in your bed Friday night."

He rode to the river, went past the old men at the landing and pulled into the spot where he and May had parked. He sat and watched the water rush past, his mind focused on his dilemma and what to do about it. A part of him didn't feel right about going to Shoal Creek and getting Karen if it wasn't fair to her. However, on the other side, walking away from Karen could be completely foolish. His feelings for May seemed to be equally foolish since she had shown no evidence of her having any feelings for him. He decided that if he couldn't get this situation with May cleared up, and that didn't seem possible based on the conversation he'd just had, he would go after Karen.

~

Walt was on the phone when Josie walked in his office. "What the hell do you mean, they said they were going to shut down the stills. Did they say why they were going to do that?"

Josie stopped in the door and was about to turn around when he motioned for her to come in. She tentatively walked to his desk and sat in a chair.

"No, I don't want you to do anything," said Walt. "I'm going up there myself and straighten their ass out." He slammed the phone down and looked at Josie. "Did you talk to May?"

"I talked to her," said Josie, "but she said she ain't gonna come back. She said if you keep on bothering her or yo' people come up there, she is gonna come after you."

Walt turned around and stared out the window. "Damn, what a mess. First May being a problem and now the Shoal Creek people say they're getting out of the whiskey business." He shook his head then looked at Josie. "Get your coat, you can ride with me to Shoal Creek.

Josie shrugged and followed him outside. They got in the car and pulled out of the parking lot.

Walt looked at her. "So, May said she was going to come after me?"

Josie nodded. "That's what she said. She seemed to be set in her mind that she ain't comin' back."

"Did you see Star?"

"I didn't see Star, just May and Alva."

Walt grimaced. "That prissy bitch, Alva. I tried to be nice to her and she threatened to have me in court." He grunted. "She is a good-looking woman though. I should have taken care of her when I had her in my room." He smiled. "I know I would have enjoyed having her and I think she would have liked it too."

Josie looked around at him. "Miss Alva is a lady, she ain't like that."

"I saw her reaction when she was watching May on stage and she got all worked up," He shook his head. "She might be a lady, but she has feelings too. She was red-faced and breathing hard that day, like any woman when they get stirred up."

Josie didn't say anything else, but she thought he was wrong about Miss Alva.

They turned through the gate at Shoal Creek. Big'un was standing by the fence. Josie waved to him. Emotionless, he stared at them as they went on down the road toward the barn.

Josie jumped out of the car. "If you don't need me, I'm gonna go see my folks."

"Go on," said Walt. "I won't be here long."

Josie ran up the road toward the houses. Walt looked around and didn't see anybody. He walked up on the porch, opened the door and walked in. Lila was sitting behind the desk. He looked around the room. It seemed she was alone.

Lila looked up when the door opened and was surprised to see Walt walk in. He had never come to see them without calling, but then she had expected he would come eventually.

"Well," said Walt as he walked toward her, "I'm surprised to find you here all alone." He walked to the desk and sat in a chair in front of her. He smiled at her. "If you were my woman, I would never leave you alone, I'd be afraid some bad man would come and take you away."

Lila looked at him and shook her head. "If I was your woman, Walt, I'd be hoping for somebody to take me away."

He reared back and laughed. "Damn, Lila, I like you, you are one hell of a woman." He leaned toward her. "Seriously, it's a shame you're stuck out here in the middle of nowhere, a beautiful woman like you. I would like to take you away with me."

Lila smiled. "I'll tell you what, Walt. When Rep comes in, you tell him that you've propositioned me and see what he thinks of it."

Walt frowned. "Rep is a hothead and wouldn't understand two grown people having a grown-up conversation. He might react badly."

Lila laughed. "Walt, you are an ass. There was nothing grown-up about our conversation. I know exactly what you meant." She stared at him. "Do you still have Josie in your bed?"

"Yes," Josie is still with me, but she's not permanent," said Walt. "I'm looking for somebody more on your level."

"Enough of this," said Lila. "Why are you here?"

"You know why I'm here. I got word you're threatening to shut down the stills."

Lila nodded. "Prohibition in going to end and we want to get rid of the whiskey before the trouble starts. You have two weeks."

"We've already been over this, Lila. You know we need the stills running. If you do this, I've already told you what will happen."

The door opened and Rep walked in. He looked at Walt, then at Lila and back at Walt. His eyes were cold when he looked at Walt. "What are you doing here?"

Walt stood up and faced Rep. "I came to talk to you about this message I got about shutting the stills down."

"Not gonna be no talk," said Rep. "You got two weeks and they're gonna be shut down."

Walt shook his head. "I told you before what is going to happen if you do that. You don't want that."

"Walt," said Rep, "I should have killed you the night yo' man shot Mose and tried to kill me. That was my mistake. You leave here right now and don't ever come back here again. You come back here again, and you won't ever leave. We'll bury you here."

"Those are serious threats, Rep. I'll have the law out here on you."

Rep started toward him. "I told you to leave."

Walt put up his hands. "I'm leaving, don't start anything."

Rep grabbed him by the arm and pulled him toward the door, Walt objecting all the way. Rep opened the door and pushed him out on the porch.

Lila came out the door. "Let him go, Rep. Let him go."

Rep shoved Walt across the porch and turned him loose.

Walt staggered and regained his balance as he put his foot on the top step. He looked back at Rep. "You're gonna regret..." He never finished the sentence. Rep slapped him on the side of his face with his open palm, knocking him off the porch onto the dirt road. Walt was stunned. He lay on his back for a minute, then rolled over and got to his knees.

Rep walked toward him. "Get your ass in the car and leave before I beat you half to death."

Walt staggered up and stumbled to the car. He opened the door, got in and started the car. Rep moved to the porch as Walt turned the car around and went toward the gate.

Lila walked over and put her arm around Rep. "You know this is not the end of this."

Rep nodded. "We will deal with what comes." They walked back in the barn.

They were settled at the desk a few minutes later when the door opened, and Josie rushed in. They both were surprised. They had no idea she was at Shoal Creek and wondered where she came from. Rep stood up and stared at her.

"Where is Walt?" she asked.

"Walt?" answered Rep. "Walt just left."

She looked at Rep angrily. "The bastard left me."

"You came up here with him?" said Rep. "We didn't know you were here, and he didn't say nothin' about you."

"He told me to come with 'im cause he was gonna talk to y'all about shuttin' down the stills," said Josie. "I told 'im I was gonna go see my folks. I didn't expect 'im to leave me."

"We did talk about the stills," said Rep. "He didn't like what we said so we told him to leave. I guess he was in such a hurry he forgot you was here."

Josie stared at Rep. "Walt was mad at ya'll and said he was gonna straighten yo' ass out." She stopped and looked at Rep. "Did y'all fight."

Rep laughed. "Wasn't much of a fight."

Lila looked at Josie. "Why are you still with Walt, Josie? You know what kind of person he is."

Josie nodded. "I know how he is, but he don't bother me much. I like being at the club and I make good money." She looked at Lila. "What else am I gonna do? I sho' don't want to come back here and work in the cotton field."

Lila smiled. "I guess you have a point."

"I'll get one of the men to take you home, Josie, if you're ready to go," said Rep.

Josie nodded. "I thank you for that."

Rep went outside and called one of the men to bring a truck around. Josie thanked them, got in the truck and they watched the truck go out the gate.

16

The man from Shoal Creek let Josie off at her apartment. She dressed and went to the club. She intended to talk to Walt about leaving her. There was no excuse for him treating her that way. She got to the club, went in and walked up the stairs to his office. He was sitting behind his desk and when she saw him, she stopped and stared. His left eye was black, and the right side of his face was bruised. "What the hell happened to you?" she asked.

"Had a little problem with Rep," he said.

"That the reason you left me?"

"Yes. He didn't give me much time to tell him you were there."

"He hit you?"

"Obviously," said Walt. He looked at her. "Don't you say anything about this."

Josie shook her head. "I don't never say anythin' bout yo' business, Walt."

Walt pursed his lips as he thought. "Sit down, Josie," he said, pointing to a chair.

Josie was surprised. He had never asked to sit at his desk before. She sat as he directed.

Walt reared back in the chair and stared at her. "You and May do a good job on stage, Josie. Y'all bring in the business and that's important. If May quits as she says, we're going to have a problem. I want you to go back to May, tell her I'll pay her twice what I've been paying if she will come back. Tell her too that her coming back will avoid any trouble for her or her people. I promise that." He looked at her. "You get her back and I'll really make it worthwhile for you."

"I'll go see her again," said Josie, "but I don't know about her comin' back."

"You do the best you can," said Walt as he put an ice pack to his face.

~

Storm was up early Friday morning. After much thought and soul-searching, he had decided his infatuation with May was not only hopeless but foolish and he should focus on Karen. She was all any man could want in a woman and in a wife. His goal now would be to get her to agree to be his wife.

Although May now said she had quit the club in Phenix City, the fact that she had gone there to begin with was damning. He had seen with his own eyes May standing in front of a drunken crowd and taking off her clothes until she stood virtually naked before them. Not only did she do such an act, but she also reveled in it, smiling and flirting with the men as they ran their hands over her body. She now said she was remorseful, but that could not undo the damage.

The fact she was a Hobb couldn't be ignored. The parents, Jack and Ruby, were sorry and had no redeeming qualities. They had four children whose lives followed in their parent's footsteps. The father and the two sons had been killed while breaking the law. The two daughters had chosen a life of sin.

As Storm considered all these factors, he could only conclude that his involvement with May would end in ruin. His future was entwined in the company and the town of River Bluff and he had to think of that solemn responsibility first. His family had said nothing to this point about May and his dalliance with her, but if it got to a higher level, he knew they would. A clean break with her was the right move.

All these thoughts were in his mind as he went to the landing, got in the boat and headed up the river. When he landed at Shoal Creek Owen was cleaning fish. Storm spoke to him and headed toward the house. He didn't see Karen's car there, so he went to the barn. He walked up on the porch, opened the door and went in. Rep and Mose were at the desk. He walked over and shook hands with both.

Rep smiled at him, "You're here mighty early, Storm. Karen's not here yet."

"I came early to talk to you, Rep," Storm said. "I wanted to tell you that I was at the landing in River Bluff last week when Sugar Boy's mother brought his body up there. She told everybody that that people at Shoal Creek killed him. She said she was going to get even."

Rep nodded. "I know that. She came to see us telling us the same thing. We got it straightened out with her and there ain't no problem."

Storm stared at him for a moment, then he decided it wasn't his business, so he shut up.

"I was going to tell you something," said Rep. "We've told the people in Phenix City that buy whiskey that we're shutting the stills down. They'll be down in two weeks."

"I thought you tried that once before and they made y'all keep them running," said Storm.

"That's right," said Rep, "but times have changed and we're shutting the stills down."

"Didn't you say the last time I was here that a man named Walt Wend was involved in buying the whiskey from you?" asked Storm.

Rep nodded. "Yes, he buys the whiskey."

"I've a strange coincidence with him," said Storm, "A girl from River Bluff is a stripper in the club that Walt Wend runs in Phenix City. Karen and I met her last Saturday and she asked us to come see her on stage. Karen wanted to go and so we went. Karen saw another girl on stage that she knew from Shoal Creek, she said her name was Josie." He looked at Rep. "Do you know her?"

Rep laughed. "We know Josie, she lives with Walt. Josie is a sight; she has never had any sense of right and wrong."

"The girl and her family from River Bluff have had a lot of trouble with Walt Wend," said Storm. "You know her family, she's a Hobb."

Rep nodded. "We know all about the Hobbs. The Hobbs are trouble and Walt Wend is trouble. He was here this week and we had trouble with him. He don't like us shutting the stills down."

As Rep said that they heard a car coming down the road. Storm went to the door and when he looked out, he saw Karen's car going up the drive to the house. He looked around at Rep. "Karen's here so I better go to the house." He went out the door.

Karen was getting her luggage out of the car when he ran up. She turned around, he grabbed her, and she grabbed him. He kissed her and held on. Finally, she turned loose and looked up at him. "I didn't know if you would come or not," she said.

He frowned at her. "Why would you say that? I told you I would be here."

She hugged him. "I know that, but you know what we talked about last week.

He held her away from him and looked in her eyes. "Don't you worry about that again. That's all done with. You're the only thing on my mind." He kissed her again.

She smiled. "I'm glad. You're the only thing on my mind too." She reached down and got her purse. "Get my bags and let's go in the house."

They went up the steps into the house. Lila met Karan at the door. They hugged and kissed and talked as the went to her room. Storm followed with the bags.

Lila looked at Storm. "I'm glad you came, Storm. It's good to see you again."

"I'm glad to be here," said Storm.

"Owen and Sassy are getting married tomorrow," said Lila. "We want both of you to go with us to the wedding."

Storm looked at Karen. "I'm good for whatever you want to do."

"The wedding is at eleven o'clock at Walnut Creek," said Lila. "We plan to leave about ten."

Storm nodded. "We'll be here at ten."

Lila glanced at Karen.

"I'm planning to stay with Storm tonight," said Karen.

Lila nodded. "That's fine. Just make sure you're back here by ten.

Lila and Karen ran down the hall to see Rip. Storm told Karen he would be outside. Karen came down the steps a few minutes later, a small bag over her shoulder. She ran over to him and looked in his face, "You said everything is cleared up across the river?"

He nodded, "That's what I said."

Her eyes stayed on his face. "There's nothing or nobody between us.?"

Storm stared back at her. "You're the only person on my mind, Karen."

She nodded and smiled. "Then I'll go with you."

They walked down the path to the landing and got in the boat.

Storm got in, cranked the motor and went across the river. They landed and Karen saw the gathering of old men at the boat ramp. She got out and walked toward them with Storm trailing behind her. All eyes were on her as she approached.

"Good morning, men," she said, smiling at them. She looked back at Storm. "Storm has told me that he's a perfect gentleman and I can trust him. What do ya'll think?"

Her question set off a chorus of comments from the group, "You better watch 'im," said one man and others joined in with similar or ribald thoughts.

Karen walked over to Storm and put her arm around him. She kissed him on the cheek and looked at the group. "I trust him," she said, as she pulled him toward the car.

This action really set the group off and they could hear them yelling and arguing as they got in the car. Storm started the car and started up the road. "Tomorrow night we're having supper with my folks," he said as he looked at her.

She smiled. Him saying he was taking her to meet his parents meant more to her than any other thing he had said to date. "That's good," she said. "I look forward to meeting them.

They went on to the house, Storm got her bags out and carried them inside. "Take them to the guest room please," she said.

Storm gave her a questioning look.

Karen saw his look and knew what it meant. "Sometimes I like privacy, especially in the morning," she said. She walked over and kissed him on the cheek. "I'm perfectly able to walk to your bedroom if I feel the need to do so."

Storm carried the bags to the guest room.

Walt sat at his desk with the ice bag on his face and fumed. He had two serious problems facing him and both situations were calling for action. May not being on stage Friday and Saturday night would affect him immediately, especially if word got out that she had quit. Shoal Creek shutting down the whiskey supply would also have serious effects, getting another supplier would be a problem on such short notice.

He had sent Josie to see May, but he didn't feel good about her changing her mind. He remembered her standing in front of his desk pointing the pistol at him and her eyes seemed determined. He knew she had shot Marvin and wouldn't hesitate to shoot him. Getting her back wouldn't be possible unless he could get rid of Star and Alva.

He thought of Star. The only person that could take May's place on the stage and generate the same or more business was Star. If he could get her to come back that would solve his problem. She might agree to come back to protect May and Alva if she thought they were in danger. The more he thought of that idea, the more he thought it might work. He knew that the two men Marvin had sent after Star and mistakenly killed her daddy knew where Star lived. He called them in the office.

The two men left after he gave them their instructions and he then thought about the whiskey situation at Shoal Creek. In the front of his mind was the treatment he'd received from Rep. He was constantly reminded of this by the ice pack on his face, the soreness of his jaw and his black eye. The more he thought of how he had been mistreated, the madder he got. He got up, walked downstairs and called two other men over. He huddled with them for several minutes and then went back upstairs. He felt good. He was going to teach several people a lesson about messing with him.

~

May had just got home from school Friday afternoon and was in her room when she heard a knock on the door. Alva wasn't in so she went over and opened the door and was surprised to see Harry Rinkley. She looked up at him. "What do you want?"

"I know what you told me last time I was here, but I wanted to at least talk to you one more time," he said. "Just listen to me for a minute."

May stared at him. *He's come all this way to see me*, she thought. What could be the harm? "All right," she said. "Come on in."

She walked over and sat on the sofa. Rink sat in a chair facing her. She could see by his face that he was trying to come up with the right thing to say to her. "I like you, May. And I think if you gave me a chance to get to know you better, you could like me too." He stared at her. "All I'm asking is for you to give me a chance."

May stared at him. He seemed like a nice young man and he was rich, she thought. Until she could figure out her feelings about Storm, she could let him be with her. There wasn't anybody else in River Bluff. Then the thought hit her. Storm had pushed Karen in her face, she could do the same to him with Rink. She smiled; she liked that idea. "All right," she said. "What did you have in mind?"

Rink was surprised, he had been ready for disappointment. "I'm ready for anything you want to do. We could go to Columbus or whatever you want."

"It's too late to do that," said May. "There's not much to do in River Bluff, but we do have a movie theater."

Rink didn't care what they did. He just wanted to be with her. "A movie suits me. Is there a place we can eat before we go?"

"There's a place in Landon," said May. "It's not far. We can eat there and then come back to the movie." She got up. "Let me dress and then I'll be with you." She turned and walked to her room.

Rink sat and waited, overjoyed that she had agreed to go with him. He got up when she walked out her room. He stood and stared at her, thinking she was the most beautiful woman he had ever seen. He shook his head. "You look so pretty," he said.

"Thank you, Rink," she said. "You're so nice."

It hadn't taken but just a few words from her, but Rink was in love for the first time in his life.

They left the room, got in his car and May told him to go to the store. She had already decided that she was going to make sure as many people as possible would see her with Rink tonight. While they might not see Storm, she wanted the word out that she was with a new man. She was sure he'd hear about it.

Jim was sitting on his bench and he was the first stop she wanted to make. She told Rink to pull over and park. They got out and walked over to Jim. "Jim, this is Rink Rinkley. He's from Columbus and I wanted you to meet him."

Jim cut his eyes at May and shook hands with Rink. "Glad to meet you," he said.

They stood for a few minutes and talked, then got back in the car and left. May knew that Jim would tell everybody, including Storm, about seeing her with a man.

They went to Landon and ate. She learned a lot about Rink. He had finished college in Tennessee and was now working in his father's business. As they talked, she found that she enjoyed being with him. He was smart, interesting and she could tell he was smitten with her. It only took a few touches with her hand on his arm or leaning her shoulder against him to have him completely captured.

They left Landon and headed to the movie.

~

Storm put Karen's bags in the guest room and walked back to her. He took her in his arms, pulled her close and kissed her. "What do you want to do now?" he asked.

"I don't want to stay in this house with you right now," she said. "I need some time to get used to being with you and get control of my feelings. Then later we'll come back and see how things work out."

He smiled. "I' thought we might see how things work out right now."

She shook her head. "I thought that also. That's why I want to get out of here."

He laughed and took her hand. "Come on then," he said, "we'll walk up the town."

As they got to the top of the hill, they saw a car leave where Jim was sitting and go up the road. He noticed it because it wasn't a car he had seen before. It was a new Ford A-Model, all fancy, red with black fenders. "That's a new car," he said to Karen.

She had noticed it too. "Yes, it is," she said. "Somebody has some money."

They walked on to where Jim was sitting. "Evening Jim," said Storm. "You remember Karen."

"Yes, I do," Jim said. "It's good to see you again."

"That was a fancy car that just left here," said Storm. "Who was it?"

Jim smiled. "That was a young man from Columbus." He paused, watching Storm's face. "May was with 'im, said they was goin' to eat in Landon. First time I ever met 'im. Nice lookin' fellow and May sho' did look happy to be with 'im."

Storm looked at Jim but knew he didn't need to make any more comments about the car. "Anything much going on?" he asked. He wanted to get away from Jim before he made any more comments about May.

Jim shook his head. He knew another comment about May would only cause problems, so he remained quiet. He intended to talk to Storm later when he was alone.

"We'll see you later," Storm said as he took Karen's hand and started away.

Karen looked up at him. "Did Jim say May was with the man in the car?"

"That's what he said."

"Had you ever seen the car before?"

"No, I've never seen it before."

She stopped. "I'm ready to go to the house."

"Are you sure, it's a while till dark."

"Is that a problem for you?"

"No, it's not a problem" He took her hand and they started toward the house.

When they walked in the front door, Karen stopped and looked at Storm. "You know I'm taken with you, Storm. I never thought it could happen like this, but it has. I'm telling you this because I find myself not in control of my feelings and you could take advantage of me if you wished to." She looked at him. "I'm trusting that you have told me the truth."

Storm walked over, hugged her and kissed her on the cheek. "Tell you what," he said, "we haven't eaten, so I have two steaks in the kitchen that I'm going to cook for us. After we eat, I want to show you the golf course. Then we'll come back t the house and see how things go after then." He led her over to the couch. "You sit here, and I'll call you when I'm ready.

Karen sat down

In a few minutes he called her. They ate and then he took her to the golf course. They walked and talked until almost dark and then they went back to the house. When they went in he led her to the bathroom. "You take your shower and get ready for bed."

She stared at him, questioning.

He shook his head. "You're on your own tonight. I'll take a shower when you get through."

She came out in a few minutes and went to the guest room to dress. He went in to take a shower. When he came out, she was sitting on the sofa. He came over, sat by her and put his arm around her. "I told you today that I was serious about you and I meant that." He took her hand, pulled her up off the sofa and led her down the hall to the guest room. "My plans for you amount to more than jumping in bed with you. If it works out that we both feel we have a future together, we'll have plenty of time for that." He kissed her. "We have to be across the river at ten in the morning, so I'll wake you early." He kissed her again. "Good night." He turned and went down the hall to his room.

Karen watched him walk away, turned and walked over to the bed. She stood there for a moment, turned around and went out the door and down the hall to Storm's room.

He was lying in the bed when she walked in. She came to the edge of the bed and looked down at him. "It was easy to walk in here from the guest room," she said. "I could slip in your bed now and stay with you tonight without a problem. It's very tempting to do that. But I'm not because it is too important to me." She leaned over and kissed him. "Good night." She turned and walked out of the room.

Storm watched her go out of the door. He lay there for a few minutes thinking about what she said, then turned over and went to sleep.

~

Rink bought tickets, popcorn and a drink for them at the movie. They went in, May guided him to a seat in the back on the side where she and Rollie had always sat. They were away from the crowd. She sat close to him and later he held her hand. When they finished the popcorn, he put his arm around her, and she leaned against him. Later she put herself in a position where she invited him to kiss her and he did. She was surprised that he knew what he was doing, and she enjoyed it with him. While they kissed several other times, he didn't try anything else. By the time they left the theater she had him conquered.

They got in the car, drove to the dormitory and pulled into the driveway and parked. May had Rink where she wanted him; she intended to keep him there. She leaned over, kissed him and opened the door. "Can I see you tomorrow?" he asked.

"If you want to," she said. "Come about two. Good night," she said as she got out.

Rink watched her walk away. He couldn't believe she had gone with him and even kissed him. He was already looking forward to tomorrow as he drove away.

17

Owen woke up early Saturday morning. It was his wedding day, and he was excited. Today Sassy would be his wife and she would come with him to the cabin. He got up, and cleaned and swept up the cabin. He wanted everything to be right when Sassy got there. He put on the suit Rep had got for him, got in the boat and headed to Walnut Creek.

He landed, got out and walked to the house. One of the sisters was on the porch. She saw Owen coming across the yard. "Sassy be at the barn feedin' the chickens," she said. "You gonna be marryin' Sassy today?"

Owen looked up at her, nodded and walked on to the barn. He went around back, and Sassy was in the pen tossing corn to the chickens feeding all around her feet. She saw him, put the pan down and came out the door. She ran over to him and hugged him. He kissed her. "I be glad you come," she said. She stepped back and looked at him. "You sho' do look good all dressed up," she said. She took his hand and started toward the house. "I gotta go get dressed," she said. "I'm gonna wear the same dress Bess wore when she married Rep. He done give it to me." They got to the house, Sassy ran up the steps and went inside. Owen sat on the steps.

~

Storm woke up early. He went to the kitchen and put coffee on the stove. He walked to the guest room and quietly opened the door. Karen was in the bed looking at him.

She smiled. "Good morning."

He walked over to the bed, lay down beside her, leaned over and kissed her. "It's good to wake up in the morning and see you here with me."

"I think so too," she said as she laid her head on his chest.

He put his arm around her. "I've only known you for about three weeks, but it seems we've been together much longer."

"Seems the same to me."

He kissed her, "How long are you staying at Shoal Creek?"

She snuggled closer. "Depends on what I have to stay for."

"Would you stay for me?"

She raised up and looked in his face. "What does that mean?"

"Would you stay and live here in River Bluff with me?"

Karen sat up and looked down at him. "You need to be careful what you say, because that sounded somewhat like a proposal."

He nodded. "It sounded like a proposal to me too."

She stared at him. "My answer is yes, but I'm not going to say that now. If you still feel the same way in three weeks you ask me again and I'll answer you.

He pulled her to him. "I'll do that if you want me to, but we could settle it now."

She rolled away and jumped out of bed. "We have to meet Lila and Rep at ten," she said as she ran to the bathroom. "I'll be ready in a minute."

Storm dressed, poured them coffee and fixed sausage biscuits. When she came out, they sat at the table and ate. They got in the car, drove to the landing and went across the creek to the Shoal Creek landing. Lila and Rep were waiting along with Mose and Hattie Mae. The group went down Back Slough to Walnut Creek.

Lick and Mattie were waiting with the two girls as were Owen and Sassy. They went up the creek to the bridge and walked up to Preacher Snow's church. He was waiting for them. They went inside, the ceremony was brief, Sassy got her paper, and everybody was happy it was over. Lila told Sassy how pretty she looked and kissed her. Rep shook Owen's hand.

When they walked outside, Lila took Rep by the arm and they went around to the cemetery. They walked to Bess's grave and stood for a moment. Rep hugged Lila for her understanding and they headed for the boat.

They all stopped at Lick's house. Sassy ran in, changed clothes and she and Owen headed up the river. The other boats followed them.

May and Alva were in the room when Rink knocked. May opened the door, invited him in and introduced him to Alva.

"I'm glad to meet you, Rink," said Alva. She thought he was a nice-looking young man, well dressed and clean-cut.

"Thank you, Ma'am," he said. "It's good to meet you."

Rink looked at May. "My parents asked if you would come to the house this afternoon. They wanted another chance to meet you."

May was surprised by the offer but she knew Rink's parent's blessing would be important if she wanted to build a relationship with him. "That would be nice," she said.

They said goodbye to Alva, got in the car and headed to Columbus. "Why did you change your mind about going out with me," asked Rink, 'when you were so against it before?"

May looked at him. "You seem like a nice person, Rink. You're smart and come from a good family. You seem to have everything." She turned in the seat and stared at him. "You saw me half naked on the stage and asked to meet me by offering me money. What was I supposed to think about you?"

Rink grimaced. "When you say it like that, I can see your point. When I saw you the first time, I was taken with you. I asked about you and the people said you were different, not like the other girls. So, I wanted to meet you and see how you were."

They rode on with May thinking about what he had said. "I come from a rough background, Rink. My family is much different than yours."

"Your father and two brothers were killed, and your sister Star was a stripper among other things," said Rink. "You are a senior in high school and will be an honor graduate. You plan to go to college and be a schoolteacher." He glanced at her. "What else?"

She took a deep breath. "You checked up on me. Why?"

He looked at her. "I'm just a boy that asked a girl for a date. Why don't you leave it at that?" He reached over and patted her on the hand. "And if you're worried about my parents, I've told them exactly what I just told you."

May didn't say anything else on the ride to his house. It seemed she had underestimated Rink and needed time to rethink what was happening.

They got to the house. When they went in Martha and Tap met them at the door. They both apologized for what had happened on her earlier visit. May assured them that they had no need to apologize. They had dinner prepared so they went in, sat down and were served by the kitchen staff. It was obvious to May that Rink's life was completely different from hers, but she already knew that. They had finished eating and were waiting on dessert.

Martha turned to May. "Rink said you have quit the club, May."

May nodded. "Yes, Ma'am, I have." She looked at Rink.

Martha saw her look. "I'm not trying to pry in your business, May. Rink said you might have trouble with the management about leaving and we were concerned. Maybe Tap could help you."

"Who runs the club, May?" asked Tap.

"His name is Walt Wend.'

Tap nodded. "I know who Walt is, but I've never met him. He lives here in Columbus and has been involved in shady dealings for years across the river. Why does he object to you leaving? Seems it's your business?"

"May was the star, the main attraction, Dad and her being gone will hurt their business," said Rink.

Tap nodded. "So, he has made threats to try to force you to come back?"

"Yes, Sir," said May.

"But you're not going back?" said Martha.

"No, Ma'am, I'm not going back."

"Good for you," Martha replied.

The maid brought in the desserts and little was said about May's trouble at the club after then.

May thanked them for the meal and she and Rink left.

"Your folks were nice to me," said May as they got in the car. She looked at him. "You're lucky to have such nice parents."

"I am lucky," said Rink. He took May's hand and stared at her. "I know we just met, May, and you don't really know me, but I like you a lot. You're a strong woman to have gone through what you have. I admire you for that. I do have a lot but it's not all that great unless you have someone to share it with."

May watched his face as he talked and knew he was serious. She smiled. "Rink, you need to understand that I'm not an angel. I was on the stage because I enjoyed it, not because I had to. That I felt like that should give you cause to worry about me."

Rink shook his head. "How could I criticize you, May? I came to the club to watch you and other women take off your clothes. What does that say about me?"

May laughed. "You have a point. Neither of us have much to be proud of, I guess." She stared at him and leaned over and kissed him on the cheek. "You know about me, Rink and my shortcomings. If you still want to be with me, then I'm all right with that. That's up to you."

He leaned over and kissed her. "I do want to be with you, May." He started the car and headed toward River Bluff.

They got to the dormitory and parked. They talked and kissed and then talked some more. May's first thought that she could use Rink for her advantage had now changed. She was beginning to like everything about him. He was somebody she could see a future with. Plus, she wouldn't have to live in River Bluff.

There was no doubt in Rink's mind as to what he wanted. He wanted May for his wife, and he intended to do everything he could to get her.

It was almost midnight. "I've got to get up early in the morning and go to church with Alva," said May.

"Why don't I pick you and Alva up after church tomorrow and take you to eat," said Rink.

"That would be good," said May.

He walked her to the door, kissed her and then headed to Columbus.

Owen and Sassy left the landing and headed up the river. They went out the mouth of Walnut Creek into the river and then went into Back Slough. Sassy sat in the front of the boat watching Owen. She had the marriage papers in her hand. They pulled into the landing on Big Island and Owen helped her out. He grabbed her bag and they headed to the house. He put her bag on the table and when he turned around, she was walking toward him. "I be Sassy Doe now, Owen, we be married," she said as she hugged him and kissed him.

"I know that, Sassy," he said, holding her close. "I got fish in the live basket I gotta clean and take to Hattie Mae," he said. "I didn't have time to git it all done this mornin' fore I left."

Sassy looked at him. "Owen, I be gonna go take off my clothes and git in the bed. Mattie made me take a bath this mornin' and put on good smellin' stuff, so I be ready." She stared in his eyes. "Them fish gonna still be there in the morning, but I might not be here if you ain't got good sense."

Owen laughed. "I be teasing you, Sassy," he said as he took her arm and guided her into the bedroom. He quickly undressed and then helped her do the same. Then he picked her up and put her in the bed. "I hope them fish can live for two days, cause I might not see 'em till then," he said as he pulled Sassy to him and kissed her.

18

It was past midnight when the truck came slowly up the road and went past the Shoal Creek sign and gate. The two men in the truck looked closely down the road toward the barn but didn't see anybody. They pulled over to the side of the road and parked. The men got out and each got a can from the back of the truck, climbed through the fence and ran down the road toward the barn. One of the men stopped at the near end of the barn and the other man went to the far end. They doused the wall with gasoline, lit a match and set the barn on fire.

The men threw the cans down and ran up the road to the gate. They went through the fence, jumped in the truck and drove away toward Columbus.

Rep was awakened by someone yelling and pounding on the front door. He jumped out of bed, ran to the window to look outside and that was when he saw the barn on fire.

Lila raised up in bed. "What is it?"

"The barn's on fire," he said as he was getting dressed.

"Oh Lord," she said as she got up and ran to the window.

Rep ran downstairs and out the front door. He could see several men bringing what they could save out of the part of the barn that wasn't on fire. It was obvious the fire was too far gone to have any hope of saving any part of the structure. He saw Mose and went over to him.

"They set it on fire," said Mose. "We found the gasoline cans."

"Walt Wend," said Rep.

Mose nodded. "That sho'nuff be the truth. He told us he gonna git us if we shut down the stills."

"I should have killed the bastard the other day," said Rep.

"That sho' be right," said Mose. "He ain't gonna stop till he be done hurt somebody."

"We have to stop him before that happens," said Rep.

The car pulled into River Bluff and drove slowly down the road into town. At two in the morning all the houses were dark, and the road was deserted. The car stopped at the dormitory. Two men grabbed flashlights, got out and went inside. They went to the first door in the hall on the right and kicked the door in. The first man went to Alva's room and burst in. She was awakened by the noise and sat up in bed. The man jumped on her. She screamed and he slapped her. He grabbed the front of her nightgown and ripped it off. He was on top of her and she couldn't move. His hands were all over her.

May was awakened by the noise of the door splintering. She always slept with her pistol under her pillow and her first reaction was to grab it. She raised up with the pistol in her hand. Suddenly her door swung open and a bright light was in her face. She heard Alva scream. She fired at the light and the form of a man standing in the door. He dropped the flashlight, turned around and started running away. May fired again. The bullet hit the man in the back and knocked him to the floor. He staggered up.

The man in Alva's room heard the shots, rolled off her and ran out the door. He saw his partner leaning against the wall and grabbed him. They went out the broken door into the hall and ran outside. They ran to their car, jumped in and headed out of town.

May jumped out of bed, turned on the light and ran to Alva's room. Alva was up, standing by the closet looking for something to put on. Her torn nightgown was on the floor.

"Are you alright?" asked May as she ran to her.

Alva nodded. "I'm alright."

"Did he hurt you?"

Alva shook her head. "I'm not hurt. He just scared me." She looked at May. "I heard a shot. Did you shoot?"

"Yes. I think I hit one of them."

"I hope you did," said Alva as she put on a housecoat.

One of the teachers from across the hall came rushing in. "I called Jim Hawke. He should be here in a minute." She looked at May. "Are you both alright?"

May nodded. "We're alright." She walked out into the other room and saw the blood on the floor and on the wall. "I did hit him," she said.

Jim Hawke came and listened to May and Alva's story. Other than knowing two men broke in and assaulted them, there was little else to go on. They couldn't identify the men; they'd never seen them clearly. They did know one of them was wounded, the blood on the floor and the wall proved that. May made it clear to Jim that Walt Wend was responsible for what happened; she had no doubt that was true. She told Jim the threats Walt had made.

Star arrived in a few minutes and told everybody that she was going to kill Walt Wend. Jim tried to calm her down, but she was adamant. After seeing that May and Alva were all right, she left. Everybody hoped that she hadn't gone to Phenix City looking for Walt.

Finally, as the sun was coming up, everybody left. A man from the mill came and installed a new door. Alva was getting ready for church as if nothing had happened. Since Alva was going, May got dressed to go too. She remembered that Rink had said he would pick them up after church to go eat.

Rep and Mose sat on the side of the hill and watched the barn burn. When the fire was discovered it was too far gone to be saved and they didn't have firefighting equipment anyway. The desk and some other furniture had been saved but not much.

"It's gonna be tough to rebuild the barn," said Rep. "Gonna cost a lot too."

"We got folks what can carpenter," said Mose. "We got plenty of timber too so we can git by. Ain't no need of buildin' no barn as big as that one was no how."

Rep agreed. "You know more about this stuff than anybody, so you take charge of building another barn."

Mose looked at him. "What we gonna do 'bout the stills?"

"Let 'em run till you fill up the warehouse so we'll have some for the other folks, then shut 'em down." He thought for a minute. "When the next truck comes from Phenix City, send them back empty and tell 'em there won't be no more whiskey."

"They be gonna come at us again," said Mose.

Rep nodded. "Walt sho' will if he's still alive. I done thought of that. I'm going to go see Lick. We gonna need him and his long rifle again." He got up and walked to the house. He knew Lila was upset about the barn.

Storm and Karen said goodbye to everybody at Walnut Creek after the wedding, got in the boat and came to River Bluff. They were going to Storm's parents to eat supper and had to hurry. When they got to the house they dressed and then went to the Gill house. It was the first time for Karen to meet them and she was nervous but after a few minutes she was at ease. They were nice people and were so kind to her.

After eating they sat around and talked. Karen was impressed with how she had been welcomed and Storm couldn't have been more attentive to her. She was rapidly falling in love with him and it seemed Storm was feeling the same way.

They came back to his house and got ready for bed. It had been a long day and they were tired. As she had the night before, Karen kissed Storm and then went to the guest bedroom.

Storm was asleep when he heard somebody pounding on the front door. He jumped out of bed, ran to the door and opened it. Jim Hawke was standing on the steps. "Sorry to bother you, Storm, but come look at this," he said and walked out on the drive.

Storm didn't understand what was going on, but he followed him. Jim pointed toward the river and Georgia. "Somethin' sho'nuff big is burning over at Shoal Creek," he said.

Storm looked where Jim was pointing and saw the fire and huge plume of black smoke filling the sky across the river. "Is that at Shoal Creek?" he asked.

Jim nodded.

"Karen is here with me," he said. "I've got to go tell her."

Jim grabbed his arm. "Wait a minute, Storm," Jim said, "I have something else to tell you." He told him about the two men breaking in May and Alva's apartment at the dormitory.

"Are they all right?" asked Storm.

"They weren't hurt, just scared." Jim chuckled. "May shot one of 'em, but he got away."

"I spect Karen will want to go to Shoal Creek," said Storm. "I'll let you know what I find out, Jim," he said as he ran in the house.

When Storm got inside, Karen was up and waiting for him. He quickly told her about the fire across the river.

"I hope it's not the house on fire and everybody's all right," she said.

"Get dressed and we'll go over there and see what's going on," said Storm.

They hurried and in a few minutes were ready. They went outside, got in the car and headed to the landing.

Storm looked at Karen. “Jim said that two men broke into the dormitory and assaulted Alva and May during the night. He said they were all right. He said May shot one of the men, but they got away.”

Karen looked at him. “May shot one of them?”

Storm nodded. “May always carries a pistol. She showed it to me.”

Karen stared at him. “May was a stripper, carries a pistol and shoots people,” said Karen. “I’m beginning to wonder about you, Storm, and what you’ve been into.”

He laughed. “I was beginning to wonder about myself too.” He got to the landing, parked and they ran to the boat. One of the old men hollered at him. “What’s all the smoke across the river, Storm?”

He yelled back. “I don’t know. I’m going over to find out.”

They got in the boat, Storm cranked up and they headed up the river. They got to the Shoal Creek landing, got out and hurried up the hill. When they got to the kitchen, they saw the smoldering remains of the barn. Relieved it wasn’t the house, they went on down the road.

Storm saw Rep and Mose near the remains of the barn, so he headed toward them. Karen headed to the house.

Rep saw Storm coming. “What happened?” said Storm as he met him.

“Somebody set it on fire,” said Rep.

Storm shook his head. “Who would do that?”

“Whiskey people,” said Rep. “Walt Wend.”

“They did it because you’re going to shut the stills down?”

Rep nodded. “That’s what we figure.”

Storm stared at Rep. “You remember me telling you about the girl from River Bluff that was working in the club for Walt Wend. She was having trouble with him because she quit.”

“Yes, I remember you saying that.”

“Two men broke into their rooms last night and assaulted her and her roommate. They figure Walt sent them to scare her into coming back to the club.”

“Damn,” said Rep. “Walt is causing trouble everywhere.”

"That seems to be the truth," said Storm. "What are you going to do?"

Rep looked at him and smiled. "It be best if you don't know nothin' bout what we gonna do. We plan to settle this for good."

Storm chuckled. "You might better hurry if you intend to get Walt. The Hobb women are after him too. You know the Hobbs; they don't fool around."

"Star Hobb and Walt met over here one time and agreed to get along. Seems that didn't last long," said Rep. "Anyway, we're not gonna wait on the Hobbs to take care of Walt. We'll take care of him ourselves."

Karen ran in the house and up to Lila's room. She was feeding Rip. "They burned the barn down," Karen said.

Lila nodded. "Rep thinks it was Walt Wend's men."

Karen then told Lila about the attack on the women in River Bluff. "They say it was Walt Wend's men that did that."

Lila shook her head. "Somebody needs to do something about him. I'm afraid Rep will do it and get in trouble."

"I have some news," said Karen.

Lila looked at her, questioning.

"Storm asked me to marry him."

Lila was surprised. "So quick? What did you say?"

"I told him to wait three weeks and make sure, then ask me again.

Lila smiled. "I'm glad for you. He seems to be a good man."

Karen nodded. "He is." She got up. "I'm going to go find him. I plan to keep him close for the next three weeks." She ran out the door.

~

Walt Wend was irate. He stared at the man standing in front of his desk. "I told you to scare them, not kill them. You kicked the door down and went in their room. Damn it, you're going to have every Hobb in the country after my ass."

"Hell," said the man. "We didn't know the bitch had a gun. She damn near killed Horace."

Walt stood up. "She should have killed both of you for being so stupid. Get your ass out of here."

The man ran out the door, glad to get away.

Walt thought about his situation. The idiots he'd sent to let May know he had the power to do harm to her or her friends had really screwed it up. He wanted to get May back but didn't want to get Star riled. He had to think of a way to get all this settled down.

The situation with Shoal Creek was different. He had threatened them before, and they had backed down. Burning the barn was severe but he wanted them to understand he meant business. He especially wanted Rep Doe to know he couldn't hit him and get away with it. He would send somebody out there to make sure they kept the stills operating.

His thoughts went back to Star. He would put a guard on the door in case she showed up at the club. He would also have a couple of his men drive him around for the next few days in case she came after him. After a few days everything should settle down and he would talk to May.

Owen was awake. He looked at Sassy sleeping beside him. They had got in the bed when they arrived at the cabin and hadn't left it. All the pent-up desire they had built up in the past days had erupted and they couldn't get enough of each other. He had thought about bedding her for days, but he'd never imagined the feelings it would generate when it happened.

He quietly slipped out of the bed, trying not to wake her. He had to go fish his hooks and dress the fish he'd left in the live basket. He was dressing when he heard her move. He looked around and she was staring at him.

"Where you be goin'?" she asked.

He walked to the bed, leaned over and kissed her. "I've got to go fish the hooks."

She looked up at him and smiled. "Maybe you stay in bed with me a bit longer."

He looked at her and shook his head. "Girl, I be bout tuckered out now. I don't know bout keepin' up with you."

She laughed and climbed out of bed. "You go fish the hooks and I be fixin' breakfast when you get back. Then I help you clean them fish." She cut her eyes at him. "Then we git back in bed."

Owen walked over and slapped her on the rear. "You ain't got good sense, girl." He walked to the door, opened it, stepped outside and saw the smoke. "Sassy, come here," he said.

She ran to the door and he showed her the smoke. "There be somethin' big on fire," he said. "I better go and see bout it."

"You wait," said Sassy. "I be going with you." She ran inside, dressed and came out. They got in the boat and headed up Back Slough. They got to the landing and ran up the hill past the kitchen where they saw the remnants of the barn, still smoking. They ran down to where Rep and Storm were standing.

"What happened?" said Owen as they ran up.

"Walt Wend's people set it on fire," said Rep. He looked at Owen. "What are you doing here anyway? I thought you'd still be in bed."

Owen frowned at him. "Be quiet," he said. "don't let her hear you."

Rep laughed. "Sassy," he said, "what you doing up here? Owen done give out on you after one night."

Sassy looked at him and walked over and hugged Owen. "He done good; we just be learning. When we git back we gonna learn some more."

Rep looked at Owen. "Sounds like Sassy has plans for you." He laughed. "You better take it now; she'll cool off before long."

Owen wanted to change the subject. "What y'all gonna do bout this?"

Rep shook his head. "Don't worry bout it. We'll take care of it."

"I gotta go fish my hooks," said Owen. "Ain't nothin we can do up here." He looked around at Sassy. "Come on, we gotta go fishin'."

"He's ready to go home, Sassy," said Rep. "You take good care of 'im now."

She looked at Rep and laughed. "You don't be worryin' bout Owen," she said as she walked away. "That boy gonna be hollering calf rope 'fore long."

Rep laughed as he watched Owen and Sassy walk up the hill.

May and Alva were in the room when Star walked in. May was relieved to see her. "I was afraid you had gone to find Walt and kill him," said May.

"I'm gonna kill him," said Star, "but it ain't gonna be easy. You know if he's killed, we're the first people they will come looking for. Anyway, I expect he's gonna have people with him all the time. He knows I'll be after him."

"You need to let the law handle this," said Alva. "enough people have already been hurt."

Star looked at her. "My daddy and two brothers have been killed, Alva. The law hasn't done nothing and they ain't gonna do nothing. We can't just sit here and let Walt do as he wants."

"I understand your feelings," said Alva, "but this is wrong to meet violence with violence. How many people have you already shot and what did it solve?"

Star shrugged. "Walt has been behind all of this and when we stop him, it all stops." She looked at Alva. "If May hadn't had that pistol and shot that man, what do you think would have happened to you?"

Alva stared at Star. "I expect you are going to do whatever you want. I worry about both of you." She turned and walked to her room.

Star looked at May. "We need to talk to Josie. She can tell us what Walt is up to."

I'll call her tonight," said May.

Alva walked out of her room. She looked at May. "I'm going to church. It would be good if both of you went."

"I'll go with you," said May. "Rink is supposed to pick us up after church." She went to her room and got her purse.

Star started to the door. "I'll talk to you tomorrow, May," she said as she left.

Alva and May followed her out the door. They were almost to the church when they saw the smoke across the river. "Something is burning across the river," said Alva. They walked in the church.

Rink was waiting when they came out of the church. He ran over, opened the door for Alva and May to get in. May told him what had happened during the night.

"They broke the door down and one man went after Alva and the other one came in my room," said May. She looked at Rink. "I had my pistol and I shot him."

Rink looked from May to Alva. "Were either of you hurt?"

May shook her head. "He never got in my room, but the other man slapped Alva and ripped her dress off. They ran away when I shot."

"That's terrible," said Rink, looking at Alva. He looked back at May. "Do you think it was that Walt Wend?"

"Had to be," said May. "Nobody else had any reason to attack us."

"Do you feel like going to eat?" asked Rink.

May leaned over against him and put her hand on his arm. "Yes, we'll be all right."

Rink, at that moment, would have done anything May asked him to do.

They went to Landon, ate dinner and came back to the dormitory.

Alva thanked Rink for taking them and went inside. May stayed with him for the next hour in the car. She had decided that she liked Rink and wanted to be with him. She kissed him and led him to feel comfortable with her. She pushed him and led him to where he had his hands all over her. He had already seen her naked on the stage, so she let him do as he wished to a point, then she stopped him.

"When can I see you again?" he asked.

"Call me Tuesday," she said, then we'll set up something." She kissed him, got out and went inside.

Rink watched her go. He was in love.

May went inside and called Josie. She told her what had happened. Josie knew nothing about it and was upset. "That bastard," she said. "He told me to come see you and tell you he'd offer you more money if you'd come back. I can't believe he done this to you."

"Have you seen him since last night?"

"No. I left the club after the show and I didn't see him again," said Josie. She paused. "What are you gonna do about this?"

"I don't know," said May, "but I don't want Alva to get hurt because of me."

"If he hurts Alva, I'll kill the bastard myself," said Josie.

May laughed. "I may want you to help me do that, Josie."

"You just tell me what you want me to do, May. I'm bout tired of 'im anyway."

I'll let you know," said May. She hung up the phone.

19

Mose and Rep were at the remains of the barn. Several men were working gathering up any wood left and burning it.

"Put a lock on the gate and put a guard there," said Rep. "I don't want to be surprised if somebody comes. Also, during the day, I want two guards with rifles in the woods covering this area. Put a guard at the landing too.

"You reckon Walt's gonna come see us?" said Mose.

"You sent that truck back with word we're shutting the stills down, didn't you?"

Mose nodded. "I sho' did."

"Then I expect Walt to come and he won't be stupid enough to come alone," said Rep.

Storm and Karen sat on the steps of the big house and talked. "What are your thoughts for the next several days? asked Storm.

"You have to work, and I want to spend some time with Lila and Rip, so I'll stay here for a few days," said Karen. "Lila is upset about the barn burning and what Rep is going to do. She's afraid he will kill Walt Wend. That's what he told her."

Storm chuckled. "After Walt's people came in on Alva and May across the river, I expect the Hobbs are after Walt too."

Karen looked at him. "I'm sure that's true since your girlfriend carries a pistol and shoots people." She looked at him. "I still have doubts about you and her."

Storm stood up. "I'll tell you what. That Brother Snow that married Sassy and Owen lives just down the river. If you still question me, you get your butt up right now and I'll take you to him and we'll get married today." He looked down at her.

"You'd really do that?" Karen said, looking up at him.

Storm was tight lipped as he stared at her. "I would."

She stood up, hugged and kissed him. "I believe you. Let's wait till the three weeks are up and then maybe we'll go see Brother Snow."

He nodded. "I'll come back Thursday and get you and you can stay with me through the weekend."

"That suits me," she said.

He kissed her, headed to the landing and went across the river.

May got home from school Monday afternoon, got in her car and headed for Phenix City. She said noththing to Alva about leaving. She got to the club and went into the parking lot. She saw Walt's car in his parking place. She got out and started toward the back door. Two men standing at the door were watching her.

She walked up to them, took her pistol out of her purse and handed it to them. "That's all I have," she said.

"All right, May," said one of the men, "you can go in."

She went inside, looked in the dressing room but Josie wasn't there. She walked down the hall, up the stairs and into Walt's office.

He was sitting behind his desk and looked up when she walked in. He leaned back in the chair and stared at her. "I trust the guards got your pistol."

"I gave it to them," she said. "If I still had it, I'd shoot your stupid ass for breaking in on me and Alva."

He stood up. "I apologize for that, May. They were supposed to let you know that I could come after you, not attack you."

"You scared Alva half to death."

"I'll have to do something to make it up to her. I really like Alva." He looked at her. "You're here, so I hope you have come to your senses and plan to come back."

"That's why I'm here," said May. "But only if you leave me and my folks alone."

"There won't be any more trouble," said Walt. He walked around the desk and came behind May. He put his hands on her shoulders. "You know I've always liked you, May. I could be mighty good to you if you'll be good to me." He rubbed her shoulder and his hands moved down on the front of her dress. May didn't move.

He unbuttoned the top of the dress and slid his hand inside. "You know I want you, May. I always have and it's not like we haven't already been together. Come on in the bedroom with me."

May took his hand out of her dress. "If you promise to leave us alone, I'll stay with you this weekend," she said. "I'll be here Friday night and I'll go with you after the show."

He pulled her to him and kissed her. She put her arms around him and returned his kiss. She stepped away and looked at him. "I'll see you Friday."

He put his arm around her and walked with her to the door. "I'll be looking for you Friday."

She went down the stairs and out the door. As she looked at the girls in the dressing room, she realized how much she missed being here and on stage. There was something about it that drew her to it. Shaking her head, she went out the door. The men handed her the pistol, she got in the car and headed back to River Bluff. She had to decide what she was going to do between now and Friday.

~

May pulled into the dormitory and parked. She got out, walked to the street and looked toward the stores. She could see Jim sitting on his bench and Storm's car parked in front of the gym. She didn't see Storm and wondered where he was. She stood there for a minute thinking about her options. She made up her mind and started walking toward Jim.

She was almost to Jim's bench when she saw Storm come out of the store with Mrs. Williams. They were standing on the porch talking. She saw Storm look toward her and his eyes were on her as she approached. Suddenly, the desire to be with him came over her. She had felt it when she saw his car and it was even stronger now. She returned his look and walked on toward Jim.

"Well, little girl, you settled down after all the excitement Saturday night?" he asked.

Out of the corner of her eye she saw Storm leave the store porch and come across the street toward her. "We're all right," she said as Storm walked up beside her. She could feel him standing so near...

He punched her on the shoulder. "Shot anybody lately?" he said, looking at her and grinning.

She looked around at him. "It's not any of your business what I do," she answered. His closeness was bothering her.

He laughed, "I'm certainly glad I'm not responsible for what you do."

Jim sat and looked from one to the other. He knew there were feelings between these two that neither of them knew existed. He decided to get out of the way and let them work it out. "I'll see ya'll later," he said as he walked to his car.

Storm stared at May. "I hear you have a new man in your life. I saw that fancy car he drives."

"That's my business," she said. "He's nice, I like him." She looked at him. "You got a woman too. Is she good to you?"

"Better than anybody ever has been."

She shook her head and smiled. "You know that's a lie."

They stood in front of Jim's bench staring into each other's eyes.

They both felt the attraction that had always been there. Each wanted to speak about how they felt but neither wanted to be first.

Storm stepped closer to her, almost touching her and looked down at her. "I have my car here."

She felt his closeness as she looked at him. "What does that mean?"

"Thought you might like to ride somewhere with me."

"Why would I want to do that?" she asked. She looked around as Jim's car pulled away, then looked back at Storm, her eyes on his face. "Like where?"

"You used to like to go to the river with me."

"For what now?"

"Maybe talk."

"Is that all?" Her eyes were boring into him, daring him to say more. She knew where she was leading him.

Storm stared at her; he could feel his heart beating. "You know I want you. I admit I do." He paused. "I think you want me too."

She took a deep breath and shook her head. "Not in a car," she said.

"What about my house?"

She nodded and they started walking toward his car. He ran over and opened the door for her, and she got in. Neither of them had any control over what they were doing, their animal desire had taken over. He started the car and drove out the road. She sat on the far side of the seat until they reached his house. He opened her door, she got out, he pulled her to him and kissed her.

"You know this is crazy," she said.

"Yes, I know."

They ran inside, each shedding clothes as they ran through the house into the bedroom. When they got to the bed, they were naked. They fell on the bed and all the feelings and pent-up, raw emotions took over. They were equally to blame for what was happening. Despite all of what they had gone through before, what was in their hearts took command.

Later they held each other tightly, wrapped up together. Despite not wanting to, they were of one mind.

"I don't want to like you," May said. "You know I can't be with you."

"I know that."

"I'm going with Rink."

"Is that his name?"

She nodded.

"You saw me with Karen. She is a nice woman."

"I'm sure she is."

They lay close with their thoughts, eyes staring into eyes.

"So, what do we do now?" said Storm.

"Like what?"

He kissed her. "Stay the night with me."

"Yes, we've gone this far," said May. "Might as well go all the way."

Storm smiled. "I would say that is true."

"I've got to go to school in the morning. Alva will think I've been kidnapped." said May.

"I've got to go to work early too," said Storm. "I'll get you up." He pulled her to him again and she responded.

They were up early, ate breakfast and got in the car. As they passed the gym on the way to the dormitory, Jim was sitting on the bench. May waved to him and he waved back. "No sense in keeping anything from Jim," she said. "He knows everything anyway.

He parked at the dormitory and looked at her. "You know we can't do this again if we're not going to be together."

"Yes, I know."

"I have to stay away from you, May. You know why."

She smiled. "I know why. I'm a Hobb."

Storm glared at her. "When you say that I want to kick your butt."

She laughed, leaned over and kissed him and got out. She smiled at him and ran inside.

When May walked in Alva was about to leave for school. "I was worried about you," she said.

"I spent the night with Storm."

Alva looked at her, surprise on her face. "You stayed with Storm. How did that happen?"

May smiled. "He wanted me, and I wanted him, so we made it happen."

Alva frowned. "May, there is a time and place for everything. You need to learn that." She walked out the door.

"They sent the truck back empty," screamed Walt into the phone. "I have two people here with me. You get three more men in your car and meet me here. We're going to teach these stupid bastards who's in charge at Shoal Creek." He went downstairs, got in the car with the driver and another man. When the other car arrived, they headed for Shoal creek.

Rep and Mose were at the kitchen when they saw the two cars at the Shoal Creek gate and men talking to the guard there. "Looks like we got visitors," said Rep as he started down the hill to the old barn area. He looked at Mose. "Go through the woods and make sure the guards are ready." Mose turned off and went into the woods.

Rep walked on down the road. He could see the guard running from the gate. He met him at the barn area.

"Them men at the gate said they want to talk to you and if we don't open the gate, they're going to shoot the lock off," said the guard. "They all got guns. He said his name was Walt Wend."

"I know who he is," said Rep. "You go tell him to crawl through the fence and he can come down with one man. I'll meet him halfway. Tell the other men if they come through the fence, I have men ready to kill them."

The guard was confused. "You want me to tell him that?"

Rep nodded. "Yes. Don't just stand here. Go tell 'im."

The guard turned and ran toward the gate. Rep walked on down and watched the guard talking to the group. Then he saw Walt and one man climb through the gate and start down the road toward him. Rep waited.

Walt stopped a few feet away from him and stared. Rep could see the arrogance in his face. The man with him, armed with a rifle, stood behind him. He also was staring at Rep.

Rep held his hand in the air and stared at the man with the rifle. "I have three men with rifles aimed at you," he said. "If I wave my hand, they're gonna kill you. You put your rifle down right now and go back to the gate. Tell those people up there that I have ten men with rifles watching them. If they start anything, they'll all be killed. Tell the four men in the second car that I want them gone. Tell them to leave right now or we'll start shooting."

Walt looked at the man. "Don't believe him, George. He's bluffing."

"Walt, you're a fool. You think I wasn't gonna be ready for you after you burned my barn down?" Rep looked at the other man. "George, if I fall to the ground, both you and Walt will be dead men. Put the rifle down and go."

George stared at him for a moment, put the rifle on the ground and started running up the road. Rep watched him until he got to the gate where he was excitedly talking to the men.

Walt looked at Rep. "Next time I'll come with more men and we'll tear this place down."

Rep shook his head. "Walt, for a man that's supposed to be smart, you act mighty stupid. You're down here with me by yo'self. Why the hell do you think you're going to leave here alive?"

Rep watched the gate. Four of the men got in one of the cars and left. "Looks like yo' army's bout gone," he said.

For the first time Walt realized he'd made a bad mistake. He was standing in the middle of the road with a man that had already blackened his eye with just a slap. "I'm sorry about the barn, Rep. I'll pay you for it. I just want to get the stills running."

Rep shook his head. "Don't you understand nothin', Walt? The stills are down." He walked forward and hit him in the jaw, knocking him backward. The second blow put him on the ground. Walt had never been in a fight with a man in his life; he had only hit women and was no match for Rep. He finally staggered on his feet and Rep hit him several times, then put him down again. His face was a mess. A blow to his midsection broke several ribs. Finally, Rep waved to the men at the gate to come get him and he walked away.

The two men came through the gate and down the road to where Walt was lying. They kept their eyes on Rep all the way. They helped Walt to his feet and had to almost carry him to the car. Every time they moved him, he moaned, the broken ribs were painful. Both eyes were swollen, and his mouth was bleeding. They finally got him through the gate, into the car and headed toward Columbus.

Karen and Lila were in the house watching the confrontation between Rep and Walt. "All of them have guns and Rep doesn't have one," said Karen.

"Mose and the other men are in the trees and they have guns," said Lila. "Rep knows what he's doing."

They watched as the man put his rifle down and ran to the gate. Then one of the cars left.

"Why did they leave?" asked Karen.

Before Lila could answer Rep walked forward and hit Walt and knocked him down. They watched the onslaught.

"My God," said Karen, "he's going to kill him." She looked at Lila. "Did you know Rep was like this?"

Lila smiled. "I've seen him in action before. People here on the farm know not to mess with him."

They watched as Rep walked away and the two men came from the gate and carried Walt to the car.

"I've never seen anything like that," said Karen.

~

May walked out of the school building and saw Storm's car parked on the other side of the parking lot. She was surprised to see him there. He was sitting in the front seat watching her. She walked around to the passenger side, got in and looked at him. "Why are you here?"

Storm smiled. "Last night was exciting but unplanned. There were things said and I wanted to make sure you were all right."

"I'm not sure what you're talking about."

"You're going with somebody and so am I. It's going to be hard to do that if every time we see each other we end up in the bed."

She looked at him. "If you're complaining, I just won't do it again."

He shook his head and laughed. "I can't believe we're having this conversation." He looked at her. "If you would marry me, we wouldn't have this problem."

"I'm not going to do that; we've already talked about it."

"I know that," he said. "Karen thinks I'm in love with you."

May looked at him. "Are you?"

"You know I have better sense than to be in love with you," he said smiling.

"What are you going to do about her?"

"I don't know. What are you going to do?" he asked.

"I'll date Rink, but I'm not getting married."

"So, if you're not married and I'm not married," said Storm, "when we see each other, we can do what we want. Is that what you think?"

She shook her head and looked at him. "Storm, you have a reputation to worry about. I don't worry about what people say, but you need to watch what you do."

He took her hand. "Come with me to the house tonight."

"I don't have much sense but I'm not going to do that." She

opened the door and got out. She leaned back in the car. "But I will sometime." She closed the door and walked away.

Storm started the car and drove away.

When May got to the dormitory, she saw Rink's car in the driveway. She had forgotten she told him to come back Tuesday. She walked on to the car; he was inside waiting. She opened the passenger door and got in. He reached for her and she held up her hands and backed away.

Surprised by her rejection, he looked at her.

"Wait a minute, Rink," she said. "I need to talk to you. I'm dealing with a personal problem right now and I have to work it out before I can be with you."

His brow furrowed and he stared at her. "What kind of problem? Maybe I can help."

She shook her head. "No, I have to get it fixed and until then I can't see you." She took a deep breath. "I like you, Rink, but I have to clear this up and then I'll let you know what's going on."

"When will you let me know?"

"I'm not sure, but by the weekend."

"You can't go with me tonight?"

"No, I can't."

"Are you in trouble?"

May smiled. "No, I'm not in trouble. It's nice of you to be concerned." She opened the door. "I'll let you know," she said as she got out. She ran down the hill and into the dormitory.

A disappointed Rink watched her go.

Josie walked in the club Tuesday evening and started toward the dressing room. She noticed a man standing on the far side of the room staring at her. She knew who he was, she had seen him at the club before and Walt had told her he was one of the owners. She had never met him.

He started walking toward her and called her name. "Josie," he said as he walked up to her. She stopped and looked at him.

"I'm Paul Witt," he said. "We've never met but I need to talk to you."

"Yes, suh," said Josie. She had no idea what this was about. She looked around. Walt was usually waiting for her, but she didn't see him.

"Josie," he said. "Call me Paul. I wanted you to know that I'm running the club now," he said. "If you need anything or have a problem, you come see me."

Josie stared at him. "Where is Walt?"

"Walt is in the hospital," he said. "He got into a fight with someone at Shoal Creek and was badly hurt." He looked at her. "Walt will not be back at the club; he has been replaced as manager."

Josie was shocked and concerned.

He saw the look on her face. "I see you are surprised by this news, Josie. I understand you had a relationship with Walt and lived in an apartment that he paid for."

She nodded.

"Don't worry about that, Josie." He smiled. "You are important to the club and we'll take care of the apartment for you."

"Walt ain't comin' back?"

"No, he won't be back," he said. "Walt used poor judgement and made some bad decisions that hurt our business and caused unnecessary trouble." He glanced at her. "It seemed he got the bad end of some of those decisions. Does Walt being gone upset you?"

Josie was surprised by the question. Men didn't usually ask her what she thought about anything. They just told her what they wanted. She wondered what Paul wanted. He was a nice-looking younger man. He looked to be about thirty-five or so, clean-cut and dressed nicely.

"Walt was all right to me," she said. "I don't really care if he's gone or not."

Paul's eyes were on her. "What if I wanted to come to the apartment to visit you?"

Her lips tightened. "Do you?"

He shook his head and smiled. "No, Josie, I don't. All I ask you to do is be on stage." He looked back at her. "But there is one other thing. Are you from Shoal Creek, seems someone said that?"

Josie nodded. "I come from Shoal Creek."

"Do you know Rep Doe? He's the man that hurt Walt."

"I know Rep. Walt was stupid to mess with Rep. Rep is sho'nuff tough."

Paul laughed. "I think Walt found that out." He took her arm. "Come in the viewing room with me and let's talk a minute." He opened the door to what had been Walt's private room, they walked in and sat down. He looked at her. "I've never met Rep, but I'm told he runs Shoal Creek. He shut down the stills and cut off our whiskey supply, because of a disagreement with Walt. I want to fix that. Could you go to Shoal Creek tomorrow morning and set up a meeting with Rep?"

"I can do that; I've done it before."

"That's good. You set the meeting up, let me know and I'll come tomorrow afternoon and meet with him."

"I'll do that," said Josie.

Paul patted her on the arm. "You're a smart woman, Josie. I think we'll get along."

"That's up to you," she said. "You know where I live."

May was in her room when the phone rang. She picked it up and answered.

"May, this is Josie."

"Hey, Josie. How are you?"

"I wanted to tell you that Walt ain't at the club no more. They fired 'im."

"What happened?"

"I talked to some of the men at the club and they told me Rep Doe beat the hell out of Walt and he's in the hospital," said Josie. "They say he's in bad shape. They say his head is messed up."

"I'm glad Walt's out of the club," said May. "He was a bastard. What are you going to do about your apartment?"

"There's a real nice man running the club now, his name is Paul Witt. He said I didn't have to worry bout my apartment, I could stay in it."

"Thanks for calling me, Josie," said May. "Let me know if you hear anything else."

"I will," said Josie.

May hung up the phone and looked at Alva, who was sitting on the couch. "That was good news. Josie said Walt Wend has been fired at the club, another man is in charge. She said Walt got in a fight over at Shoal Creek and is in the hospital."

Alva shook her head. "I don't have any sympathy for him. He is a terrible man."

"I agree," said May. "If he's not with the club, then he should let me alone."

"What about Josie," asked Alva, "will she be all right?"

"Sounded like it. She seemed to like the new man at the club."

20

Rep was at the barn clean up area early the next morning when he saw a car at the gate. The guard was talking to the driver. He watched as the guard unlocked and opened the gate. The car started down the road toward him. As it got closer, he saw a woman was driving and then he recognized Josie. She pulled on down, stopped and got out.

"Well, Josie, it's been a while since we've seen you," he said.

"Mornin', Rep," she said. She looked at the area where the barn had been. "I heard they burned your barn down."

"Yes, they did," said Rep.

"Well, you won't have to worry about Walt anymore," she said. "He's in the hospital and the people said you beat the hell out of him."

"He burned my barn down and came up here and threatened me and my people. Walt was a idiot." Rep shook his head. "He better not come up here again."

Josie laughed. "They fired him at the club. He ain't gonna be there no more."

"That's good. I don't want to ever see them whiskey people again," said Rep.

"There's a new man in charge of the club, Rep. He wants to talk to you about the stills. He sent me up here to get you to meet with 'im. He seems like a nice man; his name is Paul Witt."

Rep shook his head. "We're all finished with the whiskey, Josie. All it's done is cause trouble and we're shutting the stills down."

Josie nodded. "I know that, all the time there's been shootin' and killin'. Paul wanted to talk to you, that's all he said. He don't want no trouble neither. They fired Walt cause he got in trouble."

"You go back and tell 'im that we 're through with whiskey," said Rep. "We're just gonna run the farm now."

"I'll tell 'im," said Josie. She got in the car and went out the gate.

Josie drove back to the club, parked and went inside. She walked up stairs and into Paul's office. He was sitting at the desk and looked up as she walked in. "I went to Shoal Creek and talked to Rep, but he said he ain't gonna make no more whiskey. He say he's done shut the stills down." She watched Paul for his reaction. Walt had always reacted to bad news with cussing and raising hell. She watched his face.

Paul shrugged. "That's too bad. We'll have to find another source. I appreciate you going and talking to him, Josie." He motioned to a chair. "Sit down and let's talk for a bit," he said.

Josie sat in the chair, her eyes on him. She knew something else was coming, it always did when she talked to a man.

"I told you that the apartment was yours, you can stay there as long as you want. There's no strings attached; all you do is work at the club." He looked at her. "I want to make sure you understand that."

She nodded. "That was what you told me."

"I just wanted to make sure you understand it that way. You don't have to do anything you don't want to." He looked at her, questioning.

She nodded again. "I said I know that."

Paul got up, walked around the desk and sat in the chair next to her. "You don't know me, Josie but I've watched you on the stage and off. You handle yourself well. I also know that you're smarter than you act and talk." He smiled. "Am I right?"

She looked at him and chuckled. "You be doing the talkin'."

He laughed. "I am doing the talking. My point is this. I live alone in a big house in Columbus. I have a maid and a cook and a yardman that look after me. I have a good life. If you'd like to, I'm asking you to leave the apartment and come live in my house with me." He leaned back and watched her face.

"I can stay in the apartment if I want to?"

He nodded. "Yes, you can."

She looked at him, her eyes on his face. "I think I like you," she said. "Could I go today?"

"Whenever you want."

"I don't have much stuff, so it won't take me long to pack. Would you come to the apartment in about an hour and let me follow you to your house?"

"I'll do that," he said as he got up.

Josie stood up and quickly kissed him. "It won't take me long to be ready," she said as she started for the door.

Paul, smiling, watched her leave.

Thursday afternoon Storm rode to the landing, got in the boat and went up the river to Shoal Creek. He landed and headed to the house. He had promised Karen he would get her today and she would spend the weekend with him. He viewed his dalliance with May as just that, a one-time unplanned event that had happened and would never happen again. He intended to stay away from May in the future and give all his attention to Karen. She was the type of woman he needed for a wife.

He walked up the steps and knocked. Karen opened the door and looked at him. He stepped in, pulled her to him and kissed her. She put her arms around him and kissed him back. Finally, they both turned loose.

"I was waiting for you," she said.

He smiled. "I was hoping you would be. I've missed you."

She took his hand and led him to her room. "I'm all packed and ready to go," she said. "Let me go tell Lila bye and then we can go." She ran out and shortly was back. Storm picked up her bag and they went out the door. When they got to the landing Owen was getting out of the boat with a bucket of fish.

"How are you and Sassy doing?" asked Storm.

"We be doin' good," said Owen.

They got in the boat, Storm cranked up and they headed across the river. They landed, Karen spoke to the old men gathered around and they went to the house. They went inside and Storm carried her bag to the guest room. She took his hand and led him over to the sofa, she sat down and pulled him down beside her. She leaned over in his face and stared at him. "We've been apart for several days now and I know you've had time to think about us. I want you to tell me where you are with me right now."

"You are a mighty pushy woman," he said.

She shook her head. "Don't avoid the subject. Answer my question."

"All right," he said. "You seem intent on rushing me about this, so I'll answer you." He took her hand and looked in her eyes, his face serious. "Will you marry me?"

She gasped. She had expected him to say something to her, but his offer of marriage surprised her. She nodded. "Yes, I'll marry you."

He kissed her. "I don't have a ring but tomorrow we'll go get one and make it official."

"This makes me very happy, Storm. I had hoped you would ask me. I will be a good wife to you and make you happy."

"I know you will, Karen. I don't know what you think about timing, but I'd like to have you in my house as soon as we can." He looked at her. "What do you think?"

"I agree. I'm settled at Shoal Creek now, just across the river, so I have no reason to wait."

Storm took her hand. "My family is an important part of this town as you know. You will be part of the family and you will be living here in River Bluff. If you don't object, I would like for us to get married here and that way the people can get to know you."

"I understand that, Storm and I agree. We'll need a little time to get it planned and I'd like for my family from Atlanta to be here too."

"We'll need to talk to my folks and maybe you and Mother can decide what you want to do."

She smiled and kissed him. "That sounds perfect. We'll start on all that tomorrow." She got up and took his hand. "I spent those nights in the guest room and about went crazy. I'm not going to do that again." She led him into the bedroom and started undressing. "I intend to stay in this bed with you till morning."

Storm started taking off his shirt. "Sounds like a good plan to me."

~

Storm was up early Friday morning as usual, although he'd had little sleep. He was going to let Karen sleep as long as she wanted. He went in, made coffee and sat in the kitchen and had two cups. The night had been good. While his night with May had been exciting and passionate, this night with Karen, while also exciting and passionate, had been special. This had been the first of a long-term relationship and he looked forward to it.

In a while Karen came padding barefoot into the kitchen, walked over and sat in his lap. She took his coffee cup and drank, then looked at him grimacing. "You drink it black," she said.

"Sure, I do," he said. "Don't you?"

She turned up her nose and frowned. "I want cream and lots of sugar."

He laughed. "You are a sissy."

She hugged him. "We have a lots to learn about each other."

He nodded. "Yes, we do." He kissed her. "I learned a lot about you last night."

She looked at him. "Are you complaining?"

He smiled. "None at all."

She laughed and jumped up. "I have to take a shower."

"I'll go with you," he said, starting to get up.

She pushed him back in the chair. "No, you don't. I had enough of you last night. I need some time to recover."

He laughed and sat back down.

They dressed and left the house. Storm wanted to go see Jim and tell him the news. He knew that Jim would quickly spread it all over town. They talked with Jim for a while and then went to the mill office and saw Mr. Gill. He congratulated them, hugged Karen and welcomed her into the family.

Storm then introduced Karen to the office staff. Their last stop was to the Gill house where they told Mrs. Gill the news and she and Karen spent the next two hours discussing plans for the wedding. They decided the date would be two weeks away on Saturday. That would give Karen's mother time to make her plans and get there.

Karen was happy when they left and headed back to their house. "Everything has worked out perfectly," she said.

"I'm glad," said Storm. "You and Mother seemed to get along well."

"Yes, we did. She is very sweet."

When they got to the house Storm told Karen he had to go to the mill and take care of a few things.

"That's good" she said. "I can take a nap." She kissed him. "I can be rested for tonight."

He shook his head. "We'll see," he said as he went out the door."

When May came home from school Alva was already in the room. She looked up as May came in. "Did you hear the news?"

May shook her head. "What news?"

"Storm is engaged to Karen Hogan."

"How do you know that?" asked May, her face showing her surprise.

"Jim Hawke told me. They came up and told him." Alva looked at May. "That struck me as strange. Didn't you stay with Storm all night two nights ago?"

"Yes, I did."

Alva stared at May. "You slept with him. It didn't mean anything?"

May smiled. "Like I told you. He wanted me and I wanted him, so we did it. He liked it and I liked it so that's what it meant." She turned around. "By the way, I'm staying tonight and tomorrow with Josie. I'll be back Sunday."

"Are you going to the club?"

"Probably."

"I thought you were out of that."

"Walt is gone, and they have a new man there. Josie says he is nice and doesn't bother the girls."

"This is not good, May."

"I'm just going down to look."

"I'll pray for you, May," Alva said as she went to her room.

May left the room and went to the car. She headed toward Phenix city. She thought about Storm. She had turned him down again and he had found someone else. She pushed all these thoughts out of her mind and focused on what she was doing. She had tried to leave the club and the stage, but its attraction was too strong. It kept drawing her back. She realized her life wouldn't be what most people considered normal if she lived this way, but it seemed to be what she wanted.

She pulled into the lot at the club and parked. The guard at the door saw her coming. "Glad to have you back, May."

She went inside and all the girls in the dressing room hugged her when she came in. They all knew she was the drawing card and the crowds, and the tips had been smaller since she left. They were looking for better days with her back.

Josie came over to her. "I told Paul you were here. He wants to meet you." She whispered. "I'm livin' with 'im now."

May looked at her and smiled. She shook her head; Josie was going to survive. She followed Josie out. Paul was waiting for her. She knew who he was. She had seen him before but had never met him.

I'm Paul Witt," he said as he offered his hand. May shook hands. "We're glad to have you back."

"I'll stay as long as Walt isn't here bothering me," she replied.

"Walt won't be back, so he won't bother you."

She looked at him. "I understand the apartment is available. I'd like to stay in it on Friday and Saturday nights. It'll save me a lot of driving late at night."

"That's no problem. It's all yours."

"Thank you," she said and went with Josie to the dressing room. She went to the phone and called Rink. He answered. "Rink, this is May. I'm going to be on stage at the club tonight. Don't ask me any questions about it, I'll explain it later. But if you want to see me, come to the club. If it's a problem, I'll understand."

"I'll be there," he answered.

May dressed for the first time in some weeks and she was excited to be back. Josie went out on stage first as she usually did. When it was time for May to come out, the announcer said, "Here is May, the Princess." It wasn't planned, but from then on when May went out on stage, they announced her as "Princess".

May went out and she was on fire. The crowd erupted and she kept them pumped up. She moved to the edge of the stage and worked the men standing there holding money. She enjoyed the power she had to sway the crowd as she wished. She saw Rink standing back in the crowd and motioned for him to come to the door at the end of the stage. She stayed out through her act, then went through the curtain, ran to the door and opened it. She had on nothing but the G-string. He grabbed her and she let him hold her and kiss her.

She pulled back. "I've got to dress and then I'll meet you at the back door if you want to go with me. She turned and ran to the dressing room. When she came out, he was waiting at the door. "I'm staying at the apartment tonight. If you want to go with me, you can follow me over there," she said.

"I'll be right behind you."

She went outside, got in the car and left the parking lot. Rink was right behind her. She went across the river to Columbus and to the apartment. She got out and he ran up beside her. She opened the door and went inside.

"I've got to bathe," she said, I'm all sweaty. You sit down and I'll be out in a minute. She went to the bathroom, bathed, dried off and put on a robe. When she walked out Rink was on the couch. He started to get up, but she pushed him back down and sat beside him.

"You know that I never go out with men from the club," she said as she looked at him. "I wanted you to know you're being treated special, because I know you and I like you.

"I know that. I'm just glad to be with you."

"I told your mother that I had left the club. That was the truth when I said it, but now I've changed." May looked at Rink. "I won't be with you again unless she knows I'm at the club. I will not be sneaking around with you. Do you understand what I'm saying?"

Rink nodded. "I understand. I'll tell her."

"You're a grown man, Rink, and can do as you want, but I don't want to cause trouble in your family," said May. She stared at him. "I'm not worth the trouble."

"That's up to me to decide, May" said Rink. "Since you asked me, I'll tell Mother what you said. After I tell her, I'll make my own decision about what I do."

May smiled. "I'll be at the club tomorrow night, Rink. If you want to see me." She leaned over and kissed him. "Now it's time for you to go."

Rink got up and looked down at her. "I'll see you tomorrow night." He smiled, turned and went out the door.

~

May was asleep in the apartment the next morning when the phone rang. She struggled to get awake while wondering who could be calling. Josie and Rink were the only two people other than Paul that knew she was here.

She answered. "May, this is Paul. I'm sorry to wake you but I just got word that Walt is out of the hospital. He wasn't supposed to leave but he did, and the doctors say he is mentally unstable. They said that all week he has been ranting about killing several people, including you and myself. The list also includes your sister Star, someone named Alva and a man named Jim. You probably know these people."

"Yes, I know them," said May.

"Nobody knows where Walt is at this time and the police are looking for him," said Paul. "I'm going to send two men to your apartment. Keep the door locked and they should be there shortly. If you want to go home, I'll understand. Don't worry about tonight. Maybe they will catch Walt soon."

"I think I'll go home, Paul. I have to warn my friends about this," said May.

"Don't leave until my men get there. They'll follow you home and make sure you get there safely."

"Thank you, Paul. That is very nice of you." She hung up, got out of bed and dressed. She was watching at the window when the two men from the club got there. She went outside, got in the car and headed to River Bluff. The men followed her until she parked at the dormitory. She got out, thanked them and ran inside.

Alva was in her room. May quickly told her what was happening and then called Star. Star said she was coming to see her. May asked her to stop and tell Jim.

~

Rep was eating breakfast when the phone rang. He answered and a voice he didn't recognize said, "Rep, this is Paul Witt. You don't know me but I'm calling to warn you about Walt Wend. You may remember I sent Josie up to see you about operating the stills."

"Yes," Rep said, "I remember Josie saying your name. What is this about Walt?"

"He has escaped from the hospital. The doctors say he is all messed up in his head as a result of injuries. I understand you caused the injuries."

"That's right," said Rep.

"Well, he's threatened to kill several people, including you, so I wanted to warn you."

"I thank you for the call," said Rep, "but we're pretty well armed up here so I doubt he could get to me."

"The police are looking for him so maybe they'll catch him." Paul paused. "While I have you, Rep, I'd like to ask you about the stills. I realize it's your right to shut them down, but I'd like to ask you to work with us for a while longer till we can get another supplier. I'm not threatening you, I don't do that, but I am asking you."

"Paul, it was nice of you to call me about Walt. Why don't you come up and talk with me about it and maybe we can work something out for a while."

"Thank you, Rep. I'll get Josie to come with me on Monday if that's all right."

"That will be fine," said Rep. He hung the phone up.

Lila was sitting across the table from him. "What was that about?"

"Walt Wend has escaped from the hospital and they say he is bout crazy. He's threatening to kill some people."

Lila shook her head. "I expect your name leads the list."

"I would reckon so," said Rep.

"What was he saying about the stills?"

"He asked me to keep them open for a while longer to help them out till they could find somebody else. He's coming Monday to talk about it."

Lila nodded. "He was nice to call you about Walt.

"That's what I thought," said Rep.

Walt Wend got up in the middle of the night, found his clothes, dressed and walked out of the hospital. When the nurse discovered he was missing, one of the doctors had security call the police. He said Walt was mentally unstable and would be a danger since he had been threatening to kill people.

Sometime later, cooler heads prevailed. Walt was a private citizen and if he didn't want to be in the hospital, it was his business. He wasn't wanted by the police for any crime, so the call to them was cancelled.

The fact was Walt had been raising hell and causing trouble the entire time he'd been there, so the hospital was glad to be rid of him. His head and face injuries were serious, at times he was lucid, but then he would be like a lunatic, screaming and cursing and threatening to kill people.

The doctors had him fairly calmed down until a man came and told him he was fired from his job and that news set him off again. He tried to get out of the bed and attack this man; they later learned his name was Paul Witt. Walt was restrained and was so irate that he had to be sedated for two days. When he woke up, he was much calmer, and his mind was clearer. That was when he decided to leave the hospital.

Walt walked out the front door, caught a taxi and went to his apartment. He'd been living there since his wife had left him after her brother Marvin was killed. She had finally tired of his running around with other women and Marvin's death was the last straw. She had got the house in the divorce settlement and kicked him out.

He sat and thought about his situation. Losing his job at the club really upset him and the more he thought of it, the madder he got. Getting even with the people that got him in this situation was on his mind. He called a couple of people he had dealt with on business at the club and they quickly told him they couldn't help him. The word was out that he was not to be aided in any way. He was regarded as a leper and not to be touched. He was alone.

After the calls and the people telling him they couldn't help him, he knew the next step for these people could be to make sure he was never a problem. He packed a bag and decided to leave town for several days until he could see what was going on. He knew he had to stay away from anybody connected with the club. But getting even with the people who hurt him was still on his mind.

Rep Doe was one of them. Every time he breathed, he was reminded of his encounter with Rep. But getting to him wasn't possible, he was too isolated.

Star Hobb had got him in this mess when she stole money from the club. Everything that had happened since had its roots in her actions. He decided she was responsible and should pay for the trouble she had caused. His challenge was to decide how to do that.

He would need help and he had money to hire somebody, but he'd found out the people he normally used wouldn't help him. There were a couple of people he'd dealt with that weren't connected with the club that might help. While they weren't as capable as his regular people, they ought to be able to take care of one woman.

He called one of the men, briefly told him what he was going to do. The man said he was interested in the job and would call him back in a few minutes.

The man hung up, called Paul Witt and told him what Walt had said. Paul thanked him for the information and called his partner. They discussed the situation and decided they had no choice but to get rid of Walt. They couldn't afford to have him causing more trouble. Within thirty minutes word was on the street that a contract had been put out for Walt Wend.

When Walt didn't get a call from the man, he called Josie. Josie was surprised to hear from him. She bore Walt no ill will, he had treated her fairly, and she didn't want to see him hurt. "Walt," she said, "they're coming after you. You gotta run."

Walt slammed the phone down, grabbed his bag and pistol and ran to his car. He pulled out of the drive, looked in his rear-view mirror and saw two cars turn at his house. He sped out of town.

As he drove away, he thought through his choices. He could drive to the coast around Panama City; he had been there many times. But he didn't want to go someplace and sit in a motel waiting for somebody to find him. He wanted to stay nearby where he could focus on getting even. He tried to think of someone who would hide him and not turn him in. One of the people that came to mind was Crip Coon, who lived on the river above Phenix City.

Crip and his son, Coot, made moonshine on a small scale, among other illegal activities. On occasion Walt had bought their whiskey and once when Coot got arrested in Phenix City, he had got the police to let him go. Crip was in his debt.

He rode up the river road, turned off on a dirt road and ended up at a falling down shack in the backend of a slough off the river. Crip walked out on the porch holding a shotgun in one hand and a mason jar in the other. Walt stopped and got out.

"Damn, Walt," said Crip, "what you be doin' down here?"

"I got some troubles Crip and I want you to help me."

Crip nodded. "Hell, you know I be glad to help you, Walt. You done helped me and Coot out."

They went inside and the first thing Walt did was stack a pile of bills on the table. It was more money that Crip had ever seen. Crip would have sold his soul to the devil for much less, if he'd known he had a soul. "You'll get more than that as long as I'm with you, Crip, and the Phenix City folks don't find me."

Crip picked up the money and stuck it in the pocket of his

overalls. "Ain't nobody gonna ever find out you be here, Walt." He stared at him. "Who do you want me to kill?"

Walt laughed. "You ever been up to River Bluff, Crip?"

Crip nodded. "Have been but don't go much. It be far and that's Shoal Creek country. They be big whiskey people and Red Hogan tolt me years back to keep my ass out from up there. I ain't never seen no sense in lookin' for trouble. What be in River Bluff?"

Walt told him about Star. "We tried to get her before, but she damn near killed the men sent to kill her." He looked at Crip. "You said something while ago about messing with Red Hogan. Star got in the bed with Red and cut his throat. That's what kind of woman she is."

"I heared some woman cut Red's throat. So, she be the one?" He looked at Walt. "How you be plannin' to get to 'er?"

"We'll have to come in from the river," said Walt. "Do you know Jim Hawke?"

Crip nodded. "I be knowin' Jim for a long time back to when he be fishing baskets on the river and runnin' from the game warden. He be a crazy son'a bitch. How come you ask bout 'im?"

"Jim is the constable in the town, and he is the reason we have to go in from the river. There's just one road to that town and he watches everybody coming in town."

Crip laughed. "Jim be a lawman. Damn if that don't beat all."

"Where is Coot?" asked Walt.

"Coot done gone upriver," said Crip. "He gone up to Lost Man Swamp where Lizzie Hogg has a place with women. Coot has some gal up there he likes. He'll be back by mornin'."

"We need to ride upriver to River Bluff in the morning," said Walt. "I want to see it from the water."

21

Star was in the room with May and Alva discussing the call from Paul Witt. "He said Walt had been in the hospital but had left and had been threatening us," said Star.

May nodded. "That's what he said."

"I told Jim what you'd said, and he said he would be watching," said Star. "But Jim can't watch all night and you know the last time they came; it was in the middle of the night."

"I'm supposed to go to the club tonight," said May. "I only came home to tell you about Walt."

"I don't think that is a good idea," said Alva.

"I doubt Walt would come to the club," said Star. "You know they would be watching for him there."

"I called Josie this morning," said May. "She said Paul's people are looking for Walt, but he's left town. They don't know where he is, but as far as they know he's alone so he would be less dangerous."

"We have to keep the door locked and our pistols close till they catch him," said Star. "There's not much we can do here."

They all agreed.

. . .

Jim Hawke was worried about the threats from Walt Wend. He thought it was doubtful Walt would try anything during the day, any attempt would be during the night as they had done before. He decided to change his schedule and work the night shift for the next few days. He would especially be watching Star's house on Pot Licker Lane starting Sunday night.

Saturday afternoon May decided to go to the club. She called Rink when she was at the club, told him about Walt's threats and told him she wouldn't be able to see him because she was going home. After the act, Paul had two of his men follow her home.

The night was quiet, and she went to church with Alva Sunday morning.

Storm and Karen were up early Sunday morning. They had decided it would be good for Karen to go to church with him and his parents. That would give the townspeople a chance to see her and get used to her being part of the town. The word about their engagement and pending marriage was well known. After church, they went to the Gill house, ate dinner and then went back to Storm's house. They were settling in with each other and both felt the decision to marry had been the right one.

Late that afternoon they went to the landing and Storm took her back to Shoal Creek. They agreed he would come get her on Thursday. He admitted he might be able to stay away that long. He kissed her and went back to the boat.

Walt woke up and it took him a few minutes to realize where he was. He could hear Crip in the other room and smelled the coffee. He got up, dressed and went into the kitchen.

"I was bout to holler at you," Crip said. "There's be scrambled eggs and grits on the stove. You can help yo'self."

Walt walked over, fixed a plate and sat down.

"Coot be back fore long," said Crip, "and we go upriver if you want to."

Walt nodded. "I want to get the layout from the river," said Walt "and then we go back tonight."

"It be best we go bout sundown and git close fore dark," said Crip. "There's shoals upriver and I don't want to go through 'em in the dark."

"That's up to you," said Walt.

In a few minutes they heard the sound of a boat coming in the slough. "That be Coot," said Crip. He got up. "Come on. We might as well go to River Bluff now." They walked down to the pier.

Coot was sitting in the boat. He was a big young man, looked to be in his early twenties with a scraggly beard and long hair. When Walt shook hands with hm he decided Coot hadn't bathed recently. Walt and Crip got in the boat and they headed upriver.

When they rounded the bend on Big Island, Walt could see the town of River Bluff. Lines of small white houses were laid out along the ridge back from the river. The four-story mill dominated the landscape to the right. Walt knew that Pot Licker Lane where Star lived was on the far side of the mill.

The boat ramp and landing were straight ahead. He could see two trucks parked there and several men gathered around them. He didn't want to have to land here tonight and walk all the way into town. He told Coot to keep going on up the river. He wanted to see if there was another place to land that would put him closer.

They passed a small island and as they rounded it, they saw a boat tied up against the bank. He could see a path leading through the trees up the hill and he thought this would be perfect. He could land here, and it looked like the path led toward Pot Licker Lane.

He motioned for Coot to turn around and go downriver. He had found out what he needed. They would come back late this evening, park a bit downriver and then wait for dark. The moon was almost full so they would have some light to see by.

Jim was sitting on the bench as church let out. He watched May and Alva leave the Methodist Church and walked toward him. "What are you doing here on Sunday?" asked May.

"Startin' tonight I'll be here all night," said Jim. "I think it would be at night if them folks try anythin'."

"That's a good idea," said May, as she and Alva walked on toward the dormitory. He watched them go, then got in his car and headed toward the landing. He pulled in near the boat ramp and parked. He got out and walked over to the men around the trucks.

"Ya'll fellows ain't got nothin' better to do that stand around down here," he said.

"We seen a strange boat come up the river while ago," said one of the men. "Had three men in it. We ain't never seen 'em before."

Jim looked at him. "Where did they go?"

"Went on up the river toward the shoals. They weren't gone long fore they come back down."

"Did they look like they was fishin'?"

The men shook their heads. "They didn't have no fishin' poles with 'em. They was just lookin'. They sho' did eye us mighty close."

Jim thanked the men, got in the car and left. When he got back to the store, he called Roy Sides, the deputy in Landon and asked him to come down. When Roy arrived, he told him what was going on and asked him to help. Star had already told Roy about Walt.

"I have a feelin' that somethin' will happen tonight, Roy," said Jim. "Them folks seein' them men on the river makes me thank it sho'nuff."

Roy nodded. "You might be right, Jim. I'll be down here after dark."

~

The Sun was low when Walt, Crip and Coot got in the boat and headed upriver. They were all armed. It was almost dark when they landed on the Big Island bank several hundred yards below the River Bluff landing. They sat in the boat till midnight, sipping on Crip's moonshine. Then they pushed off and headed upriver again. There was enough light to see as they slowly passed the landing. A few houses in town still showed lights.

They reached the place where they had seen the boat that morning and landed. They had already talked about their plans. When they got to the house, Coot would go to the front door. Walt and Crip would go in the back. Walt told them to shoot everybody in the house, then run to the boat and head downriver. He planned to be gone before anybody could react.

Jim and Roy went to the Hobb house after dark. Jim had said nothing to May or Alva about his suspicions. He didn't see any sense in worrying them. Ruby didn't understand why all these people were in her house. Star didn't explain it to her, so she went to bed.

"Roy," said Jim, "if they was doin' what I thank, they were lookin' for a place above the mill to land. They didn't want to come to the regular landin', they were lookin' for a place closer to the house. You can run faster than me. How bout you go down to the end of the mill and if you hear a boat come past, you hurry back up here."

Roy nodded and went out the door.

"You really think Walt is coming tonight, don't you, Jim?" said Star.

"I don't know for sure, but I sho' got the feelin'."

Roy went down the road and settled down to wait. He'd been there about an hour when he heard a boat coming. He watched through the trees until he saw it pass by. He got up and headed to the house. When he went inside Jim told him to go to the front door. Jim and Star stayed at the back.

~

Coot landed the boat. They got out and headed up the path. Walt led the way with Crip and Coot following. When they got in sight of the house Walt told Coot to go around to the front. He and Crip would wait at the back steps until they heard him kick in the front door and they would go in the back.

Coot ran around to the front. Walt and Crip went to the back steps and waited. Suddenly they heard a loud crash, and they started up the steps.

Roy was standing in the front room when he heard someone kick the door. The door didn't open, and it took another kick to break it down. Roy saw a man coming in the door and he shot him twice in the chest, knocking him back through the door on to the porch. He ran to the door and looked. The man was lying on the floor and wasn't moving.

He turned when he heard shots in the back room and ran toward the noise. When he got to where Jim and Star were, they were both standing at the back door firing their pistols. He shoved Star out of the way and looked outside. He saw one man lying on the steps and the other was firing into the house. Roy aimed and fired twice at him. The man fell over backwards.

Roy looked at Star, then turned toward Jim who was on the floor on his knees clutching his chest. "Jim," Roy yelled as he dropped down and grabbed him. Then he saw the blood. Jim looked up at him for a second and then slumped over.

Star was beside him. "Jim," she screamed.

Roy looked at her. "He's gone, Star."

"Oh my God, Roy," said Star, tears streaming down her face. "I caused this. I killed Jim."

Roy put his arms around her and held her close.

~

The word went out quickly about the shooting and Jim Hawke's death. For the first time in anyone's memory, all the lights in town were on in the middle of the night. May and Alva came to the house to console Star who was distraught about Jim's death. Everyone tried to talk to her and tell her it wasn't her fault, but she was adamant that it was. He had died protecting her.

The coroner came along with the Sheriff and other law officials. The funeral home personnel came and took the bodies away when all the legal work was done. Roy explained to everyone that Jim had suspected there would be an attempt on Star's life and he had joined Jim in providing protection.

Walt Wend's body was identified, Star knew him, but nobody knew who the other two men were. Several people in the crowd that had gathered suggested that all three of the men be carried down the hill and thrown in the river. Most of the crowd agreed.

Finally, after some hours, the officials left, and the crowd dispersed. Roy stayed with Star and May went back to the dormitory with Alva. May looked at Alva as they walked up the road. "How will we be able to look at Jim's bench without him sitting there?"

Alva couldn't answer; she didn't know anything to say. They walked on in silence.

Paul Witt was called in the middle of the night and told of Walt's death and the death of Jim Hawke. He woke Josie up and told her. She told him she had to go see May in the morning. Paul agreed it would be a good thing for her to do.

Early Monday morning Paul called Rep, told him what had happened. He told him that under the circumstances he wouldn't come to Shoal Creek to meet with him today, but he wanted to meet soon. Rep told him to give him a call when he was ready to meet.

Rep went in to tell Lila what had happened. Karen was with her. When he mentioned that the constable, Jim Hawke had been killed in the shooting, Karen was visibly shaken. It took her a minute to get her feelings under control. Both Lila and Rep looked at her.

"He was Storm's friend," said Karen. "He was like his grandfather. We talked to him every day and Storm loved him so much." She looked at Rep. "I have to go to him, Rep. This is going to hurt him so bad."

Rep nodded and looked at Lila. "You get ready and I'll take you across the river."

The funeral for Jim Hawke was held in the Baptist Church in River Bluff on Wednesday. Everyone was invited and most attended, although many couldn't get inside the church. They came anyway and stood outside, wanting to pay their respect to Jim.

He had no direct blood family. His wife had died years before and they had no children. But he had children, all the children in River Bluff were his and he had looked after them as they grew up.

Mr. Gill did the eulogy. Jim had been like his older brother as he grew up. They were an odd pair. One the son of the mill owner who grew up in a two-story house surrounded by plenty and the wild, untamed young'un from the shack on the riverbank at Big Eddy. Despite their difference in birth, they formed a bond that lasted throughout their lives.

Mr. Gill's father, a southern gentleman in every way, allowed his son the freedom to roam the riverbanks with his newfound friend. As they grew, Mr. Gill assuming his place of authority in the mill and Jim thumbing his nose at any authority on the river, they still remained close. When Jim was ready to leave the river, Mr. Gill gave him a job and sat him on the bench in the middle of town. They talked every day.

When Storm was born, as soon as he was old enough, Mr. Gill turned him over to Jim to teach him about the river and how a man should act. Storm would never forget those lessons.

As Mr. Gill stood in the pulpit and talked about Jim, he was hard-pressed to maintain control of his feelings. He and Jim had been so close for so many years and he didn't want to think of him being gone. But all the people in the church felt much the same way he did, so he guided his words toward the memories of Jim and what he meant to everybody. But regardless, tears flowed throughout the service.

The pastor said the benediction, they carried the casket out and buried Jim beside his wife in the cemetery behind the church.

Mr. Gill, his wife and Storm stood in the cemetery as Jim's family. The people stood in line and filed by one by one. Mr. Gill shook every hand and thanked them for coming. Karen stood to the side and watched Storm. She now had an understanding of the responsibility she would shoulder when she married him.

Both Star and May were at the funeral but neither came through the line in the cemetery. Star still felt her actions had led to Jim's death, just as she felt responsibility for her daddy's death. If she had not come back to River Bluff and brought all her troubles with her, both would still be alive.

Roy took Star to the house. She kissed him, he said he would call her later and he left. She went inside, talked to the lady she had hired to stay with Ruby and gave her money. Then she went in her room, packed her bag and walked out the front door. She got in the car, drove out of Pot Licker Lane and up the road. When she passed the Methodist church she slowed down, looked at Jim's bench and then sped out of town.

After the funeral Storm and Karen went back to his house. She could see that Storm was having a hard time dealing with Jim's death. "What do you want me to do, Storm," she asked. "I'll stay with you if you want me to."

He hugged her. "I know you would." He shook his head. "If you will, give me a couple of days to deal with this. I'll take you across the river and I'll come get you Saturday. Then you and Mother can get everything ready for the wedding."

"If that's what you want," said Karen. "I'll be ready Saturday." She looked at him, questioning.

"I'll be there," said Storm.

May got out of school the next afternoon and went by to see Star. She was worried about how she was doing. When she walked in and asked the woman where Star was, she was told Star was gone. She ran into Star's room and her clothes were gone. The woman told her Star had given her money and then left. May walked out and went to the dormitory to see Alva.

"She didn't say anything to you about leaving?" asked Alva.

May shook her head. "She didn't say anything to me about it."

Alva looked at her. "I'm going to call Roy Sides. Maybe he could do something."

May left the dormitory and walked toward the store and gym. She knew she had to face seeing Jim's empty bench sooner or later. As she walked past the store, she saw Storm's car parked across the street in front of the theater. She looked around and he was sitting on the gym steps. His eyes were watching her. She walked past Jim's bench, over to the steps and sat down beside him. Neither spoke.

In a minute Storm put his arm around her and pulled her to him. She put her head on his shoulder. They sat quietly for several minutes.

"He loved you, little girl," Storm said.

"I loved him," May said as tears flowed down her face.

"So did I," said Storm.

"What do we do now?"

"We go on with life like he wanted us to."

"That's easy for you to say, Storm. You know what you're going to do with your life."

Storm looked in May's face. "Jim told me back when Star came to town that he was proud that she had paid for your college. He said, 'Now May can be a schoolteacher.'"

May stared in his eyes. "You wouldn't lie to me, would you?"

"I would never lie to you about Jim."

"I heard you're going to get married."

"Yes, I am"

She looked at him. "I don't want to be alone tonight."

He smiled at her. "Neither do I." He got up, turned to her and held out his hand.

She took his hand, stood up and looked in his eyes. "Could you just hold me, nothing more?"

He nodded, put his arm around her and they walked to his car.

The End

Thanks for reading Storm Rising
If you enjoyed it please consider leaving a review on Amazon.com
This will help the author and also help others to find books they will enjoy reading.

Coming Soon In 2021
Book #4 of the Shoal Creek Saga

Look For It On Amazon.com

Storm Rising, Book #3 of The Shoal Creek Saga

Made in the USA
Columbia, SC
09 March 2021